Just
Lizzie

Wilfrid, Karen, author.
Just Lizzie

2023
33305255584207
ca   11/07/23

Just Lizzie

KAREN WILFRID

Clarion Books
An Imprint of HarperCollinsPublishers

Clarion Books is an imprint of HarperCollins Publishers.

Just Lizzie
Copyright © 2023 by Karen Wilfrid
All rights reserved. Printed in the United States of America. No part of this book
may be used or reproduced in any manner whatsoever without written permission
except in the case of brief quotations embodied in critical articles and reviews. For
information address HarperCollins Children's Books, a division of HarperCollins
Publishers, 195 Broadway, New York, NY 10007.
www.harpercollinschildrens.com

Library of Congress Cataloging-in-Publication Data
Names: Wilfrid, Karen, author.
Title: Just Lizzie / by Karen Wilfrid.
Description: First edition. | New York : Clarion Books, an imprint of HarperCollins
Publishers, [2024] | Audience: Ages 8–12. | Audience: Grades 4–6. | Summary:
Eighth grader Lizzie's study of asexuality in science class leads her to understand
her own asexual identity as she embarks on a journey toward self-discovery and
self-advocacy.
Identifiers: LCCN 2022058494 | ISBN 9780063290297 (hardcover)
Subjects: CYAC: Self-actualization—Fiction. | Asexual people—Fiction. |
Family life—Fiction. | Schools—Fiction.
Classification: LCC PZ7.1.W537 Ju 2024 | DDC [Fic]—dc23
LC record available at https://lccn.loc.gov/2022058494

23 24 25 26 27 LBC 5 4 3 2 1

First Edition

For my first-grade teacher, Helen Jones,
and
for Tyler

CHAPTER 1

I hate running. That tight feeling in my lungs, the ache in my chest that feels like crying. Plus, running is all about being fast, and if you ask me, things move fast enough as it is. Just two weeks ago, I watched as Dad and James pulled out of the driveway, the car windows packed high with James's belongings in those stackable plastic bins that are supposedly great for dorm rooms. The world felt strange and jumbled; a breeze moved the shadows of leaves around the driveway like a kaleidoscope. My brother, leaving for college. After what happened last spring—Mr. Henckman, the restraining order, the move—I hadn't believed he would really go.

This morning, when I came down the stairs in orange running shorts and a tank top, Mom tried to hide her surprise, but she didn't stop me. *Going for a run*—I felt mature saying it. Back at our old house, Mom would commemorate the first day of school by taking a picture of James and me on the front step, with our backpacks and new sneakers. Today is my first day of eighth grade. Do I have to be in a picture by myself? The thought of that, when I woke up this morning in a room that still doesn't feel like mine, seemed pathetic and sad—so I decided to commemorate the morning my own way. I decided to go back.

The sun is still behind the trees now, the sky a faint purple-pink—but the air is hot from yesterday, with the promise of more heat to come. I want to slow down, maybe even walk, but every house's windows feel like eyes casting judgment. *Stopped already—big surprise. Doesn't look very fit.*

I pick up my pace as I approach the Jacobses' house. Part of me hopes Mr. or Mrs. Jacobs will see me running and be glad they've hired someone so motivated as their babysitter. I look up at the girls' dormer windows; no one there. I always thought a house with dormers would be cool. I mentioned that to my family back in June when we started looking for places, but Dad said they were an inefficient use of space, Mom said one of her students had gotten a concussion on a slanted ceiling, and James didn't care because Ally had just told him she didn't want to keep dating him when they went away to college. After that, I stopped saying what I thought. But I still like to dream about my own house someday.

Someone's automatic sprinklers hiss, and I jump, but it's too late—my sneakers get sprayed. This neighborhood is a newer development, with wooden fences separating square after square of chemical-green lawn. No one here has woods. No one here has an apple tree.

Our old yard had one. Set back in a small clearing at

the edge of the yard, it dropped mottled green fruit from late summer up until the beginning of October, my birthday. Mom told me those apples were wild and not for eating, but I ate them anyway. Each time, I was startled by their bright sourness, the starchy feeling they left behind on my tongue. Sarah Nan and I played in the tree, shimmying up the branches to pick the littlest fruits for our American Girl dolls. I always thought of that tree as "mine." Technically, though, as Mom later told me, it's in the part of the woods that belongs to the Henckmans. I hadn't known the woods were anyone's. I thought they were just woods.

As the sprinkler water soaks through to my skin, I run alongside a stone wall that has rocks set upright like spikes along the cement rim. Who do they think is going to sit there, and why do they care?

Maybe our wall should have had spikes.

After the wall ends, I turn onto Cedarwood, then Pleasant—then I stop. Dead end.

The neighborhood that we moved to, across town from our old one, is an offshoot of the area known as the Maze. The winding, illogical streets are meant to discourage cut-throughs, and—as one neighbor told us when she came by with a welcome basket—to prevent home invaders from getting away. She probably wasn't thinking what would happen if the invader lived next door.

I stand at the dead-end street, catching my breath.

Maybe I should turn back. Maybe I don't need to go all the way there.

When we moved, the apples were still hard green marbles. By now, they'll have grown big enough to wrap my hand around, but won't be ready yet for picking. I always felt like that tree knew me—like we knew each other. But after what happened with Mr. Henckman and my mom, I wasn't allowed to go back in the woods anymore. I didn't get to say goodbye.

I turn around and try again.

I trace my previous path, trying to look like I know where I'm going as I remember the steps. The automatic sprinklers. The aggressive stone wall. The house where the dog jumps out . . .

The dog jumps out, a beagle type that scares me three feet off the sidewalk.

"No," I say, in my best firm voice, which isn't very firm. One time I got bitten by a dog. It was a tall gray one that tugged its owner over to me as James and I were walking home from sledding behind the high school. "Someone wants to say hello!" the owner said, so I reached out—and that dog chomped straight down on my hand. Fortunately, I was wearing mittens, but I could still feel the teeth digging into the soft spaces between my knuckles. "Haha—ouch!" I said, while the owner said, "*Leave it!*" and pulled him off. James didn't even realize I'd been bitten until after, when I pulled off the mitten and we saw the skin already turning purple.

"Lizzie, why didn't you *say* something?" he demanded. He wanted to go back and find the dog walker, but I wouldn't let him. Finally, he sighed and took my sled so I wouldn't have to carry it. As I cradled my injured hand in my opposite elbow, I reasoned: I was the one who had reached out. So when the dog bit me, it was my fault.

Now that I'm back on track and the barking has faded away, it's easy. A long stretch of downhill sidewalk and I'm out of the Maze, a block away from Main Street. The traffic picks up as I jog past the cemetery and library and Village Diner, where James used to take me for waffles on Wednesday mornings when he had first-period study hall.

At a crosswalk, I get to rest. The telephone pole has a sign taped to it: *Wendover Community Center—Registration Now Open for Fall Classes!* Fall already—where did the summer go?

There's a honk; a car is waiting for me. I wave, though I would rather have waited until no one was there. As I jog across, it feels like that car and all the cars behind it are watching me in my orange mesh shorts.

A few more blocks, and I'm in a residential neighborhood again—my old neighborhood. Down the hill, around the corner, onto Deerfield Circle, and my feet stop moving. I stand across the street and look.

There's our wall with one stone upside down from how it should be. There's our front doorbell that never worked. And there, at the edge of the woods, is my tree.

I'm back, I think.

Mom and Dad don't know a lot about the family who bought our house. They moved here from Connecticut, apparently. Are they taking care of it? From the outside, it looks the same. In my bedroom window, on the second floor, I see the eyelet lace curtains I left behind. Sarah Nan and I used to wrap ourselves up in them and declare, "It's my wedding day!" That was back when I thought everyone got married.

A twig snaps overhead. I feel on edge out here in the open, and the border of the woods looks farther away than I remember. How can I get back there? I slip into the grove of pine trees that lines our across-the-street neighbors' sidewalk and peer through the needles. Looks like the new owners have backed a couch right up to the living room window. Who would want to sit on a couch that faces the wall? Connecticut people, I guess.

I lean forward to see what else I can make out, but suddenly I hear an engine grumbling down the street: Mr. Henckman's red pickup.

I drop to my knees, pressing my back against the tree trunk. *Don't let him look over here*, I think, as if the tree had the power to hear my thoughts. *Don't let him see me.*

The pickup slows as it takes the curve past my hiding

spot, rumbling through the space between my old house and me. I hold my breath. *Don'tlookdon'tlook.*

I remember the plaid shirt he was wearing that day.

I remember his hand on the door, pushing back.

The engine fades to a grumble again, turns up the Henckmans' driveway, and stops.

It's been four months since Mr. Henckman forced his way in our front door, but now, as I inhale the tang of sap and the deeper, browner smell of decomposing bark, I'm right back in that moment. Frozen. My heart pounds.

A car door slams. I wait for the *creak-bang* of the porch's screen door to tell me that he's inside, and only then do I rise to my feet, knees shaking.

Something green glistens by the curb.

Cautiously, I part the pine branches and look through. One of my apples, all the way out here? How? Maybe a squirrel, or maybe—it's a gift. Even from here, I can see that it's perfect: smooth, symmetrical, with a fine spray of brown speckles around a tiny dimple in the side. All I need is one seed. Then I can have it back.

Three, two, one—now! I tell myself, and in one movement I burst out of the trees, snatch the apple, and take off at a run. I've got pine needles stuck to my socks and hair and shoulders, but I don't stop to brush them off. I don't stop at all, even though my lungs are burning, until I'm safely back in the Maze.

There, I bend over, gasping for breath, the apple still clutched in my fist.

I know things can't go back to the way they used to be. My brother was the one who always made sure I was okay, and now he's gone. Strangers have my house, my room, my tree, everything. No part of my home is mine anymore. Because in spite of what Mr. Henckman did, he got to stay. We're the ones who had to leave.

CHAPTER 2

~

The new house is okay. Mom likes that it has a screened-in porch, and Dad likes the wide granite counters for kneading bread. My new room is supposedly a little bigger, even though the house, overall, is smaller. But as I turn the corner onto our street—walking now, not caring what anyone thinks—it feels wrong that we live here.

I pass through the porch and come inside. It's dark: earth-tone paint on the walls, and hardly any overhead lights. The first thing we went shopping for was a bunch of lamps.

The sound of ocean waves and Spanish guitar drifts down the stairs. I try to be quiet, but I'm halfway up when Mom calls, "Lizzie?"

"It's me," I say. "Sorry."

The music stops, and the door to James's room opens. Not James's room anymore—Mom's new meditation room. It wasn't his for very long, before he left. "I was just about finished. How was your run?"

The back of my neck is sweaty and my cheeks are hot. I was hoping I could shower and change before she saw me. "Fine."

She picks up a meditation cushion, slaps the imprint of her backside out of it, and returns it to the stack against the wall. James's bed has an old gray bedspread on it, no pillow. "That was ambitious for the first day of school. Where did you go?"

The apple rests in my pocket, a knob against my thigh. "Around."

"Around where?"

"Just . . . around different places."

Mom looks up from the cushion stack. "You didn't go back to the house."

It's a statement and a question. "Well . . ."

"Lizzie!"

"I just passed by it," I say, trying to push aside the image of Mr. Henckman's truck crawling up the street. A pine needle prickles inside my sock. "Nothing happened."

Mom closes her eyes, drawing a breath. Maybe she's imagining herself on the beach with the shirtless man playing Spanish guitar. I've seen the front of the CD. "I thought you understood that we can't go back there."

"But—"

"Even to see the house."

Four months ago, when it would have made sense to be worried, she missed the signals. Now we're here. "You never said that," I tell her. "You said not to let him hamper our lifestyle."

Two weeks after we moved into our new house, she found me awake at midnight checking to make sure the front door was locked. Just in case. The next morning, she sat me down and told me that, yes, it was scary what had happened, but she didn't want fear to rule our lives. Most people out there, she said, are trustworthy. She would hate to see me close myself off to the world just because of him.

I didn't think I was closing myself off, but I saw her point. My fear gave Mr. Henckman even more power over us. I didn't want him to have that.

"We have a restraining order on him," Mom reminds me. She's using her I-know-you're-having-a-hard-time-right-now-so-I'm-being-patient-with-you voice. "If you go back there, it shows we're not taking it seriously. He could appeal it. Then we'd have nothing."

"Oh." I didn't know that.

Sometimes it feels like there's so much I don't know about.

"I'm sorry, sweetheart." She puts her hand on my shoulder. "I know it's been a lot of change in a short amount of time. But we'll get used to it."

I shrug her hand off.

Mom sighs. "Hurry up and get ready," she says. "It's time for school."

I almost ask her if she's taking my picture, but then I don't. One more thing that's lost.

The bathroom in our new house is long and narrow. The counter, patterned in fake pink stones, looks strangely spacious now that all James's stuff is gone. That's at least one benefit of him going away: now I can put my supplies in the drawer instead of stealthily bringing them in one at a time from my bedroom. I did that in our old house, too. James knows what happens to girls each month—he has a girlfriend, or had one, anyway—but I didn't want him to know it was happening to *me*.

Three mirrors surround the counter, reflecting an infinite line of Lizzies in pink towels while I wait for the water to get hot. Some people don't mind seeing themselves naked. Sarah Nan says that sometimes in the summer, her mom likes to go "alfresco"—just walk around the house with nothing on. Of course, Sarah Nan's mom is also "a little bit much," according to my mom. Whatever that means.

I can vaguely remember a time when I liked the way I looked. I remember flexing my thigh and seeing the muscles there, and thinking how grown-up that was. But now when I think of how I look to people, I remember the day in sixth grade when I wore leggings and Michael Gorman said the word *squeeeeeze* as I walked by, and then laughed with his friends.

Those boys would have laughed even harder if they'd seen me running today. *Running.* What was I thinking? My chest still hurts, and I have weird, gucky stuff in the back of my throat. I should have known. Running isn't me.

This body also isn't me. It's a bunch of skin and fat and skeleton carrying around the real me, my brain or my spirit or whatever it is that makes Lizzie. Sometimes I think it was a mistake that I wound up in this body—maybe even a mistake that I wound up being human. Maybe I was supposed to be a tree. Tall, steady, solitary, wise. Watching the rest of the world run.

The mirrors are starting to fog, so I drop my towel and escape into the nonreflective safety of the shower. With my eyes closed and the spray of steam and water surrounding me, it's easy to imagine that I am not a body at all—that I am only myself, and nothing more.

Mom drops me off in Sarah Nan's driveway a little after seven so that we can walk to school together. She almost didn't let me—this year, for the first time, she wasn't sure about the two of us walking alone, and she asked me about six times to text her when we get there—but we've walked to the first day of school together ever since fourth grade. My old house was a little too far to walk from, and our new one is even farther, but from Sarah Nan's it's just a few blocks. When I get out of the car, she's there on the steps waiting for me.

"Here," she says when I reach the doorstep. She hands me

a warm scone, sticky with burst raspberries. "Mom picked them up from Village Diner."

There's a thumping behind us, and I turn to see Sarah Nan's mom, Daria, knocking on the window. "Hi, Lizzie!" she calls, her voice muffled by the glass. "Have a great first day!"

"*Mom*!" Sarah Nan starts up the driveway. "She's so embarrassing."

I think Daria is really nice, but lately she and Sarah Nan have been fighting a lot. Or Sarah Nan says they're fighting. I partly think she goes looking for fights because that's what teenage girls are supposed to do. But maybe she and her mom are just different. Like me and my mom.

At the end of the driveway, Sarah Nan glances sideways at me.

"You're wearing long pants? It's like eighty-five degrees out here already."

I break off a corner of scone. "I don't know." The truth is, I never wear shorts to school. I hate the way my thighs look squashed against the desk chair. I'd rather be hot.

She shrugs. "Whatever. Here, let me see your schedule."

I pull up my class list on my phone and hand it to her. We used to do this, compare schedules, right away to see what we had together. Last year, it was almost every class. But by the spring, it didn't really matter, because she was much more interested in spending time with her gymnastics friend Chloe. I wasn't even sure she'd still want to walk with me today.

"You've got art this term," Sarah Nan says, studying our screens. "I've got tech. Different homerooms. Oh, you have Mr. Davis for PE! No Aardvark this year—that'll make you happy."

"Tell me about it." Even after drifting apart, Sarah Nan remembers my sworn eternal hatred of Ms. Ardvinson, who gave me my only B last year, along with the comment, *Needs improvement*. Sarah Nan was the one who came up with the nickname "Aardvark."

"You're in advanced math?" Sarah Nan asks, looking up.

"Yeah."

"You weren't in it last year."

"I tested in."

Sarah Nan tested into advanced last year, the earliest you could.

"Well, we have that together, then," she says. "And did you see they moved Ms. Faraher to eighth grade?"

I take my phone back, pretending to study the schedule. "Oh, yeah." Ms. Faraher was our sixth-grade science teacher, and also my favorite teacher in the world. She's tall—the kind of tall that's staggering, even to the boys—and smart in general, not just about science. I used to hang out in her room after school. She had a long row of plants lining the counter beneath the windows, all kinds: cyclamen, jade, aloe, orchid, even an avocado tree. She'd tell me about growing up on her family's orchard in Vermont, while I gave each plant a drink with her little copper watering can.

When our schedules came out a week ago and I saw her name under science, I did an actual jump in the air, right there in the kitchen. I can't wait to see her again.

"Well, we'll see if she's finally gotten a new hairstyle," Sarah Nan says, tucking her phone away. "Do you think we'll still have to do that CARP thing? Maybe she won't make us do it."

"I think she has to."

CARP stands for Capstone Research Project, the big project all eighth graders have to complete. Anyone who wants to be considered for honors science in ninth grade has to present their findings at the annual CARP Exposition in December. *I can't wait to see what you do for CARP*, Ms. Faraher said to me one of those afternoons in her classroom while I tilted the watering can over a pot of ivy. *I'll have to find a way to get down to the cafeteria to see you.*

I shyly shook my head. *I don't even know what I'll do.*

You'll think of it, she said. *You have time.*

Not so much time now. It's two years later, and I still haven't thought of anything. But at least now I know she'll definitely see my presentation. And grade it, too.

"If you had kids," Sarah Nan is saying, jolting me out of my thoughts, "would you teach them swear words?"

I wonder what wandering route of thoughts led her to this topic. "Um . . ."

As usual, she isn't really interested in my answer. "I

think I would," she says. "I wouldn't make it a big deal. I'd just say, 'This is what the F-word is.'"

I kick a loose piece of gravel and watch it bounce toward the gutter. "I think I'd wait until they asked me."

"Of course," Sarah Nan says. "You had a big brother to tell you things—you don't know what it's like to be in the dark. I had to find out all that stuff on my own."

"I thought your mom told you everything." Daria had Sarah Nan with a sperm donor when she was forty-five, and she's always been very open about it. Sarah Nan was open about it, too, but it wasn't until we were seven, in the car on the way home from the New England Aquarium, that I asked what "sperm donor" meant. Daria, being Daria, explained it to me in anatomically accurate terms, and that was the first I learned about where babies come from. My mom was furious when she found out. I wonder when she would have told me otherwise.

"My mom doesn't know what it's like now. She doesn't even know the right words for things. I think I want to be a young mom," Sarah Nan muses. "Not too young—but young enough to be the kind of mom who's fashionable, has good taste in music, and just knows what's going on. The kind of mom who can actually *relate*."

"Mm," I say, even though I don't agree. I think Sarah Nan's lucky to have her mom. For a little while, Daria was dating a guy named Nick, and it seemed like they might get married, but then last year they broke up. Daria has always said the guy comes second and Sarah Nan comes first. I like that.

We walk in silence for a few moments, until Sarah Nan asks, "Do you ever think about having kids?"

I shrug. Traffic picks up, and cars whoosh by us as we approach the main road. "Maybe adopting."

"That's right—you don't want to do it 'the natural way.'" She says this in a mockingly solemn voice, with air quotes. Then she perks up. "Maybe this year you'll start liking boys!"

I flinch, recognizing the creeping tendrils of a conversation that keeps resurfacing no matter how many times I squash it. "Unlikely."

Sarah Nan doesn't respond to that. She exhales through pursed lips, like she's whistling without making a sound.

How do you "start" liking boys? I've always thought it was an unsettling idea: Something deep inside you, ticking down, unheard, until one day, *ding!* You go off like some kind of microwave.

We come to a stop at the intersection across the street from school.

"Hey—it's okay with me if you're gay. You know that, right?"

Sarah Nan is looking intently at me. I'm not sure what to say. "I'm glad I have your permission."

She rolls her eyes. "That's not what I *mean*. You know what I mean."

She means that she's okay with me as I am, which I guess is a step up from last year, when she barely had two words to say to me. I should be grateful. "Thanks, but I'm not gay."

We wait for the light to turn. "Well, you have to be *something*, don't you?"

CHAPTER 3

~

The first day of school always feels like one of those bad dreams: you're in a familiar place, but everything is off somehow. People you knew before look slightly different—they grew taller, they changed their hair, they got tan, they got breasts. Our school is a three-story brick building, each level laid out exactly the same for grades six, seven, and eight. As I go from class to class throughout the day, it feels like I should still be in seventh grade, but all the rooms and teachers are different. Except for PE, which, even without the Aardvark silently judging me from the sidelines, feels the same as always. Mr. Davis, an older guy with a comb-over and short-shorts, nags us about sneakers and gym clothes, assigns us our lockers, and then lets us play dodgeball for the remaining fifteen minutes. I stand near the front so I get out early—a smack to the arm from Michael Gorman, because of course he's in class with me. He gives a victory jump and shouts, "YES!" while I trudge off to the bleachers. There's a sign on the wall next to me listing the community center's extracurricular fitness classes, one of which is Women's Self-Defense. I wish I knew self-defense. I'd sock Michael right in his smug face.

Just make it to Ms. Faraher, I tell myself.

At lunchtime, I arrive at the cafeteria doors and hold my breath. There's an empty seat next to Sarah Nan—but is it for me? By the end of last year, I mostly sat at the "miscellaneous" table with other girls who didn't have a group. I wanted to ask her on our walk this morning if we could sit together, but it felt like something you didn't just *talk* about.

Sarah Nan and Chloe are sharing Chloe's carrot sticks as I approach the table. No one says anything as I sit down and unzip my lunch box.

"Hey, Sarah," I venture. Last year, Sarah Nan decided to drop the "Nan" and go by just the first part of her name. I shouldn't have been surprised, but I was. Making her just plain "Sarah" seemed like stripping away a part of her—the part that made her interesting and different. "Hey, Chloe."

"Hey, Lizzie." Sarah Nan smiles. I feel a wave of relief.

Chloe acknowledges me with a sound somewhere between *hey* and *meh*. "So," she says, turning back to Sarah Nan, "have you kissed him yet?"

Ugh—Ned. Sarah Nan started going out with him over the summer. Ned, with big ears, who's been in our class since kindergarten; he used to pretend to stick his pinkie finger in the pencil sharpener. What's so different about him now?

Sarah Nan gives a small scoff, and I'm relieved. "It's not like that, Clo. We're just talking. Plus, he's kinda shy."

Chloe sighs. "Do I have to come over there and mash your faces together?"

I wouldn't put it past Chloe to do that. She's very interested in pairing people up. It'll probably only be a matter of seconds until she asks me who I "like."

"Hey, Lizzie," she says. "Who do *you*—"

"Whoa," Sarah Nan interrupts her, leaning sideways to look past us. "Who's that kid?"

Chloe and I both look. People are going through the line with their Styrofoam trays; one of the lunch monitors yells at a boy trying to nab an extra bag of chips.

"Where?" Chloe asks—and then I see.

Standing in front of the condiment and utensil station is a student—a boy?—with shoulder-length brown hair and a flowing gray skirt that reaches his ankles, revealing only the tops of some dirty Converse sneakers.

"Oh, him," Chloe says, returning to her lunch. "He's new."

"Yeah, no kidding," Sarah Nan says. "But how do you know . . . ?"

"That he's a he? Mr. Fanopolous had us do our pronouns in homeroom, and he said 'he.'" She holds up a slice of red pepper, contemplating it. "I forget his name, though."

"Did he say why he wears a skirt?" I ask.

Chloe snorts. "Right, like anyone was going to ask him *that*."

Sarah Nan nods in appreciation. "Bold choice for the first day of school. I wonder who he'll make friends with."

"I think he's cute," Chloe says.

The boy makes his way to a table. As Sarah Nan and Chloe resume their conversation about Ned, I glance back over at him. *Bold choice.* I wish I could be bold.

After lunch I finally have science. I leave the cafeteria a little early, telling Sarah Nan and Chloe that I need to use the bathroom—but really I'm hoping to catch Ms. Faraher alone before class, the way I sometimes used to in sixth grade. I'd arrive at her door at the end of lunch to find her reading, a bagel in one hand and a book in the other. She liked to sit at the student desks rather than her own, which was covered with plants and science trinkets. I liked that. I thought it revealed something about her—like maybe some part of her hadn't grown up all the way yet.

On my way, I stop at my locker to drop off my lunch box and check my hair, which has been doing weird things in the humidity. I look in the little magnetic mirror inside my door. Droopy—figures. I try to fluff it up a little, move one strand over to even out my part. A little better. Not great.

I stare into the mirror a bit more. Is this really what people around me have been seeing all day? Sometimes I can't understand how anyone would want to be friends with this face, this person.

As I round the corner, Ms. Faraher is standing outside her classroom, beaming at a passing sixth-grade tour. "Hello," she says to them. "Are you having a good first day?" I notice with satisfaction that she *does* have the same hairstyle as always—a long brown braid down her back.

The sixth-grade teacher has stopped the tour and is joking with Ms. Faraher about how she's a traitor for leaving sixth grade to teach eighth. *Shut UP*, I want to scream. Finally, the group moves on, clearing my path—and I stop short.

"Lizzie!" Ms. Faraher exclaims.

Her arms are open to hug me—but in between those arms is a blue-striped dress that bulges roundly in the front.

How do you hug a pregnant person?

Carefully?

From the side?

Not at all, because you're not a little sixth grader anymore and it's weird to want a hug from your teacher?

Once I get close enough, she scoops me in with a squeeze. "How was your summer?"

"Um, good." She lets go, and I step back. "What about you?"

"OH MY GOSH, ARE YOU PREGNANT?!?" Chloe screams from behind me. I guess everyone's back from lunch. "When are you due? Is it a girl?"

"A boy," Ms. Faraher says, her hand resting on the bump.

I realize that I've forgotten about all the niceties—the things women say to other women who are pregnant. I've heard my mom say them. "Congratulations," I manage, but the conversation isn't really between us anymore.

"Let's all come inside," Ms. Faraher says warmly, and ushers us into the classroom.

Our names are projected on the screen to show us where our seats are. I barely have time to groan inwardly before I hear, "Lizard Burger, yes!"

It's Michael Gorman. He drops his binder on the lab table next to me, already spilling papers even though we've only had four classes. "Lab partners, all right! Can I get a high five?"

He holds up his hand. I ignore it.

"Whoa, that's mean," he says. "Chloe, did you see how mean Lizzie is?"

Chloe sits down at the table in front of ours. "I'm ignoring you," she informs him. Easy for her to say. Her partner is Aidan, who's quietly arranging his pencils so they line up parallel with the edge of the table.

Why, why, why does Michael Gorman have to be in science with me? PE I could understand; it's already horrible. Science is the one place I'm supposed to feel good.

While Ms. Faraher calls the attendance, I look around the room. Something isn't right. When Michael moves his bursting binder from the table to the window ledge with a heavy *whump*, I figure it out: Ms. Faraher's plants aren't here. In fact, there isn't a single plant in this room. Did she take them all home? Did they die? Maybe now that she has a baby on the way, she doesn't care about plants.

When she calls my name, she smiles. I smile back, but inside, I feel betrayed. Ms. Faraher used to say that her plants were her kids. She used to say *we* were her kids. But maybe that's what happens in life: You know a person, or you think you do, and then, *ding*, the microwave goes off. Something inside them changes; their life starts to go a different way than yours. You start to wonder if their new direction has a place for you—or if they ever really had a place for you at all.

CHAPTER 4

Later in the afternoon, when I get home from school, I go upstairs to my room and flop back onto the bed. It's quiet. In our old house, I could always hear James stirring across the hall—or if I couldn't hear him, I could *feel* him there. When I was little, I used to sneak into his room after lights-out and fall asleep on his floor. I even did that when I was maybe too old for it. He'd say, "You sure that's comfortable?" and I'd say, "Yeah," and sometimes, on the really good nights, he'd get up and put an extra blanket over me. We used to text each other silly things, too. I scroll through to our last exchange before he left:

Him: im hungry. you think dads cooking?
Me: Prolly mom
Him: maybe we can call for takeout

I miss him.

His phone rings and rings, and just when I'm about to give up, he answers.

"Hey, Nugget!"

"Hi, James." He and my dad still sometimes call me by my childhood nickname, born out of the two-year span when I would only eat chicken nuggets for dinner.

"How was your first day?"

I stare up at the ceiling, which is plastered in a pattern of overlapping fanlike brushstrokes. "Pretty good. Long." I trace my finger along the stitching in my comforter. "I have Ms. Faraher again."

"They moved her up? That's cool."

I smile. "Yeah." James got it about Ms. Faraher. When I was in sixth grade and talked about her all the time, he never said, *What, are you in LOVE with her or something?*—which is what Sarah Nan said once. Maybe he'd get it about her being pregnant, too.

"So that means you get to do CARP with her," James is saying. "Do you have any ideas?"

Suddenly my eyes are stinging. There are so many things I want to talk to James about—Ms. Faraher, Michael Gorman, going back to the house—and there isn't enough time. Not for all of it. Now that we don't live together, he's only ever going to know less and less about me. "Not yet," I say.

"That's all right," James says. "You will."

"I know."

There's silence as both of us breathe. It's new for us, talking on the phone. When we ate waffles together at Village Diner, or when I hung out on his bedroom floor, a lot of the time we wouldn't even talk. It felt comfortable then. Now it just feels awkward.

"How's college?" I ask.

I really do want to know, but it comes out wrong, like I'm teasing: COLL-ege.

James laughs. "Good so far. I signed up for mostly afternoon classes, so it's awesome not getting up at six. And you pick what you take, so nobody makes you do Spanish or something."

"I like Spanish."

"Of course you do."

I pick up my American Girl Molly and hold her in my lap. "Can I see your room?"

He hesitates. "Okay—but you're sworn to secrecy. It's a real mess."

"Wow, already?"

"You want to see it or not?"

"Okay, okay—I won't judge," I assure him.

He switches to video, and I catch a quick glimpse of him before the screen begins swooping around. His hair is short; I forgot he got it cut the day before he left.

The camera pans briefly around the room: concrete walls; a desk covered with papers, an orange, and a jar of peanuts; his navy-blue bedspread; and a mini fridge with an open pizza box on top. "Well, I'm glad you're not starving."

"Yeah, yeah, laugh it up," James says, rolling his eyes at

me before the screen goes dark and we're back to a regular call. "You'll see when it happens to you."

I rest my chin on Molly's head. The familiar doll smell is comforting, and I close my eyes, remembering how excited I was when I first took her out of the box and saw that she had glasses like me. Now I don't wear them anymore—I switched to contacts—but Molly still wears hers. "Is it weird? Being away?"

James considers this. "Not yet," he says. "It's only been two weeks. That's how long I was at soccer camp, remember?"

"True." I don't tell him that it feels weird here. Or that I always hated those two weeks when he was away at camp. "Is Gerald nice?"

"He's . . . interesting," James says. "Spends a lot of time gaming. Doesn't really leave the room."

"Do *you* leave the room?"

I mean it as a joke—James also spent a decent amount of time by himself when he was home—but he surprises me by hesitating. "Well . . ." His voice sounds different now. "Actually, I think I might have a date tonight."

"What?" I can't believe it. He and Ally just broke up. Is it really that hard to *not* have a girlfriend? "What do you mean, you 'think'?"

"This girl in my Calc II study group texted me if I wanted to get dinner and I said yes, but I still don't know if she meant with other people or just us."

"Can't you ask her?"

James gives a small laugh. "Oh, Lizzie."

One more thing I don't get about relationships. Irritated, I ask, "What about Ally?"

His voice hardens. "We broke up."

"Yeah, but aren't you supposed to, like . . . wait?"

"Relax, Nugget. It's just dinner. And it might not even be a date—it's at Subway."

"Then I *hope* it's not a date."

He laughs, and I feel relieved. "Well, I'll find out and get back to you. Don't say anything to Mom about it, okay?" he adds as an afterthought. "I don't want her to get all weird."

"I know," I tell him. "I won't."

I wouldn't have said anything anyway, but it warms me that he asked me to keep a secret.

"I'd better go," James says. "I've got to make a dent in my environmental science book."

"I should go, too," I say. Even though I have nothing to do. "Have fun at COLL-ege."

He laughs. "Thanks, Lizzie. Bye."

After we hang up, I stare at my dark phone screen, feeling strangely empty. Not better after talking to him. Worse. For the rest of my life, instead of saying "good night" or "where'd you put my charger?" I'll be saying goodbye to him.

The day before he left, all of us were tense. Mom and Dad were still unpacking and organizing the house, and

James was repacking the few things he'd taken out of boxes since the move. Meanwhile, I sat at the kitchen table eating cereal.

"Lizzie, when you're done, I need you to tell me which of your dolls you want to keep and which ones you want to go in the attic." Mom was on her hands and knees scouring the inside of the oven. The previous owners had only lived there for three years, but Mom thought they could have left the place a lot cleaner.

I moved my cereal around in the bowl. "Why don't you decide? You decide everything, anyway."

Mom pulled her head out of the oven. "Would you *please*—"

"Hey, Lizzie." James appeared in the doorway. "Want to kick a ball around out back?"

I didn't really, and I was mad at him, too: he'd just told us that he was going over to Ally's after dinner, even though the two of them were breaking up. But I could tell he was trying to save me from another argument with Mom. He was always doing that, even before Mr. Henckman heightened the tension between us. I slipped on my shoes and followed him outside.

James has played soccer since he was a kid; in high school he did varsity. I played for one year when I was in first grade, trying to be like him, but I hated it—too much running. That night, out in the backyard, he bounced the ball a few times from knee to knee just to show off, then passed it to me, rolling it gently across the grass.

I let it roll past. In our new, smaller yard, it was only a matter of feet before it hit the row of bushes separating our property from the neighbors'.

I trudged after it, then set myself up to kick it back.

"Hey," he said.

"Hey, what."

"You okay?"

I pushed the ball toward him, more of a shove than a kick. "Sure."

He stopped it. "Listen," he said. "You're the one I'm going to miss. You know that, right?"

"Whatever."

"I'm serious." He nudged the ball back to me, so I wouldn't have to chase after it again. "I mean, obviously I'm going to miss Mom and Dad, and Ally . . ."

I grimaced to hear her name listed alongside the rest of us, his family.

"But you're the one I'm really going to miss. I'm going to miss you."

I didn't kick the ball back. Instead, I ran forward and hugged him.

"Oof," he said, but he didn't laugh at me. He hugged me back.

The next morning, when he actually left, was different.

Breaking up with Ally had put him in a dark mood. He and Dad kept packing and repacking the trunk, trying to make everything fit, and Mom was hovering, worrying, asking repeatedly if James had remembered everything. When I hugged him, he was wearing his backpack, and I couldn't get my arms all the way around. He let go quickly. Then Mom and I stood back while Dad started the car and the two of them drove away.

I wish I had known that afternoon in the backyard was going to be our real goodbye. If I had, I would have said how much I was going to miss him, too. There's more I wish I could have told him, even though it wasn't something we normally said to each other: I wish I had told him that I loved him.

CHAPTER 5

～

A week after we moved in, Mom was out working in the garden when Bonny Jacobs came by on her bike and asked if it was true that Mom had a teenage daughter. Mom said yes, and the next thing I knew, I was babysitting for the Jacobses once a week on Saturday afternoons while Mr. and Mrs. Jacobs rode their bikes around town, training for a big fundraiser race they had in August. The fundraiser is over now, but the girls like me, and so do Mr. and Mrs. Jacobs. They say I'm a good influence. Mom, meanwhile, is glad to see me "making connections" in the neighborhood and "taking on additional responsibilities"—and after the first three times, she stopped texting me every five minutes to make sure I was okay. (Now she only texts once.)

Today, the Jacobses' side door is open except for the screen, so I don't even have to ring the bell.

"She's here!" Carly, ten and still in her karate uniform, rushes to be the first to greet me, while Sabrina, seven, does a standing long jump off the arm of the couch. Before their mom even makes it into the room, they each have me by an arm.

"Can we play pretend?" Sabrina asks.

Carly tugs me the other way. "Mom said we can do tie-dye!"

Sabrina hands me a crumpled paper with a watercolor circle on it. "I painted this for you."

It still surprises me that just because I'm a few years older, these two girls think I'm cool. I have to admit, I like it. As a younger sister, it's nice to be looked up to for a change.

Mrs. Jacobs, in bike shorts and a spandex top, laughs as she enters the room. "Looks like you have plenty to keep you busy." She turns back and calls up the stairs, "Lizzie's here! Are you ready?"

Mr. Jacobs calls down that he's trying to find his "other shorts," and then, a moment later, appears in the kitchen.

"Oh good, you found them." Mrs. Jacobs gives him a swat on the rear, and I look away.

"Mom, gross!" Carly says.

Sabrina wasn't looking. "What? What happened?"

"Nothing, I just love your dad, that's all." The Jacobses kiss each other. It's fine, but I feel uncomfortable. My parents don't kiss like that. Is that the reason my inner microwave hasn't "dinged" yet—because my parents aren't mushy?

"Have fun!" Mrs. Jacobs calls back over her shoulder as they take off down the driveway on their matching mountain bikes.

"Tie-dye!" Carly shouts, and dashes off to get the supplies. Her mom said she signed Carly up for karate to help her build confidence, but if you ask me, it's Sabrina who could use confidence building. She's still clinging to my arm, her face framed on either side by dark pigtails.

"After tie-dye, can we play pretend?"

"Definitely," I say, as Carly returns with a large plastic bucket and a pile of socks and T-shirts.

"Okay, Sabrina, pick a shirt. Not *that* shirt . . ."

Sometimes Carly reminds me a little of Sarah Nan, and Sabrina reminds me a little of me.

I haven't tie-dyed since summer camp when I was ten— and I think I missed most of it since I was busy crying about how I wanted to go home—but Carly knows what to do. She leads us out to the backyard and sets up the picnic table with bottles of dye and the bucket for soaking. Then she shows us how to fasten the rubber bands. She's dyeing a white T-shirt that reads *Wendover Soccer*; Sabrina's working on a pillowcase. Since I didn't bring anything, Carly gives me an old sock.

"Where did you get this?" I ask.

Carly shrugs. "My dad."

I decide to just watch.

As the girls eagerly rubber band their projects and some late-afternoon clouds give us a bit of relief from the heat, I start to think that this might be one of the good babysitting days. Sometimes when I come over, one of them—usually Carly—starts a fight, and the other—usually Sabrina—ends up in tears.

"Careful!" Carly exclaims, just as Sabrina squeezes extra hard and sprays her front with purple.

"Uh-oh." Sabrina looks down at her splattered shirt. Her chin drops. "I'm so *stupid*!"

"It's okay," I say quickly. "We can wash it."

"Just take it off, Sabrina," Carly says. "We're all girls."

"Oh yeah!" Sabrina yanks the shirt up, exposing her outie belly button and tiny nipples. I'm embarrassed, even though I shouldn't be. I forgot what that was like—not caring.

Sabrina twists and tugs, but the collar snags on her pigtails. "I'm stuck!" She starts running around, veering dangerously close to the picnic table.

"Hold on." I grab her by the arms, then gradually work her head out of the hole. "Go put another shirt on."

"Aw." She casts her purple-spattered shirt aside and runs off to the house, just as my phone buzzes in my pocket.

"Is it a boy?" Carly asks.

I roll my eyes. "No."

Math homework on a weekend?? AJKSIHAJAJK WHAT!!!

Of course Sarah Nan is already tackling the advanced math. She never puts anything off, whether it's homework on Saturdays or wearing a bra in the second grade. She even has a "master plan" to lose her virginity by the time she's seventeen.

Did you get to number nine?

Not yet, I reply, as Sabrina comes running back outside.

"Hey, Lizzie, do you have boobies?"

I look up from my phone. "What?"

"Sabrina!" Carly exclaims, and I think she's going to tell her sister that that's an inappropriate question, but instead she says, "Of *course* she does! She's thirteen!"

I cross my arms over my chest. "Let's finish your tie-dye."

"Mommy said boys don't get them because they have weenies." Sabrina follows alongside me as I pick up her discarded T-shirt from the ground.

"Sure," I say.

She watches as I inspect the stains. "Daddy has a weenie," she adds, "but only Mommy can see it."

I feel my face getting red. "That's nice."

Carly giggles, which makes Sabrina giggle, too. "*That's nice!*" they both say, and they laugh even harder.

I look at my phone—has it been an hour yet? Another text from Sarah Nan: Well, tell me when you get there!

The doorbell rings inside the house, making us all jump. *Bing-BONG.*

"I'll get it!" Carly pushes back from the picnic table. "It's probably Sasha with my—"

"Hold on." I put out my arm to stop her. No one's ever come to the house while I was babysitting before.

Sabrina has her dye bottle upside down, ready to squeeze. "Mommy said we shouldn't answer the door without her."

Carly ducks under my arm. "It's fine, Sabrina. Lizzie's here."

"Does that mean you're a grown-up?" Sabrina asks.

I'm trying to figure out how to answer as Carly crosses to the sliding glass doors that look into the house. Through them, she can see the screen door I came through. "Never mind," she says. "It's just some guy."

"Get back!" I say sharply. Carly backs away from the doors, startled, as the doorbell rings again. *Bing-BONG.*

Nothing is locked. We're in the backyard, completely out in the open.

What am I supposed to do?

"We're going to get under the table," I say. I try to sound calm, but my throat is clenched and my voice doesn't sound like me.

"*What?*" Carly says, while Sabrina stares at me, still holding her upside-down dye bottle. Neither of them thinks I mean it—*I'm* not even sure I mean it—until I duck beneath. Part of me knows this makes no sense. Another part of me thinks of Mr. Henckman's hand pushing against the door that day, and wants us all to be as small as possible.

Sabrina slides down off the bench and joins me. "Carly, come on!" she whispers.

"The door is open," Carly says. "He can tell somebody's home."

"Carly, just—" I feel like I can't think clearly. Not in words. "Just get under here!"

Carly sighs, then kneels and crawls over to us.

Bing-BONG. I close my eyes. My heart thuds: *Don't look. Don't look.*

"Lizzie?" Sabrina asks, her voice small. "Is it a bad guy?"

"No," I tell her—because how can I say I don't know?

"Then why are we under the *table*?" Carly demands.

Sabrina lifts her chin. "Look, a cocoon!"

There's a crunch of paper—then nothing. Several moments elapse. Carly peers around the table legs. "I think he's gone." She goes crawling off toward the house.

"Carly, wait!" I try to grab her ankle and miss.

"We can see your bum!" Sabrina giggles. Carly gives her backside an extra wag as she reaches the sliding glass doors.

"He's gone." She stands up. "There's a paper stuck in the door handle."

While Carly slips inside, I crawl out from under the table, brushing patio grit from my palms. Carly pops out again with a yellow paper.

"'Bob's Home Security Systems,'" she reads. "'Could they be right for your family? Call today for a free con . . . con . . .'" She gives up on *consultation* and looks over at Sabrina and me. "It's a *coupon*," she says loudly. "It was a guy with a coupon."

She hands me the paper. *Sleep easy with Bob!* "Technically it's a flyer," I say.

"Can I come out now?" Sabrina peers at us from behind the picnic bench.

My heart is beating in my ears; my knees are wobbly. I really messed this up. I'm supposed to be in charge. I'm supposed to be the grown-up.

I wasn't supposed to be afraid like that.

"You stay there," I tell Sabrina, forcing excitement into my voice. "We're going to play explorers! Come on, Carly, let's build a cave around Sabrina."

"Whoopee!" Sabrina says. "Can I be a dragon?"

Carly follows me to the clothesline, where a picnic blanket is hanging that looks promising. "You were scared," she says, accusatory.

I pile the blanket into my arms. "No, I wasn't," I say, but Carly isn't buying it.

"You made us *hide* under the *table*."

I look at her, standing there in her karate uniform with her hands on her hips, and I see exactly where this is headed. She's going to tell their mom. Her mom will tell my mom. My mom will start meditating even harder, knowing how everything with Mr. Henckman really did affect me, and then she'll make me talk to Mrs. Mahoney, the guidance counselor Sarah Nan and I used to call "Mrs. Baloney" because she's pretty much useless unless you want a Jolly Rancher and an easy out from PE. My newfound babysitting career will be over for sure. And what's worst of all: These girls look up to me, and what did I do? I taught them to hide.

I have to fix this.

I meet Carly's eyes. "Couldn't you tell it was all part of the game?"

She stares back. "What game?"

"Explorers!" I say. "First we hide from the monster—that guy was the monster—and now we have to escape the cave so we can find the buried freezer treasure."

"The buried . . . ?"

"Ice cream sandwiches!"

Carly narrows her eyes, considering all this. "So I can have an ice cream sandwich?"

"If we hurry up and make this cave before your parents get back."

Carly smiles. Then she grabs the blanket from my arms. "Okay, Sabrina," she shouts, "we both get to be dragons!" She runs back to the table and unfurls the blanket, letting it settle over Sabrina like a deflating parachute.

I stay behind a moment, and finally let out the long, shaky breath I've been holding. Because Carly was right: I was scared. When the doorbell rang and a man was at the door, I thought it was happening again.

CHAPTER 6

It began in January, when Mrs. Henckman hit our stone wall with her car. She took the curve too fast, slid on an ice patch, and just creamed it. Bashed the edge where it meets the driveway, toppling the highest stone and nudging all the others out of place. She was fine, and we weren't even home, so when we came back from the movies, we didn't know why the edge of our wall was in pieces until Mr. Henckman came to our door, twisting a black Bruins cap in his hands. Mom was the one who answered, while I watched unseen from the top of the stairs.

"But she's all right?" I remember Mom asking, about Mrs. Henckman, while Mr. Henckman insisted that they would pay for the wall to be fixed. "And you're all right?"

Before this, we hadn't known the Henckmans very well, even though we'd lived next door to them my whole life. They were older and had kids who were already grown up. Mr. Henckman had a small vegetable garden in a raised bed out back, and sometimes when James and I were outside, he'd invite us over to try a cherry tomato or a leaf of lettuce. Mostly, though, he kept to himself as he puttered around the yard, bending and stooping every so often to pick up stray twigs and helicopter seeds.

After the wall incident, we started to see Mr. Henckman more. The next time it snowed, he cleared our driveway. The storm had lasted through the night—school was canceled—and Dad was away visiting my grandma after her hip replacement surgery. I woke up to a snowblower revving, and there was Mr. Henckman plowing a path toward the garage. Mom waved to him through the living room window, *Thank you*.

"How did he know Dad was away?" James asked. He was grumpy because he'd said *he* would take care of the driveway, only he'd still been asleep.

"I don't know," Mom said, watching Mr. Henckman from behind the curtain as he went on to plow his own sidewalk. "But it was very generous of him."

Mom baked a batch of snickerdoodles that afternoon and wrapped half of them on a plate with foil. "Come with me, Lizzie," she said. "You haven't been outside all day." I carried the cookie plate, sulking, and Mom rang the doorbell. Mr. Henckman answered, exclaimed over the cookies, and invited us in, but Mom said we had to get going. And then we stayed there, on their front steps, for twenty-five minutes, while Mr. Henckman talked.

"Sorry about that, Lizzie," Mom said when we finally extricated ourselves and were safely down the sidewalk. "He just kept talking!"

"He didn't even ask a question," I pointed out, stomping my boots to get the feeling back into my toes. "He only talked about himself."

Mom pulled off her knit hat and shook her hair loose. "I feel sorry for people like that," she told me. "They want to connect, and they don't know how."

I felt the mild criticism in her words: I was being mean. I didn't know why I couldn't be a naturally warm and outgoing person like my mom. I resolved to be nicer to Mr. Henckman if I ever saw him again.

After the next snow, which was only a few inches, Mr. Henckman tried to plow for us, but this time Dad was home. I couldn't hear their conversation from inside, but I saw Mr. Henckman's shoulders hunching as he pushed his snowblower back along the thin path he'd made, back to his own property.

"You could have let him," Mom said later when Dad came in from clearing the driveway. Dad replied something about "boundaries" that I couldn't hear.

Mr. Henckman started bringing in our newspaper for us. Instead of at the end of the driveway, where the delivery left it, we'd find it on our front step. On trash collection days, he'd close our bin and wheel it back up the driveway. He was retired, Mom said, and he liked to have little things to do.

In the spring, Mr. Henckman appeared at our door again. This time, I was the one who answered and saw him on the front step holding what looked like a bunch of dead sticks in a burlap sack. Rosebushes, he said. They were for Mom to plant in the bare lawn where the contractors had trampled all the grass; he knew she liked gardening. They were dormant now, but when it got warmer, they would grow.

"Mom?" I called over my shoulder, because it didn't seem like the kind of gift I should accept myself. She appeared behind me, drying her hands on her apron.

"How lovely!" she exclaimed, as if she saw something more than just the sticks.

Mom planted the rosebushes. Sure enough, the sticks grew green shoots, and the shoots grew leaves. They looked strange there, the new growth stark against the older branches as if an entirely different plant were growing out of them.

Then Mr. Henckman started calling our house.

The first time, he called because he'd heard there were coyotes around. He wanted to warn us.

Another time he called because Mrs. Henckman was making cinnamon rolls, and they were all out of cinnamon. Mom sent James over with a plastic baggie.

James was back in five minutes.

"I think he was hoping you'd bring it," he said. Mom didn't answer.

Mr. Henckman usually called between four and five— the hour when Mom was home from work, but Dad still wasn't. One day, Mom and I came home from school, and while she was taking off her jacket, I saw the light on the *New Message* button blinking. I pressed it.

The voice mail started in the middle of a thought. *"—so sorry if I was BOTHERING you, I didn't realize it was HARRASSMENT to make a KIND GESTURE. I'm a kind person, Laura, like you; we have kindness in our hearts that the rest of the world can't understand. If you could just let me explain, Laura, I need to see you again so I can EXPLAIN . . ."*

"Lizzie!" In an instant, faster than I knew she could move, Mom was there in front of me, slamming the red *X* button.

"Message erased," the machine said pleasantly.

For a moment, both of us just stood there. "Mom?" I felt hot and cold at the same time.

"We're taking care of it. Dad and I are," she said. "He's not well."

Is he in love with you? I wanted to ask. But I couldn't make myself say it.

The next day, Dad came home early, and he was the one who answered the phone.

"I am asking that you not call here anymore," he said. "Or we'll have to involve the police."

I couldn't make out the words, but Mr. Henckman's voice got shriller, defensive—and then Dad hung up.

The calls stopped. For three days, they stopped. Then, on a Saturday afternoon late in May, while James and my dad were out shopping for college supplies, there was a knock at the front door.

I thought it was Sarah Nan. We hadn't hung out together for most of the spring, and I was excited that she was coming over, even if it was only to finish a social studies project. When the knock came, I was staring at myself in my bedroom mirror, trying to see if you could tell that I was wearing a bra under my T-shirt. Up until then, I'd only worn a soft pullover bra, but I'd finally asked my mom for the real kind, the kind I saw on the other girls in the locker room. It fastened in the back with little hooks, and as I looked at myself in the mirror, I thought it made my head look like it was attached to someone else's grown-up body. What was the way to wear something you *had* to wear, but didn't want anyone to think about you wearing? That's what I was wondering as I turned away and thudded downstairs.

I swung the door open wide, expecting to see Sarah Nan mid-text, asking me what was taking so long—but it was Mr. Henckman in his Bruins cap. I jumped back.

He also looked surprised. "Oh, Lizzie. Hi," he said. "Could I speak to your mom?"

I thought I should say no. Shouldn't I say no? But I remembered my mom's words: *People like that want to connect, and they don't know how. I feel sorry for them.*

I found my mom in her study, leaning over her lesson plans at the computer.

"Mr. Henckman's here," I said.

She looked up. "Where?"

"At the door."

"You answered?"

Already I had the sinking feeling of having done something wrong. "I thought . . . ."

Mom pushed her chair back abruptly. "Wait here," she said.

I waited—ten seconds. Then, cautiously, I stepped out of the room and listened from around the corner.

". . . told you that we can't be in contact anymore," Mom was saying.

"David said that, but he's away now. You can talk to me for five minutes. Please."

I peeked around the corner. Mom had the door partway open, but through the gap I could see Mr. Henckman's loose jeans, and one of his plaid sleeves.

"That isn't appropriate," Mom told him, the way she might talk to one of her disobedient students. "I'm sorry. You have to go." She closed the door—but it didn't close all the way. Mr. Henckman's hand was stopping it.

"I'm not leaving . . ."

Mom pushed harder, but the hand pushed back, followed by both hands, then a shoulder reaching through. She made a sound I'd never heard her make before: a helpless cry as she struggled, as her feet slid on the little woven mat at the foot of the stairs, as Mr. Henckman started to come inside. Was this really happening? I couldn't move, or I *didn't* move. I just kept thinking that I must have it wrong somehow, I must be misunderstanding. I couldn't be seeing Mr. Henckman trying to force his way into our house.

"James!" Mom cried out, and suddenly Mr. Henckman's pushing went slack. She stumbled, striking her forehead on the edge of the door.

"Mom!" I rushed forward. She was on her knees, one hand over her eye, as Mr. Henckman tried to help her up.

"Laura," he said. My skin crawled.

"I'm all right." Mom pulled out of his grasp and rose shakily to her feet. "Just slipped . . ." I could see blood above her eyebrow. Why had she called for James when he wasn't even home?

"Mom," I said again, but Mr. Henckman talked over me.

"Laura, I'm sorry." The sight of the blood seemed to have brought him back to his senses. "I didn't . . ."

"Please go," Mom said. She kept her hand over her face.

Mr. Henckman looked helplessly at Mom, then at me. "Lizzie . . ."

"*Don't talk to her.*" Mom's free arm shot outward to shield me, pulling me behind her.

Mr. Henckman backed away, stumbled a little over the front step, then turned and fled down the walkway and onto the sidewalk.

"Mom?" I said, and that was when she started to cry. She

held me close with one arm, shaking, while the other held the cut on her forehead, which wouldn't need stitches but would take weeks to heal, and which you can still see faintly behind her bangs, even today. "It's all right," she kept saying, which made *me* start to cry. She cried, and I cried, and I felt the new, grown-up bra digging into my rib cage, even though I wasn't grown up enough to say *hey* or *stop* or *no* or to shut the door in the first place like I should have. Later, James would see Mom's face and say, "What the hell happened?" and Dad would go out to the yard with a shovel and dig up the rosebushes and toss them onto the Henckmans' driveway—and all I would be able to think about, all I can still think about, is my mom's voice as she called out *James!*, how reflexive it was, how she had known that Mr. Henckman would stop pushing if he thought my brother was there, how she didn't even bother calling for me.

CHAPTER 7

At the end of September, Ms. Faraher does her first CARP check-in. She sits at her desk with an oscillating fan pointed directly at her, even though it isn't that hot, and calls us up one at a time. While we wait, we take notes from some ancient textbooks, with permission to talk "at a low volume"—which means Michael Gorman is low-volume annoying me.

"Hey, Lizzie." He sits sideways in his seat, kicking the legs of my chair while I lean over my composition notebook. "Lizzie. Lizard Burger. Hey."

"*What*," I finally say.

"You like me, right?"

I roll my eyes and go back to my book. The cover is teal, with a picture of a squirrel under the title *Life Science for the Middle Grades*. We're supposed to read about classification—kingdom, species, genus, all that—and answer the questions at the end of the chapter.

"Whoa, that's mean." He kicks the legs of my chair some more. "Why are you so mean?"

Just ignore them was the advice Mom always gave me about annoying boys. I wish it worked better.

I turn a page that has a chunk of the corner torn out. Normally we don't use these books. They came from the long shelf at the back of the room, next to the empty terrarium and display of reptile skeletons, and the inside covers are filled with the names of students from back when they used to lend these out for the year. Ordinarily, Ms. Faraher would have handouts for us, or she would give us something digital. I think today she just wants to keep us busy.

"Do you even like anybody?" Michael asks. *Kick, kick.* "Or you think you're too good for us?"

His kicking has gradually angled my chair so now I'm crooked at the lab table. Why doesn't Ms. Faraher see?

As Ms. Faraher continues the CARP conferences—she's on Aidan now, who wants to do something about solar energy—what began as low-volume work gradually crescendos into full conversation. Ultimately, Ms. Faraher doesn't seem to mind. She fans herself with a folded paper and calls the next person. That's when I hear Michael snorting.

"Whoa!" he says, turning around to Ethan behind him. "Check out page eighty-six!"

More laughter. I use my thumb to lift the corners to 86, and I'm right: it's the human reproductive system. In the upper corner, above impossibly colorful diagrams of testes and ovaries, there's a photo of a boy and a girl with '90s hair and shorts laughing on the front steps of a school. A caption underneath reads, *Primary sex characteristics are present at birth, whereas secondary sex characteristics develop at puberty.*

"What are you birdbrains laughing at?" Chloe asks, turning around in her chair. I'll give this to Chloe: she doesn't take crap from people.

"Mine even has a drawing in it—look!" Michael squeals. Chloe looks.

"That's disgusting," she says.

"Hey, Lizard, check this out." He shoves the book toward me.

I shake my head. "No thanks."

"Come on." He starts kicking my chair again. "What, don't you want to know what a boy looks like? Or what a *girl* looks like?"

I hunch low over my notebook. My face is hot, and I just hope my hair is covering it. I hate that boys—generations of boys—have looked at these pictures and laughed. Marked them with their own pencils, even. How is it fair for Michael Gorman to know what's inside me? *Please call my name, please call me,* I beg Ms. Faraher with my best attempt at telepathy. But she's busy with Sami, rolling her chair over to the small shelf beside her desk and pulling out some extra books. It's never going to be my turn.

"Chloe," I say, still ignoring the kicking and the book

Michael is repeatedly shoving against my elbow, "what are you doing for CARP?"

Chloe sighs, as if my question is interrupting her from some important work, not from surreptitiously texting under her desk. "Something about magnets. My stepdad's helping me." She's clearly uninterested in doing anything to save me from Michael.

Aidan turns around in his seat. "What are you going to do, Lizzie?"

My chair vibrates with one last kick, and then Michael stops. Aidan isn't popular—he won the geography bee last year, which nobody thinks is cool—but apparently his attention is enough to turn Michael back to his empty notebook page. Does Aidan know he made that happen? I can't really tell.

"I'm still deciding," I say, just as—finally—Ms. Faraher calls my name.

I walk up to her desk, where a small student chair faces her. I sit, clutching my marbled science notebook. She leans away from me, her growing belly between us. The fan blows the stray hairs at the back of her neck that aren't caught up in her braid.

"So, tell me what you're thinking," she says.

I wish I really *could* tell her what I'm thinking, which is that Michael Gorman is a creep and I don't want to sit next to him anymore. But her face is tired and serious. I don't want to use my first chance alone with her for complaining. "Um . . ." I open my notebook to the list I made there yesterday:

- Do all living things ~~reproduce~~ seek a mate?
- What does it mean to find someone "cute"? (might not be science)
- How does an organism ~~know what to do~~
- Apple trees

I hadn't meant to leave it until the last minute, but every time I tried to come up with an idea, I got stuck. I'm still stuck.

"I've got a list," I offer, hoping she'll ask to see it.

"Great." She doesn't ask.

I hesitate. "Well . . . one idea I had was to do something with apple trees."

"What about apple trees?"

Eighth-grade Ms. Faraher sometimes doesn't seem as patient as sixth-grade Ms. Faraher. Or maybe it's just pregnant Ms. Faraher who's less patient.

"My family used to have a wild apple tree. I'm trying to grow some of the seeds, but it isn't really working." Since the first day of school, the seeds from inside that tiny apple have been wrapped in a damp paper towel on my windowsill, but they haven't grown at all. Not even a sprout.

"Okay." She nods.

Ask me about my other ideas, I think. *Ask me why my topics are about mating and cuteness*. If she asked, I would answer, *Everyone else seems to know and I don't*, and then she would invite me to stay with her for lunch or after school because she would finally see how much I need to talk to her, even though I haven't asked. *Tell me what you're thinking*, she would say, and I would tell her everything.

Ms. Faraher looks up from her clipboard. "Remember that this is a research project. When you're in high school, if you take honors, then you can design and conduct your own experiment that way with seeds."

My stomach lurches. *If* I take honors? Doesn't she know that of course I would take honors science—because of her? Doesn't she think I can do it? "I know."

"So what would you like to *research* about that apple tree? What question do you have?"

"I guess . . ." I look down at my notebook. The words don't look like words anymore, just strange, cryptic symbols written by a girl who thought this meeting was going to go differently. "I was wondering why some apple trees make sour apples and some make sweet ones. Why they aren't all sweet."

Ms. Faraher brightens. "Reproduction," she says.

I feel my cheeks go a little pink. "What?"

"Reproduction in apple trees—flowers, fruit, seeds . . .

I'd love for you to explore that. Did you know that my family has an apple orchard?"

"Yes," I say—wouldn't she remember that I know?—but she's scribbling away on her clipboard and doesn't hear me. The best I could have wished was for Ms. Faraher to be excited about my idea. But what she's excited about is not what I had in mind. I didn't even get to ask her about my other ideas.

"You know, the thing about apples," she says, "is that they don't grow true to seed. If you plant a seed from a McIntosh apple, you probably won't get a McIntosh apple tree. Did you know that?"

I shake my head. I write it down in my notebook: *apples not true to seed.*

"It's because apples are heterozygous—we'll be learning about that later this year. So your seeds, if they grow, will most likely produce different fruit than the tree they came from. Of course," she adds, "that part doesn't happen on its own. It takes two apple trees to make more apples."

Now I'm turning pink for a different reason. "Oh."

Ms. Faraher sets the clipboard aside. "Is there anything else?"

It takes two apple trees. Ms. Faraher thinks I don't know how things work. But then, I don't know how things work—not really. I know, but I don't understand. Maybe I can still ask her. Maybe she *wants* me to ask her. Wouldn't a science teacher know, better than anyone?

Is it weird that I don't "like" anyone? That's what I want to ask. *Am I just sour inside, and not sweet?*

"Is it . . . ," I start. Ms. Faraher waits, and I think I should have started the sentence differently. "What if a person . . ."

There's a crash, and hundreds of tiny skitterings across the floor tiles. Michael and Ethan stand frozen in the back of the room by the shattered terrarium, which has sent blue and gray pebbles all across the floor.

"Nobody move." Ms. Faraher jumps to her feet—impressively, for someone so pregnant—but of course everyone is moving, climbing up from their seats to see what happened.

"Ohmygod, was there a fish in there?" Chloe shrieks.

"Since when do you keep fish in a *terrarium*, Chloe?" Ethan demands—but he looks scared, waiting for whatever Ms. Faraher's verdict will be.

"Stop," she says to Michael, who, even with everyone's eyes on him, is trying to inch away from the trouble. "There's broken glass."

Michael starts. "We were just—"

"I didn't ask what you were doing." Ms. Faraher crosses the room to the phone. "I asked you to stay where you are." The room is silent while Ms. Faraher calls the office and asks if Mr. Haynes, the custodian, can come. I sit awkwardly in the chair facing her desk, my question still half formed on my tongue.

Ms. Faraher hangs up, looks at Michael and Ethan frozen in place at the back of the room, and sighs. "Let me get my broom for some of the bigger pieces. Excuse me, Lizzie." She moves around me, away from me.

My meeting is over.

I slip back to my seat. Open my book. Stare at the page without seeing it. Behind my sternum, I feel the pressure of my question like something too big I tried to swallow.

After school, I wait in the front turnaround for Mom to pick me up. The elementary school lets out forty-five minutes after us, so I'm used to hanging out in the library or cafeteria while I wait. In sixth grade, I used to stay in Ms. Faraher's room and water her plants—but she leaves right away now, her classroom already closed and dark by the time I arrive.

Mom's running late today. While I wait, I open my composition notebook again. *Apples not true to seed.* When I snuck back to my old house and swiped the apple, it was because I thought I could regrow that exact same tree and have it for my own. Does this mean I never can?

"Lizzie!"

Mom has the car pulled up in front of me. She moves her purse aside as I climb in.

"How did your CARP meeting go?"

I drop into my seat. "Fine."

"Fine, and . . . ?" Mom is a speech-language pathologist,

otherwise known as a "speech teacher." She's also an extrovert, which means she's all about communication. Or the talking part, at least. Sometimes I think she's not so great at the listening part.

"Fine, *and* Michael Gorman ruined it."

"Michael? How?"

"He knocked over a terrarium."

She sighs, shaking her head. Whenever I tell Mom about the latest trouble Michael is in, she seems sorry, like it's misfortune and not his own fault. "One day, things are going to click for that kid."

Is it bad that I don't care if they "click"? I don't care about his problems. I just want to be as far away from him as possible.

Mom would be disappointed in me if I said that. I'm not supposed to know this, because it's confidential, but Mom worked with Michael back in elementary school when he had a speech impediment. She said he had *a lot going on.* What she didn't say but I understood was that I needed to be more understanding.

"He was being a jerk before that, too," I say.

"Being a jerk how?"

The AC is on, blowing cool air onto my knees. I don't have the words to tell her about the illustrations in the book. "He kept kicking my chair."

Mom doesn't answer right away. "Do you think maybe he likes you?"

"Mom."

"I'm not saying you like him back! Boys aren't as mature as girls. Sometimes the only way they know—"

"Mom, I hate him more than any person *alive*."

She sighs.

"What?"

"Nothing," Mom says. Of course, it isn't nothing. "I just hope that, when it's time, you'll give people a chance. That's all."

By "people," she means boys. "I don't see why I should give someone a chance when they haven't given me any reason to."

We're in the Maze now. Left, right, right. So many turns. "You have such a beautiful heart, Lizzie," Mom says at last. "Don't close yourself off."

I'm irritated now. I don't need to hear about my beautiful heart. "Why shouldn't I?"

"Because you might miss out on meeting a really great person."

Like Mr. Henckman? I don't say it out loud, but I think we both hear it echoing for the rest of the silent car ride.

Back at home, while Mom meditates across the hall, I lie in bed staring up at the ceiling.

Do you think maybe he likes you?

What does it mean to "like" someone?

I've been trying to figure it out ever since the start of seventh grade, which is when the boys started growing. They got taller. At first, I didn't notice, maybe because I was already so tall; it took them longer to catch up to me. Maybe it was because even though they grew taller, they didn't act any different, so when I looked at them, I saw the same shrimpy kids who flipped up their eyelids to make girls scream and laughed at other people when they tripped and fell. When Sarah Nan and Chloe talked about crushes, I didn't understand what was suddenly worth noticing.

The first time I saw the change—really saw it—was in gym class last year with Ms. Ardvinson. That class was the worst, and *she* was the worst. We were doing the fitness test that happens every spring: run the mile, see how high you can jump, show how deep you can stretch. And chin-ups. I've never been able to do one—that's what happens when your height clears the five-foot mark by fourth grade—so I didn't even really try when Ms. Ardvinson had me step up to the bar for my turn. I dropped pretty quickly. I tried not to watch as she made a note on her clipboard.

After me was Ned. In second grade, he had cried when he spilled his chicken noodle soup on the floor of the cafeteria. But that day, in seventh grade, he hopped right up to the bar, did ten chin-ups, and then did more. When he started to slow down, he let go with one arm so that he was hanging like a chimpanzee, shook out his free arm, then switched and did the same thing on the other side. Then he resumed the chin-ups. I could see the muscles stretching the sleeves of his T-shirt, and I thought, *Boys have muscles already?* I felt the same way three weeks later when I got my first period. I couldn't understand how it had happened.

I hear the guitar across the hall, the waves breaking against the sand. *Give people a chance.* Mom meditates every day, but it hasn't helped with her concern that I've closed off my heart. Have I? Sometimes it's not just Mr. Henckman but the whole world that feels like a threat: things coming at me that I don't want and don't understand, fast and hard as a dodgeball. How do I protect myself against the world?

I know one way. Mom won't like it—and maybe that makes it even better: I can sign up for Women's Self-Defense.

CHAPTER 8

~

Eight a.m. feels extra early on a Saturday. I snooze my alarm twice before finally hauling myself out of bed. I thought Mom would be the one to take me to the community center, but instead it's Dad who beeps the horn from the garage as I run downstairs, pulling my hair back in a hasty ponytail. He already has the engine running when I plunk down in the passenger seat. We start moving before I'm even buckled.

"It only takes five minutes to get there," I say irritably.

Dad cranes his neck to look behind us, taking care to avoid the hedges. Our new driveway curves around the trunk of an old tree, so you have to go slowly. "We're picking up Sarah Nan."

"*Sarah Nan* is taking the class?"

Dad glances at me briefly. "Daria thought it would be good for her, too."

I'm a little surprised that Sarah Nan's mom signed her up for a women's self-defense class. She's always saying, "The power you need is already inside you" and stuff like that.

When we pull into Sarah Nan's driveway, she's there

on the steps waiting for us. I get out so we can sit in back together, but she just says, "Thanks," and takes the front seat.

"Good morning," she says cheerfully to Dad as she sits down beside him.

"Morning," Dad says, surprised. I climb in back and shut the door. Dad catches my eyes in the rearview mirror, but mercifully, he doesn't say anything else.

The Wendover Community Center is a yellow-brick building with a big mural by the main doors. The mural is supposed to be inspirational and community-oriented, but because it was painted by kids, the heads and faces and bodies are all out of proportion, and they look creepy. Plus, somebody came by and spray-painted "weenies," as Sabrina and Carly would say, on a bunch of the figures, and whoever cleaned up afterward could only partially get the paint off. The smudges are still there.

Inside, the ceilings are high and echoey. Sarah Nan says we have to go to the locker room so she can change. I came already wearing sweats and a loose T-shirt—lockers rooms are my personal nightmare—but since she wants me to come with her, I do.

"I disagree with the whole philosophy behind this class," Sarah Nan pronounces, stripping off her shirt. She has on a gray sports bra, even though there isn't much to hold up. She's self-conscious about that. I would gladly trade places with her. "I think it's sexist."

"How do you know? We haven't even started yet."

"I mean self-defense classes in general. They teach women that *we're* the ones responsible for our own safety, and if anything bad happens, then it's our own fault for not stopping it somehow or being better prepared. You know who should be defending us? Men."

"What, like bodyguards?" I ask. "*That's* sexist."

"No, silly. I mean by creating a culture where women aren't treated as sex objects. You get more men who respect women as equals, you get more protection from creeps. It's like herd immunity."

"That sounds like Daria talking," I say.

Sarah Nan stiffens a little at having been caught agreeing with her mom. "Well, she's not wrong about *everything*."

I watch as she tugs a new shirt over her head. "If that's how you feel, then why are you even here?" I ask.

Sarah Nan looks at me sharply. "Because *you're* here," she says.

My whole face goes hot. "What?"

"Your mom called my mom and said you were set on taking this class and she didn't want you taking it alone. Didn't she tell you that?"

"No." Unexpectedly, Mom agreed pretty readily when I told her about the class. I thought she might think this was one more example of me letting fear rule my life, but her main concern was that it was for ages fourteen to eighteen, and that it might be "intense." I reminded her that I'll be fourteen in just two more weeks. I promised I could handle it.

Now I know: she actually *was* worried. Why didn't she just tell me? I slump against the lockers. "Well, sorry you got dragged into it."

Sarah Nan shuts the locker door with a rusty creak. "It's okay," she says as I stare at the bench. "Hey—Lizzie—it's okay." I look up at her. "I'm sorry. I didn't mean it like that. I'm here, right?"

True—she is here.

"Lizzie?" she asks. "When your neighbor—" She stops, her hand gripping the combination lock. "What do you think he . . . ?"

"I don't know," I tell her.

Sarah Nan puts a hand on my shoulder. "Come on," she says. "Let's go learn to kick some balls."

Women's Self-Defense is in the main gym, and when Sarah Nan and I get there, it looks as though most of the class has already arrived—there are ten of us, all high schoolers except for Sarah Nan and me. Two of them, twins, are fake-boxing one another on one of the gym's blue floor mats. As Sarah Nan and I approach, a few others look at us like we might be in the wrong place. Which it's starting to feel like we are.

"All right, everyone, gather round!"

A tall, gaunt woman with a white mullet and purple tracksuit spreads her arms wide and motions for us to join her at center court.

No, I say in my head, and then I'm saying it aloud to Sarah Nan. "No, no, no."

It's the Aardvark.

Sarah Nan starts over, but I grab her by the arm. "This is a bad dream, right? This isn't really happening."

"Let go—you're being weird." She shakes herself loose. "So what if it's Ms. Ardvinson? She's not going to give you a B here."

Sarah Nan has never had any problem with PE. Of course. "Is she even qualified for this? Doesn't she need, like, special training?"

"Why do you think she isn't trained? Ms. Ardvinson!"

She waves, and Ms. Ardvinson's skeletal face brightens with a horse-toothed smile reserved for students who can do chin-ups. "Hi, Sarah! Hi, Lizzie."

I could die right now. Am I dying? I go inside myself and try to feel my pulse, to see if I am having a heart attack, or at least feeling faint. But, as usual, I am chronically solid and healthy, even when the worst thing in the world is happening.

Ms. Ardvinson claps her hands once and rubs them together, as if we're outside on a chilly field. "Good morning," she says. "I'm Ms. Ardvinson. I teach physical education at Hillside, and as some of you know, I coach the girls' field hockey team at Wendover High. Welcome to self-defense class. I've been teaching this course for fifteen years, and I want to begin by emphasizing that the purpose of this course is not only to learn physical skills, but also to build confidence in your ability to handle a threatening situation." She pauses, scanning the circle before her. "A lot of that confidence comes from the positive feedback and support we give each other, so I hope this will be a good group. Let's begin by going around and sharing our names, pronouns if you want to, and what you hope to get out of this class."

"Why pronouns—isn't this self-defense for *women*?" one of the girls asks. A few others giggle.

"That's the traditional name for this kind of course, which so far the community center hasn't wanted to change. However, the class is open to LGBTQ+ and nonbinary individuals—and most importantly, it creates a welcoming environment to ask. Now, let's begin."

One of the twins goes first. "I'm Alexa, she/her," she says. "And I'm here because I flunked PE and I need the credits to graduate."

"Ohmygod, *me too*!" the girl across from her exclaims.

"Same here!"

As we go around the circle, it turns out that most of the

participants are here for PE credits. Ms. Ardvinson doesn't look impressed.

"You don't have to tell us why you're here," she says, for the third time. "Not everyone will feel comfortable sharing. Just what you hope to learn."

Sarah Nan is next. "I'm Sarah, she/her," she says. "I'm in eighth grade at Hillside, and . . . yeah! I'm just here to learn self-defense, I guess!"

I should have known she'd be her usual charming self. The high school girls whisper to each other: *Aw, eighth grade! So cute!*

It's my turn. I feel the Aardvark's eyes on me. She must be wondering what her worst student is doing here, on a Saturday. "I'm Lizzie," I say. "I'm in eighth grade, too. Oh, and I'm she/her." Ms. Ardvinson said we didn't have to say why we were here, but so far everyone else has. Am I the only one who's actually here for a *real* reason? If so, I don't want them to know that. "Um, I guess I want to learn how to protect myself."

My cheeks flush. What a pathetic answer.

Nobody says I'm cute.

"Okay, and—" Ms. Ardvinson points to the girl next to me, another high schooler. She's wearing a red bandanna, dark eyeshadow, and plug earrings.

"I'm Kendall." Her voice is low and deadpan. "That's all I want to say."

"That's just fine." Ms. Ardvinson nods. "Thank you, everyone. Now, this first class is going to be more talking, but I promise we'll get some movement in before the hour's up." She bends over and picks up a stack of papers from the floor in front of her. "Everyone can take a copy . . ."

She invites us to sit down on the blue mats while we go over the syllabus together. Ten Saturdays, with a break for Thanksgiving, finishing up the second Saturday in December. *December.* That's when my CARP presentation will happen, and James will come home for winter break—forever away from now.

"What's 'dynamic simulation'?" Alexa asks, flipping ahead to the last page—or maybe that's not Alexa. It might be Melissa, her sister.

"Good question," Ms. Ardvinson says. "For our last class, we'll be collaborating with the Wendover Police to bring in a trained officer for you to practice with in a simulated scenario."

Sarah Nan leans in to whisper to me, "That is *way* messed up."

When I looked up the course online, I saw those words, *dynamic simulation*, in the catalog description, but I didn't think that could possibly mean what it sounded like. Maybe this whole thing was a mistake.

One of the other girls raises her hand. "Won't that, like, hurt him?"

"He will be very thoroughly padded," Ms. Ardvinson says. "In all areas."

Kendall snorts.

"I know it can be scary to imagine," Ms. Ardvinson says. "One objective of the simulation is, in fact, to create a real sense of fear."

"You *want* us to be afraid?" Sarah Nan asks.

"The typical fear response is fight, flight, or freeze. With this class, we want you to know your own fear response, and then internalize the experience of escaping a threatening situation while in an adrenalized state. You learn that you can do it, and more importantly, your *body* learns that you can do it."

I don't need this class to teach me that my fear response is freeze. How do I know my body will do anything different after ten classes? What if I just freeze again?

"December is a long way away," Ms. Ardvinson continues. "It's my job to prepare you before then, which I promise I'll do."

I look up, surprised. The Aardvark never talks that way in PE class—like she's actually supporting us in something we don't know how to do. When it was chin-up time, she sent us straight to the bar, no pep talk.

"Now," Ms. Ardvinson says, "before we go any further, let's do a quick warm-up run: four laps around the building. Everybody up!"

"Around the *building*?" Alexa—or Melissa?—says.

"You want your PE credits, you'll have to earn them," Ms. Ardvinson says. "Four laps! Go!"

"Are you serious?" Kendall is still on the floor as everyone else rises clumsily to their feet.

"Go! Go! Go!" A whistle emerges from behind the zipper of Ms. Ardvinson's jacket, and she's blowing it at us.

This is more what I expected.

My legs are half-asleep from sitting cross-legged, but I hurry to catch up with the pack as they burst through the gym doors and take off down the hallway.

"Not jogging—*running*!"

I catch up to Sarah Nan.

"I can*not* believe we're going to be doing this until *December*," she says.

"I'm not," I say. "After today, I'm quitting."

Sarah Nan stops short; I skid to a stop, too, almost falling over. "Are you kidding?" she asks. "You can't leave me here by myself."

We're outside now, on the sidewalk that circles the building. It's sunny, but still cool; I can feel my arms prickling with goose bumps. "You can quit, too," I say. "You don't even want to be here."

"After everything my mom went through to get me out of morning gymnastics? She'd kill me. Plus, did you see those high school girls? They're going to *remember* us next year. Do you want them to see us as those two little eighth graders who couldn't—" She cuts herself off as Kendall puffs past us, cursing to herself, the wide cuffs of her pant legs swishing.

Sarah Nan continues, "You've got to let go of this Ms. Ardvinson thing. So she's not all sunshine and hugs like Ms. Faraher—big deal. Are you really going to quit just because she gave you a B that one time?"

I prickle at the comparison to Ms. Faraher. "No, I'm quitting because she's the worst."

Sarah Nan, long-suffering, rolls her eyes. "Look: You were the one who wanted to take this class, right? Not your mom, not my mom—you."

I nod.

"So are you really going to let some Aardvark with a mullet ruin this for you? She's the one who can teach you what you want to learn," she says. "So learn it."

You learn that you can do it, and more importantly, your body learns that you can do it. If there really is a way not to freeze, then Sarah Nan is right: I do want to learn. "Okay," I say.

"Okay, good." With that, Sarah Nan picks up running again, before the other girls can lap us. I follow.

"You should give Ms. Ardvinson a chance," Sarah Nan says as we round the corner toward the back parking lot. "Maybe you have something in common."

"Like *what*." I've got a stitch in my side already. My chest aches.

"Well, I'm pretty sure she's not married," Sarah Nan says, and then she picks up her pace, leaving me behind to wonder if it's true that the Aardvark—although I would never, ever ask her—might have even more answers for me than I thought.

CHAPTER 9

~

Ms. Faraher is absent today. "Baby appointment, probably," Chloe says, which for some reason irritates me. She doesn't know for a *fact* that it's a baby appointment.

What is a baby appointment even for? I feel really clueless sometimes.

I worry briefly that we'll be assigned more note-taking from the vandalized textbooks, but instead, the sub, a young guy named Mr. Le, announces that he'll be taking us to the library to work on our CARP research.

The library is downstairs and past the main office. As we file through the lobby, the boys jump to try to touch a low beam that runs across the ceiling. What is it that makes them *have* to do that? I follow behind Chloe and Sami, close enough that I'm not alone, but not so close that I'm actually with them.

"She's kind of old to be having a baby, isn't she?" Sami asks.

"Not that old, I don't think," Chloe says. "But yeah, her biological clock must be ticking. She probably told Mr. Faraher, 'It's now or never, mister!'"

Ms. Faraher kept her last name, so there is no "Mr. Faraher." But I don't tell them that.

As soon as we're in the library, Michael and Ethan start chasing each other around the stacks; Chloe and Sami claim the quiet corner by the reference section where they can secretly be on their phones. Aidan goes to the circulation desk to ask the librarian for help. I head for the magazines.

I tried researching Ms. Faraher's idea about apple reproduction. It was interesting, learning about how my tree might have gotten there—probably not wild, in fact, but planted long ago for making hard cider. I don't think I want to spend the next three months on that, though. I'm still stuck on one of my other questions: *What does it mean to find someone "cute"?* Maybe I could research what attracts one moose to another moose, or snake to snake, or bird to bird. Is it just the size of their antlers, or the brightness of their scales? But even the plainer birds still find someone. Is it all just hormones? Is there really any thinking, any deciding?

All this leads me to wonder if maybe I should start with the most mystifying organism of all.

Most of our school's magazine collection is educational—*National Geographic* and *Discover*. But there are also a few sports and celebrity magazines meant to appeal to middle schoolers. I scan the display, and I see the type I was looking for: *Teen Girl*.

Fall Fashion Issue: You'll Never Guess What's Back!

The Ultimate Skincare Routine!

Quiz: Is it a crush?

I glance around to make sure no one's looking before

I slide the issue from the shelf. A girls' magazine might not seem like a scientific source, but it feels like research to me.

I open to "Is it a crush?"

How often do you think about him?

("Or her," I can imagine Sarah Nan adding indignantly.)

How do you feel when you are around him? (Shy? Outgoing? Flirty?)

Are you putting more effort into your appearance?

Ugh. I flip past the quiz. The next page I land on is "Ask *Teen Girl*!"

Dear Teen Girl, the first person writes. *I'm thirteen. My friends are getting crushes on boys. It's all they talk about. I go along with them, but I actually really don't get it! Is there something wrong with me?—Left Out*

My heart pounds. I could have written that exact letter. I even do a brief memory scan: *Did* I write this letter? It sounds so much like me.

"Ugh, Michael, get *away*!"

Michael is standing over Chloe and Sami with a hardcover human anatomy book opened wide. The cover shows a human-shaped silhouette with a heart and various paths of veins and arteries. The page it's open to clearly shows something else.

Before Mr. Le can go over, Michael slams the book shut, laughing, and dashes off.

I look down and realize I'm holding the magazine to my chest. I have to read this before Michael or someone else interrupts me. What advice did they give to "Left Out"?

I slink back behind the magazine rack.

Dear Left Out,

There is nothing wrong with you! In fact, it's good to wait on dating until you're definitely ready. What's the rush? Once you're ready to put yourself out there, boys will be looking for someone new, so you'll be fresh and exciting! You may also be questioning your sexuality at this point, and that's okay, too. Please reach out to a trusted adult, such as a parent, teacher, or guidance counselor, if you feel like—

I stuff the magazine back onto the shelf. Then I cover it with an issue of *National Geographic* about the International Space Station and hurry away toward the computers.

Boys will be looking for someone new. As if girls are the latest Xbox or something. And what did they mean "once you're ready"? What if you're never ready?

I spend the rest of class aimlessly googling about apple trees and the history of the Granny Smith.

When Mr. Le dismisses us, I'm the first one out the door— and I nearly walk straight into the Boy in the Skirt.

He dodges me just in time to avoid a collision. "Whoa."

"Sorry," I say, but he's already moved past me down the hall, his spine straight and purposeful, his gray skirt billowing, clearing a path around him.

It's not even that he's being bold, I think as I gather my books closer to my chest and head to math. He's just doing it. He's an eighth-grade boy wearing a skirt. Why can't I stop worrying about the ways I'm different?

I wish I'd said more than "sorry." I wish we had even one class together so I could find a way to talk to him. I wouldn't even ask him about the skirt. Not at first.

As I turn the corner, Sarah Nan and Ned walk by across the hallway. They don't see me. Sarah Nan is talking animatedly, and Ned has his arm around her waist; her T-shirt is short enough that his thumb is touching her skin. Since we were little, she's dreamed of being part of a couple, always wanting to play pretend as a princess finding her prince. I played those games, too. But until Sarah Nan started dating Ned, I didn't know she really *meant* it.

Is there something lying dormant in me, like those rosebushes, just waiting for the right shift in season?

Or is something inside me missing?

CHAPTER 10

～

"No!"

It's our second self-defense class, and Kendall is shouting. The rest of us are on the floor doing push-ups because we *didn't* shout.

Ms. Ardvinson is very emphatic about the importance of shouting in an attack situation. Last class, after our run around the building, she told us that too often, women don't shout because they're embarrassed, or because they second-guess themselves. *We've been socialized not to be loud*, she said. I guess she's right. Even practicing here, everyone is shy, each of us afraid to be the only one shouting out. Kendall doesn't mind being the only one, though, which is why she's practicing her moves in front of the mirror while the rest of us are struggling on the floor.

". . . ten!" Ms. Ardvinson finishes counting, and I collapse as my arms give out underneath me. I don't know how I'm going to make it through today. On top of the push-up punishment, I have my period, which means the cramps are raging. I've seen some girls use cramps to get out of PE class—whether they actually had cramps or not—but I think it would be way more embarrassing, and not even worth it, to have someone know the private thing going on inside you.

"Now, let that serve as a lesson," Ms. Ardvinson says, as the high school girls groan on the floor. "*Yet another lesson* on the importance of shouting. It can save your life, and it can save you from push-ups. Now, let's practice the blocks and parries from last week."

While everyone grumbles, Sarah Nan sits up, dusting off her palms. She, of course, wasn't winded by ten push-ups. "I am *so sick* of all this blame-the-victim stuff."

"What do you mean?" I ask, even though I'm not interested in more of her thoughts about why self-defense is worthless.

Sarah Nan grabs two strike pads for practicing and goes over to the far wall with me. "Punishing us when we don't shout? Come on. It's like saying that if you don't scream loud enough, then it's your own fault if you get attacked. Want me to go first?"

"Sure."

Sarah Nan hands me the pads, which I swipe at her from various angles so she can block me with her forearms. *Thud. Thud. Thud.* So far, we've been doing a lot of work with blocking, and learning how to escape different kinds of holds—like if someone tries to put their arm around your shoulders, how to spin away and snap their wrist back. It's exciting to know that there's something you can do, no matter how awkward or out of shape you are. But I also get a sinking feeling sometimes. Does all this mean that Mom and I could have done something differently that day with Mr. Henckman? Does it mean we *should* have?

"You can go faster, you know," Sarah Nan says, so I take a sudden swipe at her head that she has to duck to avoid. "Hey!"

"Just so you know," I tell her, "my mom didn't shout. Okay? And I didn't, either. So the Aardvark is right."

"Lizzie!" Sarah Nan's expression is pure surprise.

I let my arms drop to my sides. "What."

"Lizzie," she says again. "He tried to break into your *house*. He hurt your mom. That's not your fault."

I want to believe her—she sounds so sure about it—but I can't really think about it as my insides start clenching up into another cramp. I grit my teeth.

"Are you crying?" Sarah Nan asks.

I shake my head. "Cramps," I say, and this one is so bad, I have to crouch down.

"Is this normal?" Sarah Nan kneels in front of me. "I'm pretty sure it's not."

I try to concentrate on my breathing. Puberty must be a baffling experience for Sarah Nan, who's never had any of the things in the books—growth spurts, pimples, awkwardness—actually happen to her.

"It's fine. I'm better now." I start to stand, but Sarah Nan puts her hands on my shoulders and forces me back down.

"Tell Ardvinson you need a break. It's just going to happen again."

"I don't want her to know."

"She's a woman, too."

"Who's *old*," I point out, as Ms. Ardvinson comes up behind us.

"Taking a rest, ladies?"

I pop up from the ground, and this time Sarah Nan can't stop me. "No, I just have a—"

"Cramps," Sarah Nan interrupts. "She has cramps."

"Sarah!"

Ms. Ardvinson studies me as my cheeks blaze. Maybe she's evaluating the likelihood that I'm faking, the way she would for any kid in her usual PE class. Maybe she just likes to make me sweat.

"Here," she finally says. "Try this." She picks up a long, flat cushion from against the wall. Sarah Nan urges me back to the floor, and Ms. Ardvinson sits down cross-legged in front of me.

"Sit like this, then bend forward and rest your head on the cushion."

She shows me. She's really flexible for someone so old. How old *is* she, even? Her hair is all white, but looking at her up close, she's not totally shriveled.

She passes me the cushion. Then, rising back to her feet, she turns to the rest of the class and bellows, "I still want to hear SHOUTING!"

"I hate you," I tell Sarah Nan, tucking the cushion under me.

She pats me on the head. "You're welcome."

I feel silly hugging a giant pillow on the floor while everyone else is up shouting and punching—but Ms. Ardvinson is right. The pressure of my folded legs on my abdomen eases the cramps.

Kendall appears at my side and presses a bottle of ibuprofen into my palm. "That's the other kind of self-defense, you know," she says.

I pop open the bottle. Usually I choke when I try to swallow pills without water, but today I don't even care. "What?"

Kendall drops to the floor next to me and Sarah Nan, stretching her legs out as she leans against the wall. Her sneakers are tattered and colored in with black Sharpie. "Talk about your period," she says, swishing the bangs out of her eyes. "Guys get grossed out and leave you alone. I do it all the time. That's how I got out of English yesterday—told Mr. Leary I needed a tampon." She laughs.

"Guys shouldn't be grossed out," Sarah Nan says. "It's natural."

Kendall shrugs. "I'm just saying, it's a secret weapon. Use it if you need to."

Sarah Nan and Kendall watch the other girls practice for a moment, while I rest my face on my folded arms.

"You're really good at all this," Sarah Nan tells Kendall.

"Yeah, I've taken self-defense before. It was different, though. It wasn't just about fighting back—it was also about relationships and stuff, setting boundaries, communicating, all of that. And we *definitely* didn't do push-ups. Like, at all."

"What did they say about relationships?" Sarah Nan asks, but then Ms. Ardvinson calls out for everyone to finish their drills and come back to the circle.

"Except you, Lizzie," she adds.

Sitting out for a while isn't so bad, or even that embarrassing. It's different watching the class than being in it. Ms. Ardvinson begins by reviewing the first move she ever taught us, the defensive stance: one foot dropped back; one hand raised to block or parry, the other held close to the body in a fist, prepared to strike. After that, it's practicing hammer fists on a boxing dummy: an orange man-torso with no arms and a scowling face. Kendall volunteers to go first.

"Nice work!" Ms. Ardvinson exclaims as Kendall's fist slams down and the dummy vibrates on its post.

I can't remember ever hearing her compliment people that way in PE. There she always acted as though we were the last few obstacles between her and retirement somewhere on the Cape. But here, as she nods with approval while each girl takes a turn, I think I see a flicker of happiness. Maybe self-defense is what she actually *cares* about teaching.

After about ten minutes, I'm ready to join in again. I approach the circle around Ms. Ardvinson, who's demonstrating sweep kicks and snap kicks. She sees me take my place next to Sarah Nan and meets my eyes, but doesn't say anything.

She has us practice kicking the air a few times, all of us shouting "No!" simultaneously.

"No need for the flourish, Sarah," she says. "That's just wasted energy."

Sarah Nan sulks off to the side with me as we pair up for practice. Now we're using the cushion I was hugging as a block to kick.

"You go first this time," Sarah Nan says, hoisting the cushion up in front of her. "Go ahead, kick me."

I shift my weight, draw my leg up, and kick, trying to make the action come from the knee the way Ms. Ardvinson showed us. "No," I say, shyly.

Sarah Nan rolls her eyes. "Ugh. Lizzie, if you're going to buy into this shouting thing, the least you could do is *actually* shout. Do you even know how to do that?"

"Sure I do." Her question makes me think, though. When *was* the last time I really raised my voice—at anyone?

"Okay, so? Do it!" Sarah Nan hunches her shoulders, hopping from side to side. "Come on, kick me. Kick me."

I try to ignore her and concentrate. I think about Michael Gorman calling me "Lizard Burger." "No!" I say, and I kick the cushion.

"Keep going! I'm a bad guy, grrr!"

I remember how I felt on the playground when Michael said *squeeeeeze*: So surprised I couldn't even believe what he meant. Then so ashamed. I kick the bolster again. "No!" Again. "NO!"

"*Good*, Lizzie," Ms. Ardvinson says as she passes by, and I'm so surprised I almost fall over.

"Did that just happen?" I ask Sarah Nan as Ms. Ardvinson continues on.

Sarah Nan smiles at me. "See?" She does her "bad guy" imitation again and gets me to go a few more times, but I'm distracted now and can't concentrate. Good, Lizzie. She really noticed me.

After class, Sarah Nan and I stand just inside the front entrance to the community center, waiting for Daria to pick us up. Sarah Nan's busy on her phone—probably with Ned— while I watch the sparrows hopping in and out of the gaps in the chain-link fence that separates the community center from the retirement village next door. Kendall's sitting on a wooden bench next to the fence, curled into herself against the wind.

I'm wondering if I should suggest to Sarah Nan that we go out and sit with Kendall when a beat-up sedan pulls up in front of her. Kendall stands—must be her ride—and a tall girl with blue-dyed hair emerges from the driver's side, smiling.

She says something to Kendall that I can't hear, and the

two of them kiss each other. It's a kiss that lasts awhile. When it's over, Kendall is smiling, too, in a way I haven't seen her smile before.

Sarah Nan hasn't even looked up from her phone, so I don't say anything as the two of them get in the blue-haired girl's car and drive away. I'm surprised—not that it's a girl Kendall kissed, but that it was anyone at all. The way she stands apart in class, the way she rolls her eyes and says everything with such blunt seriousness . . . I didn't expect her to be interested in kissing. I guess all kinds of people can be.

"What's it like?" Sarah Nan asks abruptly.

"What's what like?"

She doesn't answer right away. She sways a little where she stands, working her lips around like she's trying to hold something in. "Your period," she mumbles finally.

"You still don't have it?" Sarah Nan and I stopped talking about this stuff last year, when she got closer with Chloe. I assumed she'd gotten it and just hadn't told me.

Already, she's back on her phone. "Never mind."

"No, sorry, I didn't—" I remember that when we used to talk about it, Sarah Nan was always excited about this thing that was going to happen to us. I wasn't. I kick my sneaker against the tiles, and it squeaks louder than I meant it to. "It's not very interesting," I assure her. "Just happens."

"Try telling my mom that," Sarah Nan says, still focused

on her screen. "She's all 'Yay, womanhood!' and 'Cycle of life!' That sort of thing. If I don't start soon, I think she's going to have a meltdown. She's afraid I work so hard at gymnastics that I've thrown everything off and, like, stunted my growth or something."

"In that case, sign *me* up for gymnastics."

She laughs. "Oh, Lizzie." She holds up her phone. "Here—self-defense selfie."

We put our heads together and make look-at-us smiles. When she shows the photo to me, my head looks bigger than hers, and one of my eyes is squinched more than the other. But it's okay. The fact that she took our picture means she isn't embarrassed to show that she spent her Saturday hanging out with me.

CHAPTER 11

October fifth—my birthday. When Mom picks me up in the front turnaround at school, she barely waits for me to buckle my seat belt before pulling away. It's parent-teacher conferences tonight, so she has to be back at the elementary school by six thirty.

"Let's go!" she says, pausing to wave along some hesitant sixth graders at a crosswalk. Once they've gone, we lurch forward onto the main road, where she calms down a little.

"How was your day?" she asks.

"Fine." I scan through the details I'd want to share. "Sarah Nan invited me to sleep over on Saturday." She also offered to "tutor" me in math while I'm there, which I was less excited about, but I decided to focus on the fact that she remembered my birthday and wants to celebrate it.

"That's great," Mom says. It seems like she only half heard me.

When we walk in the door, Dad is at the counter, licking chocolate off the side of his hand. Two cake pans, freshly filled with batter, are propped on wire racks over a countertop with a heavy and likely accidental dusting of flour. He must've come home from work early.

"You didn't finish yet?" Mom sets her briefcase on one of the kitchen chairs.

Dad adjusts one of the pans on the rack and says cheerfully, "They're just about to go in."

"Now?" Mom repeats. "They won't be ready in time."

"It's only twenty minutes. I checked."

"You have to let them *cool* before you frost them."

Dad's shoulders deflate a little as he looks at the shiny round faces of the cake batter. "I guess we can have it later . . ."

I feel sorry for him. "I don't mind," I say, but Mom is already banging the cupboards around getting ready to heat up the meat sauce for tonight's spaghetti.

"Can you move, please?" she says to Dad, who's blocking the utensil drawer.

Maybe it's my own fault that my birthday doesn't feel special. I told Mom it didn't matter that she had to go out tonight for conferences. I told Dad it didn't matter what kind of cake he made. I told James it was fine that his present would be arriving late because he didn't get it to the post office in time. I tried so hard not to make a big deal out of it. Maybe I tried *too* hard.

Mom shakes a fistful of spaghetti out of the box. "I thought you were starting it as soon as you got home."

"I was, but it called for espresso powder, so I had to go back—"

"What recipe are you *using*?"

"It had five stars . . ."

It's my birthday, I want to say to them, as they stand in the kitchen with their backs to each other. *Can you please not do this on my birthday?*

I clench my backpack strap. The clenching reminds me of the way Ms. Ardvinson told us to position our hands for a hammer fist strike to the nose. Her voice pops into my head: *I still want to hear SHOUTING . . .*

"Hey," I say, and it comes out louder than I expect. Mom and Dad look up at me. "It's my birthday."

I can't make myself say the rest, but they look at each other, and it seems like they understand. "You know," Mom says, "it was a fall day just like this when you were born." She salts the spaghetti water. "Sunny. Clear. Crisp."

"It was the prettiest drive to the hospital," Dad says.

"The whole thing went much quicker than James—"

"I know, I know," I say, embarrassed to hear the part about how I came out bright red and screaming, with my tongue sticking out. That's why they named me Lizzie— for "lizard." I used to like the story until I shared it one day in fourth grade and Michael Gorman made fun of me for it.

"Go put your stuff down," Mom says gently, noticing me

there with my backpack still in hand. "I'll finish getting all this ready."

"We can stick a candle in a meatball!" Dad exclaims. Mom laughs, and I smile with relief.

I head upstairs to my room and drop my backpack by the door. On the window ledge are my apple seeds from the old house, still hopefully rolled in a damp paper towel. I unroll it to see if anything is happening, any tiny green sprouts. Not yet.

My phone buzzes—James.

"Happy Birthday, Nugget!"

I smile. "Thanks." With his afternoon classes, he doesn't usually call at this time of day. "I thought you were going to call during cake and presents."

"I am, but that's not the same as talking just to you. Plus, I feel bad for being a scumbag and not getting your present in the mail in time."

When James went away to college, I was scared that he would change—that his life would be full of newer, bigger concerns, and he wouldn't care about me anymore. But maybe it's true, what he said to me the day before he left: *You're the one I'm really going to miss.*

"It's okay," I say, and it is. "Hey, James?"

I hear crunching in the background. Maybe James is eating those peanuts I saw on his desk before.

"Yeah?"

"Did you and Ally have sex when you were together?"

The crunching stops. "Get out of here."

"Well, did you?"

"Where the heck is this coming from?"

I look down at my feet. One of my blue socks has a tiny hole in the toe. I wiggle it. "I don't know."

"Did they show *Miracle of Life* in health class or something?"

"I'm not taking health."

"Okay, well, take this: you're my little sister, and we are *not* talking about that."

"I'm not little!" I hear a pot lid clanging downstairs—Mom checking on the spaghetti sauce. I lower my voice. "Other people's brothers tell them things. You hardly tell me anything."

"Whose brothers? What 'things'?"

"I don't know!"

"You're really asking this on your *birthday*?"

"When else am I supposed to ask it? You're not here!"

James sighs. Is he giving in? My heartbeat quickens.

"We did . . . some things," he says slowly. "Not everything."

"Did you want to?" I'm staring hard at my sock, at the individual threads.

James's voice is quiet. "I guess I hoped we could, sometime."

"Why didn't you?"

James gives another frustrated sigh that crackles through the phone. "I don't know. First she wasn't ready, then I wasn't ready. We talked about it, but . . ." I hear the part he doesn't say: *But then we broke up.*

I don't reply. I thought I would feel relieved knowing that they didn't do it, the way I felt relieved when I found out Sarah Nan hadn't kissed Ned yet. Instead, I just feel heavier inside.

"Is something happening?" James asks. "What's all this about?"

I'm not sure what it's about. Or why I suddenly needed to know. "Nothing."

"Well, did I answer your question?"

"Yes." Only now I have a hundred more. When James looked at Ally, what did he see? And what did she see when she looked at him? What does it mean to be "ready"—for any of it?

After James and I hang up, I go to the window and look out onto the street. It's getting dark so early now. In class, Ms. Ardvinson warned us about being backlit in front of street-facing windows—how we should keep the shades down after dark, especially if we're home alone.

Someday, I'll be home alone all the time, because I'll *live* alone. Does Ms. Ardvinson live alone? I wish I could ask her. But that's not a polite question. It's not even the *right* question, really. Sometimes I feel like I have this question deep inside me that's so big, I can't even put it into words. I don't know how to ask it. Which is maybe just as well, because as far as I can see, there isn't anyone I can ask.

CHAPTER 12

The first part of my belated-birthday sleepover with Sarah Nan is math homework.

"We don't have to do this now," I tell her as she unzips my backpack and roots around through my clothes for my math notebook.

"If we can get it done, then we can enjoy ourselves and not worry about it," she says. She's always been a do-it-right-now kind of person, while I'm a think-about-it kind of person. "Here, page thirty-four."

After twenty minutes of polynomials, Daria comes into the kitchen.

"You two are growing up so fast," she says, shaking her head. "Math homework on a Saturday night?"

"Don't worry, Mom, we'll do something wild later," Sarah Nan says without looking up. She's busy erasing half of what I just did. "You factored it wrong here, so now you have to go back and fix it."

Dinner is takeout Thai, and its arrival is what finally convinces Sarah Nan to clear our books and papers off the table and put the math to rest for the night.

"I'm sorry it's not homemade," Daria says, placing the takeout containers in the spot vacated by our homework. "I would have liked to do something special for your birthday."

"It's all right," I tell her. "This is great." It *is* great. It's great to be back at Sarah Nan's house—almost like it used to be, when we would have sleepovers all the time.

While Sarah Nan carefully picks the bean sprouts out of her pad thai, Daria tells us about the year she spent teaching English in Thailand after college. Dessert is chocolate raspberry cupcakes from a bakery in town, top-heavy with frosting. Sarah Nan eats half of hers and says she's full; Daria eats the whole thing, so I feel okay doing the same.

"Want to go downstairs?" Sarah Nan asks me when we're done.

"Don't forget it's your job to run the Liberator tonight," Daria reminds her. That's what she calls their dishwasher— the Women's Liberator.

"But we've got company!"

"Lizzie's not company," Daria says, clearing our plates. "She's family."

I've never been happier to load a dishwasher.

Once the Liberator is contentedly rumbling, Sarah Nan and I head down to the basement.

At our early sleepovers, when we were eight years old, we slept in Sarah Nan's room. She has a trundle bed that used to belong to her grandmother. Daria would make up the trundle part for me with blue-flowered sheets, and we would stay up giggling until Daria came and told us to shush or else she would be sleeping in there with us.

Then we got older, and Daria let us move down to the basement. The basement had the added novelty of a foldout couch, and of being two floors away from Daria. It was down there that Sarah Nan told me about her first crush (the older brother of a gymnastics teammate; it didn't last long), and where we read one of those *What's Happening to My Body?* books and giggled together under the tent of the covers.

Tonight, we tug open the couch together—the metal bars make a reverberating *thwangggg*—and then we get the air mattress going on the floor for me.

"You sure you don't mind?" Sarah Nan asks, helping me pull the fitted sheet over it. It's the blue-flowered one, a little worn and pilled, but still pretty. "I just really hate air mattresses."

"It's fine," I say, even though I can tell my feet are going to be hanging off the end. Neither of us mentions the possibility of sharing the foldout couch. I guess those days are over.

While Sarah Nan goes upstairs to put her pajamas on, I lie back on the air mattress and stare at the ceiling. That's what we used to do back when we slept on the couch together: stare up and look for faces in the swirled stucco. Usually we found them once and could never find them again, but there was one we called the Windswept Lady that we always told stories about because she was easy to see: a big swoosh that looked like hair, and a foot in a pointed shoe stepping out from under a cloak or blanket. I try to spot her, scanning the swirls.

There's a buzz on the floor beside me—Sarah Nan left her phone behind. I roll over.

Ned.

Maybe at my dads house. Hes gone a lot.

I lie back again, draping my arm over my face. What's happening at Ned's house with his dad gone? I wish I hadn't looked.

"Are you asleep?"

Sarah Nan is back in flannel pajama pants and a T-shirt that says *Wilma's Dance Academy*. She's holding her nail polish collection. "I need a touch-up. How about you?"

"I'm okay."

She sits cross-legged on the unfolded couch and begins inspecting the colors, settling on a pale green. She's fastened her dark, curly hair on top of her head in a messy bun that flops forward as she bends to apply the first coat. Probably the reason people like Sarah Nan can get boyfriends so easily is that they look cute even when they're not trying.

"Hey," I say, looking across the room. "What's Priscilla doing down here?"

Priscilla is Sarah Nan's American Girl doll. Daria would only get her one after she begged for two years and paid for half of it with her own allowance. It's one of the ones you can get to look like you—only Sarah Nan chose one with straight blond hair and green eyes, which is what she's always wished she had. Somewhere in a bin of doll clothes is a bathrobe-and-pajama set that we used to put Priscilla in whenever we had sleepovers. My Molly doll has the same set.

Now, though, Priscilla is wearing her "winter ski lodge" outfit, and sits smiling from the top of a small end table.

"Oh yeah," Sarah Nan says. "I needed some more room, so I moved a bunch of old toys down here."

"I've gotta do that, too." I pluck Priscilla from the table and bring her over to the air mattress. She has some dust in her hair. I run my fingers through it.

Sarah Nan looks up. "Her brush is in the cabinet underneath."

"Okay."

Sarah Nan paints her toenails, and I brush Priscilla's hair. There's a special way you're supposed to do it so the hair doesn't get tugged loose: little strokes, starting from the bottom.

"Hey, you know what?" Sarah Nan asks after a little while. "Those self-defense moves really work. I tried one on Ned."

The brush catches in a snag, and I go extra carefully. "What?"

"You know the one where they try to put an arm

around you? Yeah, I tried it out! I told Ned I was going to do something, though, so he was scared I was going to hurt him. Ha!"

I focus on the doll's hair, on the beginnings of a braid. "You told Chloe you guys were just talking."

"Yeah, a *month* ago! Plus, I'm not going to tell Chloe anything about it," she says, blowing lightly on her paint job. "She's still jealous about me going out with Ned when she and Jeremy just broke up."

"They were going out?"

"All summer! You were in tech with us last year—don't you remember them flirting?"

I remember Jeremy kicking the release lever on Chloe's desk chair every day so that her seat dropped six inches in the middle of whatever she was doing. I remember her whining, *Oh my* God, *Jeremy*, stop it . . .

"*That* was flirting?"

Sarah Nan laughs. "Oh, Lizzie."

I swallow back my annoyance. *Oh, Lizzie*—like I'm a little kid. Am I the only one who thinks it makes no sense at all that the way to show your interest in someone is to torment them?

I'm about to ask Sarah Nan if she can explain it, but her phone buzzes again. She fastens the lid back on the nail polish before she types her reply.

"Ned?" I ask.

"Yeah. I was asking him if we could ever go to his house sometime. My mom's always butting in—she's so awkward. Here, look at what Ned just sent me."

It's a video of Ned and some friends, including Jeremy and Michael. They're on a swing set, making faces as they sway in and out of focus. "Ba-ba-boieeeee!" Ned shouts before the video ends.

"Boys." Sarah Nan shakes her head, but she says it with warmth.

I pass the phone back. "Are you sure it's a good idea to show him the self-defense moves?"

"Why?"

"I thought they were supposed to be, like, secret."

"Yeah, from creeps and *predators*."

I don't answer.

Sarah Nan sighs. "Seriously, Lizzie, when are you going to give up this idea that all boys are jerks? James is a boy—do you think he's a jerk?"

I run my fingers through Priscilla's hair, undoing my attempt at a braid. "That's different." I know James will never look at me or treat me the way Michael Gorman does.

Sarah Nan tosses the nail polish back in the basket. "Okay, I'm not trying to be annoying, I'm really asking: Isn't there *any* boy you think is kind of cute?"

I do think about it. I play a quick slideshow in my head. "No."

"And you're sure you're not gay?"

"*Yes,*" I say—even though I'm not sure. When you don't feel anything, it's hard to know which way you'd go if you did. Sometimes I'm jealous of Sarah Nan—not because I want a boyfriend or what she has with Ned, but because she's always known that was what she wanted. I'm jealous of other kids in the same way: Kendall, kissing the blue-haired girl in the parking lot; the Boy in the Skirt, being so comfortable the way he is. I know what I *don't* want. Is that the same?

"Sarah Nan," I say abruptly, "what are we doing here?"

She's stretched out on the bed, inspecting her finished toes. For whatever reason, she doesn't scold me for not calling her *Sarah.* "What are you talking about?"

"I mean . . ." I keep my eyes focused on the doll, which is the only way I can make myself ask the question. "Why are you hanging out with me again? Last year it seemed like you didn't even want to be friends anymore."

There. It's out.

Sarah Nan exhales, a slow breath. "Okay, look." She turns toward me on her side, still being careful not to smudge the polish. "If we're being honest . . . I was kind of mad at you after my mom and Nick split up. I felt like you didn't really care."

My face goes hot. I remember how she told me about it when I met her at her locker one morning last fall. *Well, Nick and my mom are breaking up.* She was putting on lip gloss and didn't look at me as she said it. *They decided they're better as friends.*

So now it's just you again, I said, thinking she'd be glad that it was just her and her mom, like normal. She used to complain about Nick a lot, how having a "boy" in the house threw everything off.

"I didn't know you were that upset," I say.

"I was." Sarah Nan toys with a loose string in the bedspread, and I think back to the days when Nick was dating Daria. He taught Sarah Nan to make ravioli from scratch. He went to all her gymnastics tournaments. "I guess part of me hoped he would want to be my dad or whatever. But I get it now, why they couldn't get married. My mom is too . . . *Daria* to get tied to one guy. Even if they love each other."

They loved each other? I didn't know that. "I'm sorry."

Sarah Nan rolls over. "Then I started getting in more with Chloe and her crowd—she has a stepdad, you know? So I felt like she got it, about Nick." She sighs. "But toward the end of the summer, Sami sent me a screenshot of these texts Chloe had sent her, saying how I'm spoiled and self-absorbed, and Nick wouldn't marry my mom because of me."

She says those words so casually.

"That's awful," I say.

She doesn't meet my eyes. "When that happened, I just had this thought: Lizzie wouldn't do that. I know I can be strong-willed"—I recognize the word Daria always told us to use rather than *stubborn* or *bossy*—"but you've always put up with me."

"It's not putting up with you," I tell her honestly. "You're my friend."

She smiles, satisfied, and plops back against the pillow. "You're mine, too."

Maybe Sarah Nan hasn't changed as much as I thought. I feel warmer inside, and a little bolder. "You're still friends with Chloe, after that?"

"I kind of have to be," Sarah Nan says, looking up at the ceiling. "We're on the same team. But it's tense between us. Haven't you noticed?"

"No."

"That's because I'm good at being fake," she says. "You're not. Everyone can tell what you feel."

"Really?" I don't know if that's a compliment or not.

"Like, I can tell you don't really like Ned."

I look away. I want to deny it, but it's too late. "I just don't . . . get it, I guess."

"What don't you get?"

I shrug. *Crushes. Flirting. What you're supposed to feel inside.* The answer to her question is too big to explain.

"You're doing that braid wrong," Sarah Nan finally says. "Let me fix it."

I hand the doll over.

While Sarah Nan fixes Priscilla's hair, I go back to the

cupboard. I sift through doll clothes until I uncover the paja-mas and bathrobe.

"Here," I say, climbing on the foldout mattress beside Sarah Nan. "Then she can join the sleepover, too."

Sarah Nan looks at me. I wonder if it's true that she can see everything I feel.

"Tell anyone we did this, and you die," she says, taking the tiny pajamas.

Together, we dress Priscilla for bedtime. Then the three of us lie back on the mattress and search the ceiling for stories.

In the morning, Sarah Nan and I emerge from the base-ment to the smell of pancakes and Daria at the stove in her bathrobe and slippers. The pancakes are her usual weird-tasting kind with buckwheat and bananas, but I've gotten used to that. Anything will taste fine with enough butter and syrup.

"Here's your homemade birthday meal!" Daria puts a platter down in front of me. "And here"—she produces a small, wrapped box from the pocket of her robe—"is your belated birthday gift."

"Don't open it," Sarah Nan advises me.

"Sarah!" Daria swats her on the back of the neck with an oven mitt, then turns back to the stove to flip another round. "It's just something small."

Sarah Nan shakes her head. *Trust me*, she mouths. But I don't want to hurt Daria's feelings.

I slide my finger under the tape, unsticking it without tearing the rose-patterned paper. The back of the box is facing up. *Directions for insertion*, it says, and some other stuff in small print. I flip it over.

"Told you," Sarah Nan says.

The package says *Moon Catcher* on the front. Inside, through a plastic panel, I see a clear silicone cup. "What is it?"

"It's—"

"Mom, come on." Sarah Nan snatches the box from me. "You can't give Lizzie this for her birthday."

"It's a menstrual cup," Daria finishes. "We're all women here, Sarah. There's no need to be embarrassed by our bodies—"

"We're not embarrassed. We just don't want to talk about it at *breakfast*." Sarah Nan leans in and lowers her voice. "I told her I wouldn't use one, so now she's trying to give it to you. You're supposed to put it *in* you to, like, catch stuff. Stuff that comes out." She gives me a significant look.

"Oh." I feel myself blushing. I can't imagine my mom giving a gift like this. We hardly ever talk about periods. "I've never seen one before."

"Don't even get me started!" Daria says, which means she is already started. "Men own and run most of the menstrual product industry—can you believe that? But these were designed by women, for women. I use one—right, Sarah Nan?"

Sarah Nan has her face in her hands. "*Mom . . .*"

"Economical, less waste, more comfortable . . . and, you know, it makes you more familiar with your own body." Daria flips the next round of pancakes, and the griddle hisses. "Some women don't even know what they look like down there."

Sarah Nan just moans. "Are you finished yet?"

I stare down at my plate, not sure what to say. When Sarah Nan and I read that *What's Happening to My Body?* book, there was a part that told you how to use a pocket mirror and take a "guided tour." We laughed at it then. Now I wonder if I'm one of those women Daria is talking about. While boys like Michael are laughing at pictures, I'm too embarrassed to look at the real thing.

"I know it might be early for you still," Daria continues, setting an empty mixing bowl in the sink, "but it's good to have one around for when the time comes."

Sarah Nan rolls her eyes. "The time already came, Mom."

"What?" Daria turns around.

"Lizzie got hers, what, like six months ago?"

Now I'm embarrassed.

"You did?" Daria asks, and I nod. "Lizzie!" She rushes over and hugs me, leaving the pancakes unattended. A greasy spatula is dangerously close to my face. "Congratulations, sweetheart! And what a coincidence, just in time for the ceremony . . ."

"Ceremony?" I repeat. I had a mouthful of pancake when Daria hugged me, and now my cheeks are smooshed up in the hug.

"Mom, I told you, nobody wants a coming-of-age ceremony." Sarah Nan is carefully picking all the bananas out of her pancake. "People don't do that."

"People do that all over the *world*." Daria shakes the spatula at us. "You're fourteen now, such a threshold year—high school, puberty, young adulthood . . . I've been planning it since you were little. It'll be all you girls who were in the same playgroup when you were babies—that's where you two met, you know."

"We know, we know." Our moms can't quite agree on the origin story of our friendship, but they know it involved terrorizing each other at playgroup. My mom says it was when Sarah Nan saw me get snack first and promptly bit my arm; Daria says it was when I beaned Sarah Nan over the head with a Cabbage Patch doll.

"What happens at the ceremony?" I ask.

"Oops!" Daria rushes over to the stove; the pancakes are burning. She scrapes them off the griddle, looks at the undersides, and dumps them directly into the compost bucket. "Sorry, girls, that was the last of them."

"We have to walk through the woods in the dark," Sarah Nan starts, "and then—"

"Hush, hush, hush," Daria says. "You're not supposed to know about that. How do you know about that?"

"I heard you telling Nora's mom on the phone." Nora was another baby in our playgroup. She goes to school in a different district, so we don't see her anymore. All I really remember is that she used to eat the Play-Doh. Chloe was the fourth baby—I guess that means she'll be there. Great.

Daria looks briefly deflated, then brightens again. "Well, the last part of the ceremony is something no one else knows because I haven't told any of the other moms yet. All you need to do is think of an object that represents your child-hood, and bring it with you. Something you don't mind parting with for a while."

"Are we going to burn it?" Sarah Nan asks dryly.

"We are not *burning* it."

"Come on, Lizzie." Sarah Nan pushes her plate away. "I lost my appetite. What about you?"

Ordinarily, I would say yes. It's easier to go along with Sarah Nan even if I disagree; maybe that's why she doesn't bite me anymore. But this morning, I feel different. When it came to my period, Mom gave me supplies and told me what was happening inside me, but she didn't tell me about being a woman. Sarah Nan's mom is excited for me—like something good happened. I want to know what she thinks is so special.

"I'm almost done," I say coolly. "I'll meet you upstairs."

Sarah Nan's jaw drops. But she doesn't like to act taken by surprise, so she says, "Fine," and leaves her syrupy plate on the table.

I'm alone in the kitchen with Sarah Nan's mom. Daria scours the burn-crusted griddle, cursing to herself while the sink runs noisily in the background. I've only got a sliver of pancake left, so I try to make it last a long time while I wait for her to finish. Finally, she turns off the faucet.

"Thanks for the present," I offer.

Daria smiles as she takes Sarah Nan's plate away. "It's okay if you don't want to use it. We all have to do what we're comfortable with."

I want to tell her that I'll use it, but I'm not sure that's true. "Okay."

Daria begins wiping down the counters with a rag. I see her muscles flex beneath her sleeve, and suddenly I think, *Of course*. Sarah Nan's mom never married. She and Nick decided to stay just friends. She has a job and a house and Sarah Nan, and she does it all herself. She's the one I can ask.

My lungs suddenly fill with questions, but before I can ask them, Daria turns around. "Lizzie, can I ask you something?"

"Sure," I say, surprised.

"I'm wondering what you think about . . ." She glances back toward the staircase, then cups her hand to her mouth and whispers so that only I can hear, "*Ned*."

"Oh." I press the back of my fork against my plate, tracing squiggles in the syrup. "Um . . . he's fine. Funny. I don't know."

She pulls up a chair across from me. "I guess what I mean is, when he and Sarah are together, are they . . . I mean, they've only been boyfriend and girlfriend for a month. I guess I don't know, these days, what it means to be 'going out.'" She gives a nervous laugh.

"They text a lot," I say, which feels like the safe answer.

Daria seems reassured. "Sometimes a person can get consumed by a relationship. They lose their identity. I just don't want that to happen to Sarah Nan."

Hearing her call Sarah Nan by her real name makes me bold enough to lift my head. "Neither do I."

Daria smiles. "I'm glad she has a friend like you to remind her who she is."

I blush, feeling suddenly guilty that I didn't tell her the whole truth of how I feel about Ned, or about the fact that Sarah Nan is trying to find a place to be alone with him. But Sarah Nan is my friend. She's the one whose secrets I have to keep.

"I don't totally get why she likes him," I confess. That, at least, is the truth.

Daria nods. She reaches out and squeezes my wrist. "No one's ever good enough for the people we love the best."

CHAPTER 13

~

When we enter Ms. Faraher's room on Monday, we find her desk covered with greenery: the jade, the orchid, the ivy.

Her plants are back.

"So," she says, smiling pleasantly, "I heard that some of you have been showing a lot of interest in anatomy books. You must have a lot of questions, if you're using class time for that purpose. Of course, it's *very* normal to have questions about your body . . ." A few people giggle, hearing her mock the conventional grown-up-to-kid puberty talk. "But that's certainly no excuse to distract others or make them uncomfortable."

Ms. Faraher's voice is serious now. Michael squirms beside me. Who told her about what he and Ethan have been doing with the books?

"So, to settle any questions, I thought we'd depart from our current curriculum for the day and spend some time talking about sexual reproduction—"

Everyone in the room lifts their heads.

"—in the plant kingdom."

Sighs of both relief and disappointment sweep across the

rows of lab tables as Ms. Faraher cups an ivy leaf in her palm. For my part, I'm relieved. I couldn't imagine sitting through "the talk" with Michael Gorman beside me.

"That's not sexual!" a voice behind me calls out.

Ms. Faraher looks up from the branch. "Who said that?"

Nobody will own up to it at first, until Ethan raises his hand. "I mean, don't you need, like, body parts and stuff?"

"Interesting point." Ms. Faraher smiles—and then she calls us to gather around her desk and look closely.

One by one, she tells us about the different types of plants and how they reproduce. She shows us the fern's bumpy spores, and the cones on a cut pine branch in water. Mostly, though, she tells us about flowers—about how the pollen, the male part, fertilizes the ovule, the female part, which is how a plant embryo—inside the seed—develops.

When she says "embryo," pretty much the entire class looks at her belly, which is bigger than ever now in her pink-striped shirt. I can even see her belly button poking through. It must be so embarrassing to be pregnant.

"So when you get allergies, in the spring," Ethan says, "that means you're, like, allergic to plant sperm?"

"That's right," Ms. Faraher says, over a backdrop of giggles. Michael doesn't laugh; he's sulking, his hands in his sweatshirt pocket. "Though I should remind you that while these reproductive organs are *analogous* to human anatomy, they are not *homologous*. Who remembers what that means?"

Chloe touches the blossom of a paperwhite, which Ms. Faraher earlier tricked Ethan into sniffing. ("Not all scents are meant to attract humans," Ms. Faraher pointed out, when he gagged and said it smelled like garbage.) "It means we aren't related to flowers," Chloe says.

Ms. Faraher nods. "It means that our organs may share similar functions to a plant's, but they don't have the same evolutionary source."

The day's lab is to dissect flowers. ("Mr. Watt's class gets to dissect *frogs*," Ethan complains.) Back at our lab tables, we use tweezers to peel them apart carefully on an aluminum tray, then draw and label the parts: sepal, pistil, stamen.

"I feel like a mortician right now," Aidan says. I laugh, as Chloe says, "Aidan, you're so weird."

Aidan's ears turn red, and I feel sorry for him.

Could he be the one who told Ms. Faraher about Michael and the books?

Michael and I have a Peruvian lily, *Alstroemeria aurea*, white petals with pink tips and a yellow swatch in the center. The stamens are the parts that stick out from the center, topped with the anthers—some of which are still capped, while others are coated with yellow pollen. After we've removed and labeled the anthers, Michael takes one and smears it on my sleeve.

"Hey, Lizard, guess what you've got on you."

I ignore him.

Chloe turns around. She didn't see what Michael did, she just sees the yellow smudge. "That doesn't come out, you know."

"Whatever," I say. It would be worse if I showed that I cared.

After we've all cleaned up, Ms. Faraher calls us back to the front of the room. "What do you make of this plant?" she asks. She draws another flowerpot out from behind the rest. It has thick, spiny leaves, like a succulent, and each spine is tipped with what appears to be a tiny bud.

"A cactus?" someone guesses.

"Something creepy," Michael says.

Ms. Faraher tells us the name, and everyone exclaims, "*What?*"

She writes it on the board behind her, then says it again, "*KAL-an-KOH-ee*. This plant is different than the others I've shown you. Any guesses why?"

Aidan, closest to the plant, leans in to inspect the leaves. "It's got more tiny plants growing off it."

"That's exactly right!" Ms. Faraher gives one of the leaves a flick, and several buds fall off. Each of them is made of two or three tinier leaves, with thin white roots at the bottom. "The kalanchoe is a plant that reproduces *asexually*; it creates offspring without fertilization. Each of these tiny plants can grow on its own into a new plant—no pistils or stamens here. No sexual reproduction needed."

My heart starts to beat a little faster. I didn't know that was a thing that could happen.

"I have a spider plant at my house that does that," Aidan says.

Ms. Faraher nods. "Same idea. Of course, asexual reproduction means there's no genetic variation—no potential for adaptation to its environment. The genes of this kalanchoe are exactly the same as the genes of every kalanchoe plant before it—excepting random mutations, of course."

"Isn't that bad?" Ethan asks.

"Asexual reproduction isn't good or bad," Ms. Faraher says. "It's a strategy, with its own advantages and disadvantages."

Did Ms. Faraher plan this lesson for me? Even though I couldn't ask her what I wanted to during my conference, did she somehow know?

"As you can see," Ms. Faraher concludes, "we have several baby kalanchoes to spare. Would anyone like one to bring home? If so, you can take one on your way back to your seat."

Aidan takes one. A few others do, too.

"*It looks like a bug*," someone whispers.

I hang back until I'm the last one, and then I let Ms. Faraher put a kalanchoe in my palm.

It *is* about the size and shape of a housefly: green leaves for wings, and tiny white roots sticking out, eyelash thin. I look up, and her eyes meet mine. She smiles.

"They're naturally drought resistant, so they'll last awhile outside the soil," Ms. Faraher tells us as we go back to our seats. "You'll probably want to plant it when you get home."

When I get home, I check my apple seeds on the windowsill—still no growth. In fact, they're starting to grow a pale fuzz of mold. I don't have a green thumb like my mom does. How am I going to keep alive the little sprout that Ms. Faraher gave me? I plant it in a tiny pot from the garage, but I don't know what to do next. I sit down at my computer with my marbled notebook and search *kalanchoe*.

"Caring for Your Kalanchoe"—I click on that. Succulent houseplant. Warm temperatures. Plenty of light. My bedroom window above the radiator will be perfect.

It turns out that *Kalanchoe* is actually a genus of plant, rather than the name of an individual species. There are many types, and many common names to go along with them. Chocolate Soldier. Felt bush. Alligator plant. Widow's-thrill.

I click on the widow one, but it's different from Ms. Faraher's. Wider, rounder leaves, and flowers. Ms. Faraher's kind is asexual; it wouldn't have flowers or anything to fertilize. Right?

I try *alligator plant* next. *That's* what Ms. Faraher gave me. I recognize the narrow, pointed leaves, which are the inspiration for that common name. It's also called devil's backbone.

Not very friendly names. I guess it's not a very friendly looking plant: lots of sharp edges. "Kalanchoe" isn't a bad name. Too bad the end of it looks so much like "Chloe." I laugh to myself, imagining Chloe's reaction at being compared to a plant. It ought to be the kalan-Lizzie.

Are there other asexual plants?

I search some more, and I learn that there are many kinds of asexual reproduction. Vegetative. Apomixis. *No intermingling of male and female gametes.* There are even insects that produce asexually: water fleas, aphids, parasitic wasps . . . Certain species can be parthenogenic, reproducing with eggs that need no fertilization.

I'm feeling excited. Maybe *this* could be my CARP project: how not every living thing needs to find a mate. Some organisms—the asexual ones—really can survive on their own. I thought that wasps lived together in papery nests like the one Dad had to spray in our new garage when we moved in. But this article says that those are "social wasps"; solitary wasps live on their own, boring holes in wood to lay their eggs.

"New Mexico Whiptail Lizard," reads the title of one *National Geographic* article. "How an Asexual Lizard Procreates Alone."

Lizard. My fingers type almost on their own:

Can a person be . . .

"Lizzie?"

I jump in my seat, snapping the laptop shut. "Mom! Can't you knock?"

"Sorry, I didn't mean to scare you." Mom is always calmer after meditation; otherwise she would definitely be more attuned to the fact that I'm hiding something. "Are you working on CARP?"

My skin is tingling. "Yeah." It's not *exactly* a lie.

"When do I get to find out the top-secret topic?"

"Soon." All this time, I've been telling her it was a work in progress. Which is code for: I still have no idea.

"What's that?"

She's looking at my kalanchoe, which, now that it's planted, looks like two green beads in the dirt.

"Ms. Faraher gave it to me," I say.

"Huh." Mom watches me press on the damp soil. "Well, don't keep it in that little pot for too long. It'll need plenty of room to grow."

I wait until my parents go to sleep before I search again. I want to be alone when I ask my question, finally.

"Good night, Lizzie," Mom says, stopping in my room to kiss the top of my head. I look like I'm reading, but I'm not taking in a word.

My parents' light goes out. There's murmuring for a few moments, then silence. I make myself wait five more minutes. Then, soundlessly, I extract my phone from its charger at the foot of the bed.

Last year, our technology teacher, Ms. Hughes, told us that the internet has made the world smaller. She said that she remembers the days when the only way you could communicate with your brother in the Peace Corps was by letter, and could we even imagine what that was like?

These days, no one is ever so far away, she said, while we waited for her to turn off the screen lock so we could go back to playing games when she wasn't looking. *One tap, and your brother's face is right there in front of you, no matter where he is.*

It seems like she might have been overestimating how easy it is to get in touch with your brother. I haven't heard from James since my birthday. Not even a text.

I type my question, and this time I don't hesitate: *Can a person be asexual?*

Asexual: experiencing little or no sexual attraction.

Maybe Ms. Hughes was right that the internet made the world smaller—but tonight, huddled in my blankets with the glow of my phone, I feel my world open up.

CHAPTER 14

~

"What are you smiling at?"

"Huh?"

I'm at the cafeteria table with Chloe and Sarah Nan, barely listening to them. The word *asexual* keeps repeating itself over and over in my mind. All day, I've had the vague, happy feeling that something is going right; sometimes, in the midst of things, I'll forget what, and then I'll remember. *Asexual.* The prefix "a-" means "not." Hasn't my life always been about what I'm not? Not pretty, not athletic, not interested, not ready—but now here's this word that tells me that what I am not is actually what I *am*. Something—I'm something.

Sarah Nan waves her hand in front of my eyes. "You were just, like, smiling off into the distance."

"It was kind of freaky," Chloe adds, twirling her fork in her cafeteria stir-fry noodles.

I shrug. "Okay."

I was up until three in the morning reading and watching videos. "Asexuality: The Other Orientation"; "What Does It Mean That I'm Asexual?"; "Five Things Asexuals Want You to Know." Each of them was like hearing my own voice and thoughts through someone else. People talked about feeling out of place, about not relating to their friends' feelings, about discouraging things others have said to them: *You just haven't found the right person yet.*

"There's a lot of us," one person said.

Some people call it being "ace." I like that. The ace is the playing card that could mean just one, or it could mean the highest value of all.

Both Sarah Nan and Chloe are looking at me now.

"You are really out to lunch," Chloe says.

I'd better compartmentalize a bit. "What?"

"I said, you're going trick-or-treating with us, right?"

I nearly choke on my sandwich. "I am?"

Surprised at *my* surprise, Chloe frowns. "Sarah Nan said you were."

"Remember, Lizzie?" Sarah Nan gives me an urgent stare that Chloe couldn't possibly miss, except she's just turned to wave at Sami at another table.

"Oh. Right," I say.

Chloe turns back, and Sarah Nan gives a small laugh at my forgetfulness.

Irritated, I add, "I thought maybe we were too old for that."

Sarah Nan's smile fades. Last year, when I asked Sarah Nan what we should dress up as—every year before that, we'd gone as a team, like M&M's, or bacon and eggs, or the

chicken and the egg (Sarah Nan loved her egg costume)—
she told me that trick-or-treating was for kids and that she
was going to stay home and give out candy. Now that I think
about it, though, maybe she only said that because she was
mad at me for what I said about her mom's breakup with
Nick. Not because she actually believed it.

"It'll be a last hurrah before high school," Sarah Nan says.
"We're going to try for the biggest candy haul *ever*."

I almost point out that Daria makes Sarah Nan give away
half her candy every year because "too much sugar cuts your
life span by seven percent"—but I bite my tongue in time.
"Great."

"Ned knows all the best neighborhoods," Sarah Nan says,
then blows delicately on a spiraled noodle from the cafeteria's chicken soup. "He's going to show us his top-secret
itinerary."

"Ned's coming?"

Sarah Nan looks up. "We're going with him and his
group."

"Who's in his group?"

"Not too many people. Just Jeremy—"

Chloe gives a little hiccup, and I remember how Jeremy supposedly broke her heart over the summer. Now this
whole plan is starting to make sense to me.

"And Michael."

"What?" I say, but Chloe shouts over me.

"Sami, wait!" She grabs a notepad from the table and hurries across the cafeteria.

Now I can talk to Sarah Nan. "What's happening? Why are we trick-or-treating with those guys?"

"I need you to come with me," Sarah Nan says. "My mom said I can only go if you do, too."

"I hate Michael Gorman," I remind her. "Why would I go trick-or-treating with him?"

"You won't even have to talk to him. It's a big group. You can talk to me."

"You and *Ned*."

"Argh, Lizzie, *please*." Sarah Nan puts her face in her hands. "You act like I'm making Ned your stepdad."

"That's not what I'm acting like."

"Then why won't you go with me? Last year you wanted to go."

Last year, I did want to go. I cried on Halloween, as our doorbell rang and rang with kids having fun with their friends. This might be—*is*—my last chance.

"I don't have a costume," I say feebly.

"I'll help you think of something. Ned and I are doing a fifties theme—I'm wearing my poodle skirt!—but you could maybe be . . ."

Chloe and Sami approach our table. "Hey, Lizzie," Sami says, holding up a manila envelope. "So you know how Ms. Faraher's going away right before Thanksgiving?"

"She is?" My stomach plunges even further. I knew she'd be leaving, but I didn't know when. Thanksgiving is soon. I want her to be the first one I tell about being asexual. Will I even have the chance?

"Um, yeah, for her baby?" Chloe gives Sami a sideways glance that clearly means, *Seriously?*

I don't bother defending myself. "Oh, right."

"Anyway," Chloe continues, "we were thinking we could all chip in a couple of bucks and get her some baby things, like maybe onesies or something, and give them to her on her last day."

"Like a baby shower," Sami adds unnecessarily.

"Yeah," I say. "That's a good idea."

It *is* a good idea. I kind of hate that Chloe was the one to come up with it.

"So do you want to pitch in?" Chloe asks.

"Sure," I say. "I have money in my locker."

"Great!" Chloe says, and the two of them flounce away.

I turn back to Sarah Nan. She's trying to catch Ned's eye across the cafeteria, where he's sitting with Michael and some other boys.

"A lizard," I say abruptly.

She turns back to me. "What?"

"A New Mexico whiptail lizard. That's my costume."

Sarah Nan's forehead wrinkles with follow-up questions—like how I'll get a lizard costume on short notice, or why on earth I would dress up as the nickname that Michael Gorman has taunted me with since elementary school. But she knows she can't ask those questions. She can only ask, "So you'll go?"

"Yes."

I've never been trick-or-treating in a group. Before this, it was just me and Sarah Nan—and before *that*, when James was still young enough to think it was fun to go out with his family, he would take me around the block. I was so little then that I don't really remember it. What I mainly remember is that James would hold my hand as we walked up to each door, while Mom and Dad hung back at the sidewalk. He would let me be the one to ring the bell.

My lizard costume turned out pretty well, for something last minute. Mom helped me paint stripes running from my forehead to my nose, like the whiptail has; I took my winter gloves, which will be good to wear anyway in the cold, and added some felt to the fingertips to make them extra long and lizardy; and when I get to Sarah Nan's house, she lends me the tail she wore for some dance performance a long time ago and pins it to the back of my leggings.

"I can't remember the last time I saw you wear *leggings*," she says around the safety pin in her mouth. She's in her poodle skirt, her hair bobby-pinned back.

The last time I wore leggings was sixth grade, when

Michael Gorman said *squeeeeeze* as I walked past him at recess. If he says anything to me tonight, I won't just keep walking. I know what I am now. I don't need to care what he thinks.

"I can't believe this will be your last time trick-or-treating together!" Daria stands in the doorway, wearing her usual witch's hat. "I remember taking you girls around in your sweet ballerina costumes . . ."

"You wouldn't *let* me be a ballerina," Sarah Nan says, tugging on my tail to make sure it stays. "You made me be Ruth Bader Ginsburg."

Ned and Michael meet us at Sarah Nan's house, and then we wait a few more minutes for Chloe's mom to drop her off before we set out into the night. It's after seven, and younger kids have been hitting the streets for a while now. That's part of the plan.

"The strategy is late hours and side streets," Ned says as we leave Sarah Nan's neighborhood. He's wearing a big unicorn onesie that a boy with less confidence wouldn't be able to pull off. (Apparently Sarah Nan's fifties theme was "too hard.") "You want to hit the people who bought too much candy, and now they're trying to get rid of it. There's this one place I know—last year they were giving out king-size Toblerones." Ned's eyes go dreamy.

Chloe just looks annoyed; at the last minute, Jeremy said

he had hockey practice and would try to join us later. "What's your costume, Chloe?" I ask, trying to cheer her up.

"I'm a spirit," she says glumly.

She's wearing a spaghetti-strap top and gossamer skirt, with shadows painted under her eyes. And she's shivering. When her mom dropped her off at Sarah Nan's house, she was wearing a sweater over the top, but before we left, she took it off and left it in Sarah Nan's room. All she's carrying now is a small sequined purse. "Don't you need a bag for your candy?"

She stares ahead, wobbling slightly. Apparently she's the kind of spirit who wears platform heels. "No."

"Michael has an extra," Ned says. "You can use that."

"That's my overflow bag!" Michael says, but Ned swipes one of Michael's two pillowcases and hands it to Chloe.

"Thanks, Ned!" Chloe smiles. Sarah Nan regards her suspiciously and takes Ned by the hand.

"Let's go," she says.

The three of them walk ahead, taking up the full width of the sidewalk, leaving Michael and me at the back. He's not even dressed up. All he did was put on a Darth Vader mask.

"Nice costume," I remark.

The mask turns to face me. "At least I'm wearing one."

My ears go hot, and I feel the surge of anger inside me. "Look, just don't talk to me tonight, okay?"

"What? You started it. You insulted my costume."

I ignore him and hurry ahead to walk alongside Chloe, even if it means being partly on the grass.

Ned might not be the brightest bulb in some ways, but his Halloween strategy is airtight. We knock on several doors where the person who answers says, "Oh, thank goodness!" and dumps fistfuls of candy into our bags. Ned is polite, too. After we say "trick or treat," he always asks, "How are you doing tonight?"

"People like that," he says when Michael tries to tease him about it. He pops a malted milk ball into his mouth. "It's called manners."

Maybe Ned isn't so bad, I think. Then I remember the text—*Maybe at my dad's house*—and I feel my wariness rising up again.

With all the decorations up and the roads mostly empty of cars as families wander the streets, I almost don't recognize where we are. But then I see us approaching the hill where Windy Ridge slopes down until it becomes Deerfield Circle, and I slow to a stop.

Sarah Nan notices. Realizes why.

"Hey," she says, hurrying forward to tug the sleeve of Ned's onesie. "Let's skip this one."

"But this is the place I was telling you about," Ned says. "The one with the Toblerones!"

"This is Lizzie's old neighborhood," she says. "She can't go back there."

Michael butts in. "Whaddaya mean, she can't go back? What's the big deal?"

Sarah Nan glances at me, sees my horrified speechlessness. *Please don't tell them*, I beg her with my eyes. "It would be weird," she says at last. "All the memories."

Michael gives an aggravated sigh. "Then have her wait here while the rest of us go. Come on, I've only got until nine before my mom starts tracking me." He holds up his phone. I'm not surprised his mom doesn't trust him.

"I don't want to split up . . . ," Ned says, clearly torn between his girlfriend and the promise of king-size Toblerones.

"Girl huddle," Sarah Nan announces, taking Chloe and me by the shoulders. "We'll be right back."

She guides us to the other side of the street, where Chloe finally shakes her off. "What is going on?"

"Lizzie can't go this way," Sarah Nan says. "Want to split up? We can go back to my place."

I can't believe Sarah Nan would suggest it. My heart warms with relief—but then Chloe speaks up.

"Before Jeremy even gets here? Sarah, that's the whole reason I came. Do you think I'm actually going to eat any of this stuff?" She shakes Michael's pillowcase. "I'm allergic to half of it! You promised you'd help me get him back. We can't just leave!"

"Okay, okay, don't freak out," Sarah Nan says. "Let me think."

I don't like where this is going. "Sarah . . ."

"I said let me *think*."

Chloe and I both watch the thinking. Nothing seems to come of it.

"What's the big deal, anyway?" Chloe asks, unwrapping a stick of gum that she's decided is safe to eat. "It's just a house."

Sarah Nan glances at me. Her look says that it's my secret to tell, if I want to get us out of this.

"We have a restraining order on our old neighbor. Two hundred feet," I add, as if that's the important part.

To my surprise, Chloe's impatience dissolves instantly. "Well, why didn't you say so? Is that why you guys are in the self-defense class?"

I nod mutely, my hope renewed that maybe we can split off from the boys.

"My mom had to get one of those once—some creepy professor when she was in law school. But a restraining order doesn't mean *you* can't go places." She looks at me, puzzled. "Right?"

"I don't know," I say. "Just, my mom doesn't . . ."

"I've got it!" Sarah Nan strides back across the street to the boys and snatches the Darth Vader mask off Michael's head.

"Hey!" He rubs his ears. "That hurt!"

Sarah Nan triumphantly hands me the mask. "Now no one will know it's you. You can come with us!"

"Perfect!" Chloe claps her hands. "Come on, let's go."

It's far from perfect. For one thing, this mask has been on Michael Gorman's face for the past forty-five minutes. For another, it still doesn't solve the fact that I'm really, *really* not supposed to be here.

"*How*, exactly, does this fix the problem?" Michael demands.

"Here, I've got wipes." Chloe reaches into her sequined spirit-purse and produces a tiny pouch. "For the germs."

"Hey!"

"Come on, Michael," Ned says, nudging him in the arm. "*Toblerones*."

Suddenly, it's all of us against Michael, and *that* feels perfect. I take one of Chloe's wipes and sanitize the inside of the mask. I pull it over my face. "Let's go."

"Woohoo!" Ned pumps his fist and takes off running. Meanwhile, Michael digs into his bag for a candy bar, grumbling. "What am I even supposed to *be* now?"

"You can wear my ballet skirt, Michael," Chloe offers. Everyone laughs.

"Hey now," Sarah Nan says. "Let's not be gender normative."

We start the circle counterclockwise, heading away from my old house. It's nice to see my former neighbors, even though I can't say hi to them: the people with the quadruplets (they're out trick-or-treating, but four equally butchered jack-o'-lanterns line the front steps); the people with the beagles; the people with the pool who host a block party every summer. Then there's Marge, who got divorced a long time ago and every year hangs her wedding dress from a tree like a ghost.

"She sounds like a freak," Michael says, when I point out the dress. He's grouchy because people keep asking him why he doesn't have a costume. Marge almost wouldn't give him a Laffy Taffy from her bowl.

I ignore him. I've been getting questions at every house, too: "What are you supposed to be?" The first time, I faltered, "A lizard?" before Sarah Nan jumped in. "Darth Lizard!" Now that's the running joke at each house. "I'm Darth Lizard!" I say, and we all fall apart laughing while the candy-bearer gives an indulgent, "Okay . . . ," and hands us our treats.

After the house with the Toblerones, we round the corner, and my heart starts beating faster. I remember his truck rumbling past me. His hand on the door.

"Are you okay?" Sarah Nan asks from beside me.

I can't really see her through the slits in Michael's mask, but I nod. "I'm fine."

As it turns out, the Henckmans' porch light is off. All their lights are off, actually. No one home. We pass right by them. I breathe a sigh of relief.

When we come to my old house, I try not to think too

hard about it. The stone wall out front is lined with tiny decorative pumpkins, and an inflatable black cat sits in front of the living room window, one paw raised. If I let my eyes drift out of focus, I can almost pretend that this is just another house on the block, not the place where, until recently, I felt most at home.

It's me, I tell the apple tree. But it's too dark for me to see that far back into the woods.

Chloe presses the doorbell. "It doesn't—" I start, then stop myself at the gentle *bing-bong* that chimes inside. I guess the new people fixed it.

There are footsteps. The door opens, and the Boy in the Skirt stands there with a large metal bowl full of fun-size Snickers.

The Boy in the Skirt is the weird Connecticut family?

The Boy in the Skirt lives in my old house?

"Trick or treat!" Sarah Nan shouts, with just as much enthusiasm as she has at every other door.

"How are you doing tonight?" Ned follows up, but Chloe shouts over him.

"Will! I didn't know you lived here."

Boy in the Skirt—Will?—shrugs. "Gotta live somewhere."

He's wearing his usual gray skirt and Converse, now with a long cape over his shoulders. His hair is wet, like he just washed it. Behind him, our old hallway is painted a different color, a pale mossy green, and the walls are densely packed with photographs in all sizes of frames.

"Why aren't you trick-or-treating?" Chloe asks.

He shrugs. "My dad took my sister. I stayed to do candy." He glances around at the rest of us. "What are you supposed to be?"

He's looking at me. The Boy in the Skirt is looking right at me, but he doesn't know it's me. He doesn't know that his house used to be my house, or that if he ever talked to me, he'd find out how much we have in common. How different we both are from everyone. "I—Darth Lizard," I stammer.

No one laughs this time. Sarah Nan looks at me strangely.

"What about you?" He nods at Michael, who's hanging back with one hand in his pocket, the other bunched around the pillowcase slung over his shoulder.

"I'm your *mom*," Michael says.

The Boy in the Skirt shifts the bowl into the crook of one arm. "My mom died."

Chloe gives a stifled "Erk!" in the back of her throat. Michael says, "Uh . . . sorry." The others say nothing. All the air has deflated from our group.

"So, you want candy?" the boy asks.

None of us knows what to say—I know I don't want to take candy from him anymore—but Sarah Nan finally makes the executive decision and holds out her bag. "Thank you!" she says, with a brightness that sounds fake. Chloe does the same.

"Thanks," I say as he drops a Snickers into my pillowcase. I try to make eye contact with him through the slits in my mask, try to tell him sorry, but he doesn't look at any of us as he doles out candy and then shuts the door.

We are barely back to the sidewalk when Chloe squeals, "Oh my God, *Michael*!"

"How was I supposed to know, okay?" Michael's voice is higher pitched than usual. "Obviously I wouldn't have said that if I'd known his mom—"

"Shush," Sarah Nan says. "He can still hear you."

"He can*not*."

"Let's get out of here," Ned says, checking his phone. "There's one more neighborhood I want to get to. These people there have a wheel you spin, and if it lands on 'Jumbo'—"

"Hey!" Michael exclaims. "Which one of those houses was the Lizard's?"

"None of your business," I say. Letting Michael know about my old house feels as personal as showing him a baby picture, or introducing him to my grandma.

"I think it *is* my business," he says. "You're wearing my costume just so no one would recognize you. Now I want it back."

He reaches to take it, but I step away. We're not out of the neighborhood yet, and there are still families out in the streets. Someone could recognize me. Or the Henckmans could come home. "Back off."

"This is like 'Who wore it better?'" Chloe says. "I think Lizzie did."

Michael scowls. "Give it *back*."

I block his hand with something like the moves that Sarah Nan and I have been practicing with the Aardvark. That makes him angry. He lunges again, and this time he manages to grab the mask off my head. It catches on my ears, scraping. "Ow!"

"Michael!" Sarah Nan exclaims.

Ned looks back and forth between us. "Hey, man . . ."

Michael ignores them both, pulling the mask back over his own head. "Ugh! It smells like a ferret died in here."

The anger rushes up inside me, and this time I can't stop it. As Michael settles the helmet over his head and walks past me, I kick him.

It's a dud of a kick. I barely make contact with the side of his leg—but I kicked him. And because the kick wasn't enough, I add, "Asshole."

Michael whirls around faster than I thought he could and shoves me, both hands, so that I go stumbling backward. "Bitch."

Before anything else can happen, Sarah Nan is at my side and Ned has Michael by the arm. "Dude, you pushed a *girl*."

"She kicked me!" Michael struggles to get free, but Ned holds on to him tight. "She swore at me and she kicked me!" He sounds incredulous. I am, too.

"I've had enough of him," Sarah Nan says. "We're going home."

Michael shakes off Ned. "Good. I don't know why I went trick-or-treating with a bunch of girls."

The streetlight casts shadows across Ned's crestfallen face. "But the house where you spin the wheel—"

"You do whatever you want," Sarah Nan says, pulling out her phone. "We're going."

"What about—?" Chloe says, but before she can say *Jeremy*, Sarah Nan just looks at her, and that's that.

"I guess we'll go home, too." Ned sighs, dropping Michael's arm. "It's not really fun anymore."

"Hey, I'm fun!" Michael says. Ned ignores him.

The boys stand on the street corner while Ned texts his mom for a ride; Michael calls something back at us over his shoulder, but I don't listen closely enough to hear it. Sarah Nan, Chloe, and I start walking to the street where Sarah Nan asked her mom to meet us—far enough from my old neighborhood not to raise suspicion.

"Wow." Chloe is shaking her head. "I never imagined Lizzie would be the one to teach Michael Gorman a lesson. *Wow*."

"Chloe," Sarah Nan says, after the fifth *wow*. "Do us all a favor: shut up."

CHAPTER 15

〜

For our sixth self-defense class, early in November, Ms. Ardvinson teaches us "ground defense."

As she explains what this means, the room goes silent.

"Ground defense means that you're on the ground—a very compromised position," she explains. "However, just because you're compromised doesn't mean you're powerless. There are several positions of strength that you can draw from even here."

She demonstrates the first move for us, which involves lying on one side and pivoting from the hip and forearm while kicking at an imaginary attacker's shins. It surprises me a little to see Ms. Ardvinson on the floor. In gym class, she doesn't usually demonstrate the thing she's teaching us. She definitely didn't do a chin-up to show us how.

"Your turn," she says, standing up and brushing off her hands.

A few of the girls look suspiciously at the floor. "Do they clean this, you know, regularly?" one of them asks.

Ms. Ardvinson crosses her arms and doesn't dignify that question with an answer.

Sarah Nan is away at a gymnastics tournament this weekend, so I'm all alone as I lower myself to the floor. The polished wood is cold on my forearm. Ms. Ardvinson was right: it actually isn't too hard to pivot this way, to kick and kick and kick. Next, she shows us how to get back to our feet using only our legs, no hands—that's harder to do. Once we're up, we review some of the skills: escaping choke holds, bear hugs (which seems like too nice a way of putting it), and other attacks from the front.

Mr. Henckman attacked from the front.

Mom fell to the ground.

What if Mom hadn't thought to call for James?

What if she'd been strong enough to push the door closed?

What if *I* had done something, instead of just standing there?

"Any questions?" Ms. Ardvinson asks.

I feel my hand go up.

She looks a little surprised. "Lizzie."

"For . . . when it happens from the front." I can't say the word *attack* out loud. "Could you ever, like, pretend you saw someone and shout for help, even if there was no one there?"

"You mean as a distraction?"

My face feels hot. I nod.

Ms. Ardvinson thinks for a moment before answering. "I have two responses to that," she says. "Girls, knock it off." Alexa has Melissa in a headlock, but lets go. "The first response is that I don't typically recommend techniques that involve tricking."

"Yeah, what if it didn't work?" Alexa says.

It did work, I think. But I don't want to say it.

"My second response," Ms. Ardvinson says, raising her voice louder than Alexa's, "is that I don't want to give the impression with *any* of these techniques that there's a 'right' move for every situation, or that any of this is easy. It's not. Even freezing is the body's natural, physiological response that's meant to be protective. It's not a weakness. Sometimes people think that self-defense classes are about blame, and what we should or shouldn't do in a situation. The person who deserves blame isn't you. It's the perpetrator—right?"

"Right," Kendall says forcefully, the way she shouts "no" during every practice. The other girls mumble in agreement.

Ms. Ardvinson looks at me. "Did I answer your question, Lizzie?"

The person who deserves blame isn't you. I nod.

I know the words are true. I know that all of this—my being here, selling our house, the cut on Mom's forehead—all of that is Mr. Henckman's fault. Not Mom's, and not mine.

I just wish I could *feel* that it's true.

"We're going to try all of those again in a few minutes," she says. "First, we have two more moves to learn."

The new moves are ground defense for when an attacker

is on top of you: one move if you're on your back, one if you're on your stomach. Ms. Ardvinson shows us what to do.

"All of these moves are meant to come from a place of power," she says, perhaps sensing the discomfort in the circle. "Many women have strength in the hips and legs. You can do this, but you have to practice in order for the movements to become natural. Find a partner, and give it a try."

Of all the days for Sarah Nan not to be here. I literally have to sit on top of someone, and then have them sit on top of me—and then, once I throw them off, pretend to hammer fist them in the groin.

I hang back, waiting for all the pairs to form so I can have whoever's left.

Alexa and Melissa are sisters, so they have no problem fake attacking one another. Most of the other girls already know someone who they've partnered up with in the past. Kendall approaches the girl who asked if the floor was clean.

"Oh," I hear the girl saying. "No offense, but I feel like it would be a little weird. You know?"

Kendall doesn't respond, but turns away from the girl, who finds herself a partner who doesn't kiss other girls. Kendall makes eye contact with me and mumbles something that ends with ". . . partners?"

I nod. "Sure."

She doesn't smile, exactly—not like she did with the

blue-haired girl—but the edges of her mouth soften a little bit. She's relieved.

I've never really known a gay person. I mean, I know they're *out* there. The women on our old block with the beagles, they're a couple. When I was a kid, I didn't know that. I thought they were friends who lived together, and that made sense to me. I only found out because I told my mom when I was ten that I hoped Sarah Nan and I could live in a house together one day like "the beagle ladies." That was when Mom told me that the beagle ladies were more than friends.

It makes me kind of annoyed thinking about it. She explained it all to me as if that was a reason Sarah Nan and I couldn't live together. But even if Sarah Nan and I don't love each other that way, my mom didn't *know* that at the time.

She also doesn't know that I'm asexual. No one knows but me. For now, I like it that way, especially since I feel like I don't have it all figured out yet. When I was reading online, I learned that some people identify as aromantic, which is different from asexual—they don't experience romantic attraction. Some people are both aromantic and asexual. Am I?

If Kendall smiled at me the way she smiled at the blue-haired girl, would I like it?

Sometimes I just want to scream: *How does everybody KNOW??*

Maybe, like that other girl, I was a little worried that

ground defense with Kendall would be awkward, but it isn't. "If I accidentally squash you, it's been nice knowing you," she says before sitting on me. I actually laugh.

Even though I'm smaller than her, I manage to catapult her off me just like Ms. Ardvinson showed us, by jolting my hips and throwing her to one side.

"Whoa," she says, lifting herself off the mat. "You're strong."

"No, I'm not," I say, out of habit, but I can't help smiling.

Next, Kendall catapults me. She's strong, too. I hit the mat with an *oof*. "Good job," I tell her.

It must sound odd for an eighth grader to tell a high schooler *good job*, but Kendall smiles—a friendly smile. "Thanks."

Later, after class, I wait in the lobby for Mom to come get me.

"How was it?" she asks as I climb in the car. Kendall's sitting on the bench again, waiting for her own ride, and she gives me a little wave as our car pulls away. I wonder if her girlfriend is coming to get her again. It was so easy to be her partner. If you feel more comfortable around girls, does that mean you *like* girls? Or is it the opposite?

"Fine," I say.

"Did you learn anything new?"

"Just some more moves."

Even freezing is the body's natural, physiological response . . .
It's not a weakness.

The person who deserves blame isn't you.

148

When Mom does her meditation, does she think about that? Is she trying to believe it, too?

We edge out into the street. "That girl on the bench?" I say abruptly. "I think she's gay."

"Mm?" Mom merges into traffic. She's trying to play it cool, to see what I'll say next.

"Yeah. I saw her kissing another girl before."

"That's nice," Mom says.

"Yeah," I say.

We drive along some more. We're almost home.

"If you ever thought you were gay, you'd tell me, right?" Mom asks.

"*Yes*."

"All right, all right." She glances sideways at me. "I just want you to know that you *can* tell me."

My stomach twists, feeling the lie. Everything I've been trying to figure out about myself, I haven't told her. How am I supposed to? In some ways, I've been telling her this entire time. She just hasn't been hearing me.

"Lizzie?"

"Can we talk about something else?" I stare straight ahead at the dashboard.

"Okay, sure," Mom says—but instead, we talk about nothing.

With our CARP outlines due before Thanksgiving, suddenly everyone is getting serious about research, with extra trips to the library during class and check-ins with Ms. Faraher. I'm getting serious, too—seriously petrified. Ms. Faraher still thinks I'm researching apple reproduction. I haven't told her that my project has morphed into much more than that. At this point, I have notes on reproduction for all kinds of asexual organisms: the kalanchoe, the whiptail lizard, the green anaconda. Maybe it's too big a topic. I can't explore every asexual species there is. I feel like there's some piece I'm missing that would tie it all together, or help me see it all more clearly.

On a Tuesday afternoon, Sarah Nan comes over to work on her index cards with me.

"Hi, Sarah Nan!" Dad says from the kitchen counter. He turns around and blinks at us, his eyes running. "Sorry, onions!"

"She goes by Sarah now," I remind him, but Sarah Nan quickly interrupts: "It's okay."

She follows me up the stairs. Mom's doing her meditation; the ocean sounds and acoustic guitar follow us as we tiptoe quietly into my room.

"It's like the *Twilight Zone*," Sarah Nan says, once we've shut the door behind us.

"What do you mean?"

She drops her beaded bag and plops down on the foot of my bed. "It's like, at first everything seems familiar—same furniture, same family—but actually, it's completely different. Your mom's meditating, your dad cooks now, James is *gone* . . ."

"Your mom meditates, too," I point out.

"My mom always did."

Sarah Nan is probably one of the few people who knows my family well enough to notice a change. The things she's saying are things I've noticed, too—but somehow it feels impolite for her to say them out loud.

"What about me?" I ask. "Am I different?"

Sarah Nan studies me. Sometimes I wonder if I could tell her about being asexual. Isn't that the kind of things friends share with one another? But something always stops me. After all those times she's asked me, *Isn't there anyone you think is kind of cute?*—I guess I'm not sure she'd believe me. She might think it was one more excuse for my stubbornness about boys.

"Something's different," she says at last. "I just can't say exactly what."

Sarah Nan's CARP is about Alzheimer's. Her aunt works as a researcher for a pharmaceutical company—"Big Pharma," as Daria would say—and sent her a bunch of scholarly articles on recent treatments. "Look at all this stuff I have to read," she says, producing a thick folder. "So many articles—I don't know where to start!"

"I know what you mean. I've been trying to read this." I hold up James's old AP bio textbook, which I borrowed from his bedroom over the weekend. The first section I opened to was about how the octopus reproduces when the male "introduces" a packet of sperm into the female using one of its tentacles. Sometimes, the female latches on and rips that whole tentacle off. I slammed the book shut after that and waited awhile before picking it up again. What I don't get, and what no resource has been able to tell me, is how any animal—octopus, insect, human—knows what to do. Like, why would an octopus ever think to do *that*? No one had "the talk" with the octopus.

"Mm," Sarah Nan says. I'm about to tell her about the octopus, but she's not looking at me. She's on her phone.

She texts for a while, then awhile more. I flip through the textbook's glossy pages to the section about the fungi kingdom: mushrooms, fungi, molds. The part I was just reading was about mycorrhizae, which literally means "fungus roots"— the network of microscopic fungi that extends through the soil around a plant's roots, interconnecting trees in forests and supplying them with more water and nutrients than their own roots could access alone. Meanwhile, the plants supply the mycorrhizae with food obtained through photosynthesis.

Experiments have shown that mycorrhizae greatly enhance plant growth in comparison to plants lacking fungal partners.

Fungal partners? Ick.

"Sorry." Sarah Nan puts the phone down. "What were you saying?"

"Nothing, just—lots of reading to do."

Sarah Nan squints at the title. She probably should get glasses, but doesn't want to. "What's your project, again?"

My stomach jumps a little. I haven't told Sarah Nan anything about my new idea. She still thinks I'm doing apple trees, too. "It's about plants and animals that . . ."

Her phone lights up, and she picks it up again. Reads.

"Hey," I say.

"Sorry, Lizzie . . ." She punches a fast message, then lowers the phone and lets her head drop back against the bed. "Can I tell you something?"

"Sure."

She sighs. "I don't know if Ned and I are going to work out."

"Work out?" I repeat. Sarah Nan isn't meeting my eyes. "You mean like you might break up?"

"I don't know." She motions to her phone, facedown on the rug. "He's texting me all this BS about how he hardly gets to play basketball because he's with me all the time . . . and I'm trying to tell him that relationships take *work*, and it's not all about basketball and fun . . . and he texted me back that he wants to spend more time with his friends."

I can't believe Sarah Nan is telling me this. It seems like the sort of thing she would ordinarily discuss with Chloe. Probably because I don't quite understand what she's talking about. "Relationships take work?"

"I mean . . . yeah!" She takes a binder clip off some index

cards and shuffles them. "You get out of it what you put into it. If we give up now just because we hit a rough patch, then what was the point of the last three months, you know?"

"Right." I watch as she picks up her phone and starts texting again. "What are you saying now?"

"I'm telling him that he needs to communicate better and tell me when he's feeling like he needs more space."

Rough patch. Communicate better. More space. Were those things she heard Daria say about Nick? Or maybe she heard them on TV. That's where I've heard them. "Do you think he can do that?"

She looks at me. "What's that supposed to mean?"

"Nothing. Just, Ned doesn't seem very . . ." I struggle to find the right words, remembering Ned in his unicorn onesie shouting about Toblerones. "Communicative."

"Well, what else am I supposed to do, Lizzie? Just say, 'Okay, fine, let's break up'?"

Sarah Nan's brown eyes are shooting off sparks at me.

Yes. I feel the answer deep down in the bad, selfish part of me. I want them to break up. Even though it would hurt her, even though it would mean losing something that matters to her, I still want it. I want things to be the way they were before, when I didn't have to share her and the relationship that mattered most was *ours*. Being friends didn't take any work.

"I don't know," I finally say.

She picks up her note cards. "Never mind."

I settle the biology textbook in my lap. It's heavy, and keeps sliding down. "I'm sorry."

"What are you sorry for?"

"About Ned. I'm sorry."

She pulls a loose page out of her folder and says softly, "No, you're not."

Her voice is quiet enough that I can pretend I didn't hear her, and that's what I do. For the rest of the afternoon, we work on CARP together, but separately. Downstairs, my dad clatters around with pots and pans; across the hall, waves wash in and out of the imaginary shore of my mom's meditation. I want to know what Sarah Nan sees that's changed about me, if there's anything—or if the divide between us is that I haven't changed enough.

CHAPTER 16

The Friday before Thanksgiving is Ms. Faraher's last day.

She has us finish up the group presentations we've been working on about photosynthesis, but there's lots of time left over before the end of the period. So that's when Chloe and the other girls bring out the onesies.

"You all shouldn't have!" Ms. Faraher exclaims. Chloe pushes the rolling desk chair front and center and invites Ms. Faraher to sit down while she hands her the boxes one by one, beaming. Other kids get out of their seats to have a closer look, but I stay off to the side, feeling far away.

"So cute!" Ms. Faraher exclaims over the first onesie, which says *Little Man* with a picture of a mustache. She holds it over her belly, joking, "Look, it fits!"

Last night I made a card for Ms. Faraher with a teddy bear on it. Inside I wrote something about how I would miss her and congratulations. I wasn't sure how to sign it, so I wrote *Best wishes, Lizzie*. Best wishes? What was I thinking? Now, as Ms. Faraher gently lifts the lid on the next box, it seems obvious that "best wishes" is not what you say to someone who's about to have a baby. I stick the card in my notebook, and I leave it there.

The next onesie is powder blue with a duck on the front. Again, as I watch the reactions of the girls around Ms. Faraher, I wonder how they know what to *do*. They coo over each onesie. They ask her questions like when she's due, if she's chosen a name, and what the baby's room looks like. Sometimes I wonder if there's a guide to womanhood that I didn't get, one that includes all the things you're supposed to be excited about, all the things you're supposed to say.

Maybe the guidebook also would have told me what to say at lunchtime, when Sarah Nan tells us that she and Ned made up—big time. She says they "took it to the next level."

"*Finally*," Chloe says. I don't say anything. My peanut butter sandwich has turned to glue in my mouth.

"Only for a few minutes," Sarah Nan adds. "His mom kept checking on us."

James and Ally used to make out in our basement. Only, Mom would send *me* to check on them—interrupt them, really, like the innocent little sister who doesn't know what she's interrupting. "Go see if James and Ally want some popcorn," she would say, or "Can you ask James if he has any books to return to the library?" Neither of us acknowledged the real reason she was asking me to go down there. I would make a big noise at the top of the stairs and clomp my feet going down so they had lots of warning. Ally's cheeks would be pink, and James would be sitting up awkwardly straight with his arm draped over the back of the couch. I would mumble whatever it was Mom had sent me down there to tell them and then hurry back upstairs.

"So," Chloe asks, leaning in. "How was it?"

"A little weird." Sarah Nan smiles. "But also fun."

Chloe raises her eyebrows. "Any touching?"

"A little," Sarah Nan says, pretend-casual. "Above the waist. Everything on."

I glance across the cafeteria to Ned's table, where he and some other boys are shoving potato wedges up their noses. I try to swallow the tasteless peanut butter but can't get it past the back of my mouth. I feel sick. I feel sick and sad and protective and angry and scared at the same time, and it's all building up in my chest and I can't do anything about it because nobody in the world would understand what makes it so terrible. *Ned, touching her above the waist?*

"Don't *look* over there!" Sarah Nan whacks me in the head. "He'll know we're talking about him."

I rub the place she hit me; she actually hit kind of hard. "Why, does he think you ever talk about anything else?"

Sarah Nan sucks in a breath. Did I just say that? Her face hardens. "Just because you aren't interested in boys doesn't mean the rest of us can't be," she says. "Why don't you quit acting like you're so much better than us and just *grow up*?"

Chloe sits there looking back and forth between us, her mouth still open, waiting for a carrot stick that is stuck half-way in transit. For once, she's speechless.

All the really terrible insults rush through my mind: *At least I'm grown up enough to reach the top of the refrigerator. At least I'm not a spoiled only child who can't talk about anything but herself. Did Ned even find anything to feel up there?* Instead, I stand, grabbing the loose pieces of my lunch and stuffing them into my lunch box.

"I'm more grown up than you," I say, and rush out of the cafeteria before anyone can stop me.

I remember James telling me once that if you act like everything's normal, like you're doing exactly what you're supposed to be doing, no one will suspect anything is wrong. So I walk purposefully through the hallways back to my locker, and no one stops me. Nobody cares that I'm a girl alone.

When I open my locker, my puffy winter coat pops off the hook that it shares with my backpack and falls out onto the floor. I pick it up and hang it, and it pops off again. I want to punch something. I want to punch something the way we all practiced punching the man-torso in self-defense class. Instead, I ball up my coat and lunch box, stuff it all in my locker, and slam the door shut. Then I kick the door, but that doesn't really help.

I stand there breathing. What now? Lunch won't be over for probably another ten minutes. I can't just stand around. I can't go back. *Why don't you just grow up?*

Grow up.

When I look at Sarah Nan and Chloe giggling about Ned, I feel so distant from them; it's as if I'm decades older, more mature. Or are they the ones who are more mature than me, because they've experienced this thing that I haven't?

Is this what it's like to be asexual?

Will it be like this forever?

There is nothing wrong with you. That's what I wish somebody would say to me. *Lizzie, you're fine the way you are.*

My feet are taking me down the hall and around the corner to Ms. Faraher's room. All this time, I've wanted to talk to her, and today is her last day. She's the one who gave me the kalanchoe plant. She's the one I can ask.

Her door is open, but she isn't reading like she used to. She's just sitting there, her desk chair swiveled away from me to face the parking lot outside. The onesies are neatly folded on her desk, the boxes and wrapping paper tucked into the recycling bin. Her plastic fork hovers over a bowl of noodles.

I rap gently on the doorframe. It takes a moment for her to pull herself back from wherever she is.

"Lizzie." She smiles. "I thought I wasn't going to get to say goodbye. Come on in."

She's the same as before, I remind myself as I weave between the rows of lab tables to stand opposite her. *She looks different, but she's the same.*

"Have a seat," she says, and I lean against one of the tables, not quite sitting. "Did you finish your lunch already?"

I nod. "I had a question. About what you were telling us before. About the plants?"

She waits, still holding her bowl of noodles. "Okay."

I take a breath. "You know what you said about the kalanchoe plants? How they don't . . . you know."

"Don't sexually reproduce?" she prompts.

"Yeah." My palms are sweating. I open and close them. *Get to the point.* "I was thinking . . . I might be like that."

Ms. Faraher lowers the fork back into the noodles. "Well, that's a little different," she says slowly, and maybe with some surprise. "Humans are sexual beings, Lizzie. We're born with primary sex characteristics, and the way we spread our DNA is through sexual reproduction."

I can't help but look at her belly as she says that. I drop my gaze to the floor, hoping she didn't notice. "No—I know," I say. "But what if . . ." Faltering, I try to figure out what I'm asking. "What if you don't . . . feel that way?"

"Feel what way?"

She doesn't understand what I mean. My face goes hot as I force myself to say the word. "Sexual."

"Oh, Lizzie," she says warmly, and I think she's going to say it: *You're fine the way you are.* Instead, she continues, "It'll happen with time. Everyone grows and matures differently. Just because you don't feel something now doesn't mean you never will. You're a smart, beautiful girl—I know you'll find a partner someday, when the time is right."

She doesn't get it. What she shared in class, it really was just about the plants. My heart sinks. I should have known. She's married, she's having a baby . . . I should have known she wasn't the person who would understand about being asexual. But I really, really wanted her to be.

My eyes sting with disappointment, and I have to blink hard.

"Does that help?" she asks.

I nod, hastily. I try to give a fake smile, but my face muscles won't go that way. I remember what Sarah Nan said to me when I slept over: *Everyone can tell what you feel.* I have to get out of here.

"Thanks," I say, and I turn to go. "Good luck with the baby."

Good luck—that's even worse than "best wishes."

"Lizzie?"

I turn back. Ms. Faraher looks at me. There's a question in her face that I can't read.

"Do you need a pass back to the cafeteria?" she finally asks. "I don't want you to get in trouble."

I shake my head. "I'm okay," I tell her. Even though I am not okay at all.

That night, in bed, I try to do what the book said—the body book that Sarah Nan and I giggled over in her basement when we were eleven, the book that thrilled her and frightened me. I get a little pocket mirror and make a tent with the blankets over my head. I pull my pajama pants down, blushing; I already feel self-conscious. On the wooden chest across the room, my American Girl dolls watch me fumble around. *What is she doing?* they wonder. They're all stitched up down there, nothing to see. Smooth, flat fabric.

Some women don't even know what they look like down there, Daria said. I don't want to be like that. I don't want to be a girl who doesn't even know herself.

I tilt the mirror and look.

I can't see anything. It's too dark. I stick one arm outside the tent, fumble for my phone on my bedside table, and tap the flashlight on.

Hair—didn't-used-to-be-there, not-a-part-of-me hair—and some pink, and then suddenly I'm throwing off the blankets because it's too hot and I can't breathe and I feel ridiculous. I'm blushing, even in the dark. Who else's body makes them blush when they're completely alone?

I wiggle my pajama pants back up to my waist, and then I lie down, arms at my sides.

Humans are sexual beings, Lizzie. Was I meant to be something other than human? I used to imagine what it would be like to be a tree—tall, flat, straight—but now I know that even trees don't stand alone. Above the earth, they send out their pollen in flirtatious bee kisses, and below, their roots are interconnected networks of mycorrhizae that twist and curl together. Then I thought I was like the kalanchoe plant, but Ms. Faraher said that's not the same thing. So maybe I'm not even like a plant. Maybe I'm just a rock. Cold. Unfeeling. Everyone else changes, but the rock never does. Even in a billion years, when the sun dies the death of a star and incinerates our small blue planet, the rock will just keep right on floating through space. Nobody can touch it.

CHAPTER 17

The day before Thanksgiving is a half day at school. When Mom arrives to pick me up, a little flurry of snow is starting to come down. I like the swirling patterns it makes on the roads as the passing traffic blows it around.

"When is James supposed to get here?" I ask. He's getting a ride with Gerald, who has a car and can drop James off on his way—cheaper than the bus, James said, though he's not thrilled about the quality time with his awkward roommate.

"Any time now," Mom says.

I can't wait. After Ms. Faraher, more than ever I just want to be with my brother, and hear him tell me that I'm okay. James has always liked me exactly the way I am. He's never asked any questions. I could tell him about being asexual and he'd probably just say, "That's cool."

Maybe I will tell him.

After a quick stop at the grocery store for some last ingredients, we're home. Mom drops me off at the foot of the driveway to check the mail, and when I come inside, she's on the phone.

"Well, of course we're disappointed," Mom is saying,

"but we understand. You sure you'll be—? All right, yes. Go ahead. I'll talk to you later, sweetie."

I freeze where I am, reaching into the fridge for a brick of cheddar. There's only one person besides me who Mom would call "sweetie."

Mom holds the phone tenderly for a moment before setting it down on the table.

"That was James."

I shut the fridge. "What did he say?"

Mom clears her throat. "He decided not to come home for Thanksgiving after all."

The kitchen floor seems to tilt beneath me. "What?"

"He says he has too much work to do—a big paper that's due the first week of December. It *is* a long trip for such a short stay." Mom's trying to sound calm and rational, but the busyness of her hands at the sink as she dumps a bag of potatoes and goes about scrubbing them gives her away. "We'll just have a nice, quiet dinner with you and Dad and me."

"I don't *want* a nice, quiet dinner." Mom's quiet resignation makes my outrage burn even more brightly. "I want James to come home."

"Gerald already left," Mom says. She's peeling the first potato, the peeler flicking rapidly. "He couldn't change his mind now even if he wanted to."

"Dad could go get him. I'd go, too. Why didn't he say anything until now?"

"Lizzie."

"He was supposed to come home. You don't even *care*."

"We'll see him at Christ—" Mom says, but I refuse to hear the rest. I sweep my arm across the tabletop and send the remaining grocery bags tumbling to the floor. Onions roll and scatter in all directions; a jar of artichoke hearts shatters. A can of corn somersaults, then somehow lands upright.

Mom's mouth falls open. "Lizzie!"

"If you don't care that he's not coming home, then I don't care if we even have Thanksgiving!" I shove a chair out of my path and run up the stairs into James's bedroom, his new room that isn't really his, and I throw myself at the bed and start punching a meditation pillow with everything I have, not using any of the training or coordination that I've learned in two months of Women's Self-Defense, just pummeling and pummeling until I collapse against the pillow and let the tears come.

He's not coming, I keep saying to myself, trying to make the words sink in—but that isn't even the worst part. The worst is that when he called, he didn't even ask to talk to me.

Mom doesn't come to find me. She's mad, probably, and waiting for me to apologize for making a mess. I shouldn't have shoved the groceries; I know that. It's not the onions' fault that James isn't coming home. They're just stupid onions in the wrong place at the wrong time. I picture them rolling under the table, bumping into each other, looking so pitiful that I almost start crying all over again.

I hear Dad come home from work: the door opening, the murmuring of his voice and Mom's in the kitchen. She's telling him about James, and then she's explaining the mess on the floor that hasn't been cleaned up yet. The next thing I know, there's a knock on the doorframe.

"Mom told me you were upset," Dad says. I lift my head. James's bedspread is all wet with my snot and tears. Good.

"I'm sorry."

"Tell Mom that."

"I will." I wipe my eyes with the back of my arm and sit up on the side of the bed. "I just don't get why he wouldn't want . . ." My voice starts to break. "*I'd* want to come home."

Dad steps into the room, looking around like a visitor who hasn't been here in a while. He sits down on the bed beside me. "I'm sad, too. But it was his choice to make. He's growing up."

I look down at the carpet, at Dad's feet beside mine. His shiny work shoes look monumental beside my yellow socks with the toes turned under. "But we're his family. He's supposed to be here."

Dad doesn't respond to that. He puts an arm around me.

"I remember when you were born," he begins.

"Come on, Dad." I don't need to hear it again: the beautiful fall day, me with my tongue sticking out.

He ignores me. "When we brought you home from the hospital, James came running out to meet us."

"He wanted a brother."

"He couldn't wait to meet you." Dad hugs me to him, but my shoulders stay stiff. "We sat him on the couch and put you in his arms, and he took one look at you and said, 'Look, Mumma, she's so pretty.'"

I still don't say anything. I reach around and hug my dad. He holds me there, in James's room, and both of us are quiet.

Thanksgiving morning, I pull back my bedroom shades to find a light covering of snow on the front lawn. The sun is out, making everything bright, but also melting the snow away before I can enjoy it. I wanted more.

Soon, the house fills with the familiar smells of turkey and roasted squash, as well as a new recipe for cornbread stuffing Dad wanted to try. Mom grumbles as she moves everything around in the oven to make room for it while the turkey settles on the counter. I'm in charge of potatoes, but when Mom sees how slowly I'm going, half-heartedly churning with the masher, she takes the pot from me and whips it all up in about ten seconds, then sets it back on the stovetop with a noticeable *clang*.

We eat in the dining room, even though there are only three of us. The serving platters, bowls, and gravy pitcher get piled up at the end of the table, where James would have sat. Dad's cornbread stuffing is too sweet. When Dad asks if it's too sweet, Mom says it's fine.

"Well," Mom says at the end, as we clear the last of the dessert plates, "that was a little different, but it still was a nice day."

Dad's at the sink, starting the dishes. "Yep," he agrees. "Dry for me, Lizzie?"

I take a towel and silently begin polishing a wineglass.

"She said those brownies had beans in them?" Dad says after a few minutes.

One of Mom's students gave her an aluminum tray of brownies, which Mom put out with the pies for dessert. "Black beans," Mom confirms.

"Huh." Dad swishes soapy water around one of our casserole dishes. "I never heard of that before."

I want to scream. What is it about adulthood that means you can't just *say* what you're actually thinking?

Fortunately, Mom's phone buzzes on the kitchen table. "It's James," she says. "Lizzie, why don't you talk to him?"

"I don't want to talk to him. He ruined Thanksgiving."

Mom ignores me. "Hi, honey!" she says. "Yes, we just finished up; now's the perfect time. Here, talk to your sister." She takes the dish towel from me and hands me the phone. "You can bring it back when you're done."

I sigh. I *do* want to talk to him. "Hi, James."

"Hey, kiddo."

Something's weird. He never calls me cliché nicknames like "kiddo" or "squirt." He calls me "Nugget" when he wants to tease me. Otherwise, he just calls me Lizzie.

"Hey," I say. My throat feels tight, so I stare hard at the wall calendar, which says it's only thirty-three days until Christmas. "Happy Thanksgiving."

The words sound bitter, which I didn't mean them to, but either he doesn't notice or he doesn't care.

"You too," he says. "Are Joe and Lisa still there?"

I start up the stairs so I can talk to him alone. "They're with Grandma this year. It was going to be just us."

"Oh."

Now he hears it. I start to feel bad. "Did you even get Thanksgiving food today?"

"Yeah, the dining hall had a dinner at noon, so we went over there for some turkey and potatoes."

"Who's 'we'?" I say, just as a voice emerges in the background. It asks a question that sounds like, "Where's the ham?" But that's probably not it.

"Oh—I meant 'we' like everybody, all the students still on campus."

I go into James's room and sit down on a cushion. It's been a long time since I had one of those sibling mind reading moments with James, but right now I know there's something he's trying to hide. "Who's there with you?" I ask. "I thought Gerald went home." Also, I thought Gerald was a man, which the voice in the background was not.

"Um . . ." James doesn't answer. In his silence, I figure it out.

"Is Ally there with you?" Again, James is silent. "She is—I

heard her voice. Oh my God." I stand up from the cushion. "Ally's there."

"Don't tell Mom," James says urgently. "She won't understand—"

"*I* don't understand. What the hell is she doing there?" I feel melodramatic, but also grown up, saying *What the hell* like that to James.

"Can you calm down and let me explain? Are you in your room?"

"I'm in *your* room," I tell him, shutting the door because I know that's what he wants. I know what he wants even when he doesn't ask—that's how well I know him. "What's she *doing* there? I thought she was in Ohio."

"She was," James says, and I hear him moving around, maybe shifting on his creaky dorm bed, or maybe cradling the phone so Ally can't hear what we're talking about. "She couldn't go home for Thanksgiving because she still had classes yesterday, and then we realized it was just a quick bus ride . . ."

"But you were broken up," I remind him. "You *broke up.*"

"Yeah." James ponders this, as though he's only just thought about it for the first time. "I guess we're not anymore."

A cold, hard rock hits the bottom of my stomach. "You had sex with her."

"Lizzie, come on."

"You did—I can tell you did, I know you did it!" My voice is rising, my chest tightening with panic.

"Lizzie." He's calling me by my name now.

"I thought you said you didn't want to do 'everything.' I thought you weren't ready."

"We are *not* talking about this."

"You were supposed to come home."

He sighs. "Can you give me back to Mom?"

"No!" I'm pressing the phone so hard to my ear that it will leave a mark on the side of my face. "I didn't get—I wanted . . ." I cover my face with my hand. This wasn't supposed to happen. He was supposed to give me advice on Michael Gorman. He was supposed to tell me that Ms. Faraher was wrong. He was supposed to be here so I could tell him that I'm asexual, and he could tell me it's okay.

"What did you want?" His voice is gentler now. I wipe my eyes with the heel of my palm, trying to think of something else to tell him.

"I wanted to tell you . . . I got high honors on my report card." The words are deflated and lifeless.

"That's so great!" he exclaims, as if our conversation of the past three minutes never happened. Maybe Ally is still in the room with him. "Wow—that definitely blows my eighth-grade report card out of the water. Congratulations!"

"Thanks." Suddenly, I just feel tired. "I'm giving you back to Mom now."

"Okay," James says. "Have an extra piece of turkey for me—oops, I mean an extra chicken nugget!"

"Ha, ha." I never thought I would feel the exact moment when my heart split in half.

"Hey, Lizzie?"

"What?"

"It'll be okay," he says. "Everything will."

I don't answer that. "Here's Mom," I say, even though Mom's nowhere near. "Bye."

He says "bye" as I'm already lowering the phone, so I just barely hear him.

After I hand the phone off to my parents, I go to my room, lie back on my bed, and stare up. *It'll be okay.* James's old room had glow-in-the-dark stars on the ceiling that spelled out *It's okay*. I stuck them up there for him. It was after he and Ally broke up once before, when they were sophomores—after she said she needed to "focus more on school." He was sixteen then, and I was eleven, and he spent a lot of time lying flat on his bed and not talking to any of us. When I tried to sneak into his room after lights-out, he told me to go away. I didn't know how to make him hear me, so one afternoon, while he was out at soccer practice, I wrote it in stars. He never said anything about it, but the next morning, a Saturday, he came downstairs and had breakfast with us.

I wonder where those stars are now.

CHAPTER 18

The Saturday after Thanksgiving is Pumpkinhead Day. It's a silly town tradition that people get excited about: everyone brings their decorative pumpkins, squash, and other gourds to town hall, where there are tents for kids and anyone else who wants to draw Sharpie faces on them and add them to the display along Main Street. Some people come with their pumpkinheads already decorated, wearing off-kilter baseball caps or other accessories. At the end, the town takes all the pumpkins and sends them off to the municipal compost, doing away with everyone's fall-time decorations just in time to usher in the Christmas lights and inflatable Santas.

Sarah Nan and I usually look at the pumpkinheads together, but we haven't spoken since last Friday at lunch. The past few days of school, I was back at the "miscellaneous" table in the cafeteria—my own choice. I know I should apologize; she and Ned were obviously going to go there eventually. James and Ally, too. I'm the one who has to get used to everyone else changing. I'm the one who has to grow up.

On Saturday morning, I text her. Pumpkins?

Come on over! she writes back.

While we're walking around laughing at pumpkins will be a good time to talk. I'll show her that I can be okay about Ned.

Mom is getting caught up on paperwork for school; Dad is outside raking. I tell them that I'm walking to Sarah Nan's.

"Are you sure?" Mom asks. "It's a good twenty-five minutes."

I'm sure.

It feels good to walk. Cold, but once I'm moving, it doesn't really bother me. The trees are mostly bare; the reds and golds have turned to brown now. Sometimes the wind picks up and makes a little leaf whirlwind in front of me. Here and there, I smell the smoke from people's woodstoves. In our old house, we had one of those. When I was little, I'd sit and watch in the wintertime when Dad would put on a big, thick glove and add more logs, sending little sparks. Maybe my future house will have a woodstove.

It actually only takes me twenty minutes to get to Sarah Nan's. Daria's car is in the driveway. I scrape my boots off on the welcome mat, even though the bristles are worn flat and don't really do anything. I give a few small kicks to the top of the step, and then I open the door.

"Sarah Nan?" No one answers. Maybe she's trying to remind me that she'll only respond to her new, adult name. "Sarah?"

"Is that you, Lizzie?" Daria comes into the kitchen, fastening her bathrobe. Her hair is wet; she just showered.

"Hi—sorry." I realize suddenly how weird it is that I just let myself in. Usually Sarah Nan is right here waiting for me. "Sarah Nan said we could look at the pumpkinheads together."

Said we could. As if I were her little sister, asking permission.

"You know what? She just left to see them, with Ned."

The slush in my boot treads is melting, forming a puddle around my feet. "Oh."

"You can probably catch up to them," Daria suggests. "Text her and she'll wait for you."

"Okay," I say, but the word catches in my throat. I turn around quickly. "Bye."

"Lizzie?"

I stop, my hand on the knob.

"Do you . . . want some tea?"

She feels sorry for me. I tug my hat down lower, as if that will somehow hide the fact that I'm crying. "No, that's okay."

"Come here. Sit down." She pulls back a chair from the table. "Stay and have tea with me."

I can't find my voice to say no. While Daria busies herself at the stove, I dry my eyes with the backs of my mittens. *Get it together, Lizzie. It's just the pumpkinheads.* Sarah Nan and I spent half the time making fun of them, anyway. But that was kind of the point.

"Here you are." Daria sets a mug in front of me, one that I recognize, with a calico cat painted on in light brushstrokes. Sarah Nan and I decided to use it to catch tadpoles in the stream behind her house one day. There weren't any tadpoles, and we chipped the mug, and Sarah Nan cried all the way back up the hill about how we were going to get in trouble. But we put it back in the cupboard without saying anything, and Daria never said anything to us. I turn the mug a little to see if the chip is still there. It is.

"What kind do you like?" Daria offers me a wooden box packed with colorful paper pouches.

"Any kind."

She chooses lemon for me, Earl Grey for herself. The teakettle whistles, and she uses an oven mitt to bring it over and fill my mug.

"This is exactly what I needed," she pronounces, tugging the string of her tea bag up and down. The front of her bathrobe is popping open a little, and I try not to let my eyes focus on what's there. I bring the mug to my lips. It's too hot to drink.

"So—how is James? It must be nice to have him home again."

"He didn't come." I inhale the steam, wishing I had the

glasses I wore when I was nine so they could fog up and hide my eyes. "He said he had too much work to do."

"Oh, Lizzie . . ." Daria sets her mug down and puts a hand on my arm. "I'm so sorry, honey. That must be really disappointing."

I feel the tears coming back again. I'm so sick of this—all of it. Screw James, screw Sarah Nan, screw everyone.

"What's so great about sex?" I ask.

Daria sits up a little. "What?" There's a laugh in her voice, but she isn't laughing at me. Just surprised.

"I just don't get it," I say. "I don't get what people do it for."

"Well," she says, "it's how—"

"I don't mean that." I surprise myself a little, interrupting an adult. But I know what she was going to say. "I mean . . . I don't get why any person would want to do that with another person. Why it's fun."

Daria's face changes suddenly to alarm. "Is Sarah Nan . . . ?"

"No! No—it's not that." I wave my hand as if to erase the air between us. It was foolish of me to think I could ask her. This is *Sarah Nan's* mom. She has her own daughter to think about without worrying about me. "Never mind."

Daria doesn't say anything, just sips more tea. The shoulder of her bathrobe is wet where her hair drapes over. She was probably going to blow-dry it before I walked in the door. Instead, she made tea for me. And now she's looking at me, waiting, like she knows there's more to come out.

"It just seems like you lose yourself," I say. I run my finger in circles along the mug's rim, feeling that old chip interrupting every revolution. "It's like suddenly you can't see anything else around you in the world. All you can think about or talk about is this one person—and you don't even care about *them*, you just care if they *like* you, if you're *pretty* to them, if they *want* you, and nothing else matters, no one else matters—" I cut myself off, biting my lip so I won't cry again.

I hear Daria's voice. "Are you talking about sex, or relationships?"

"It's the same thing."

"No, it isn't the same thing."

I try to think of a response to that. I can smell the lemon tea in front of me, but more than that, I get the smell of Sarah Nan's home—which has been my second home ever since I was a year old. Sarah Nan's house was the first place I noticed that other people's houses could smell different. That breakfasts could taste different. That moms could be different.

"I've been thinking . . ." I cut myself off, look down at my tea again. The color in the mug is growing stronger as it steeps. ". . . that I might be asexual."

Daria sets her mug down on the table. "Sure," she says. "I can understand that."

I can't believe I just said it aloud. I picture Ms. Faraher

with the kalanchoe. *Humans are sexual beings, Lizzie.* Sarah Nan saying *grow up.* "You can?"

"Sure. It makes sense, right? Some people are attracted to men, some to women, some to all genders, some to none—a whole spectrum. I always thought it made sense, anyway."

Some to all, some to none. "Is that what you are?" I ask hopefully.

Now she really does laugh—almost a guffaw, she laughs so hard. That was a silly question. I forgot about Nick. "No—I am not. But I know a few people who are. It's an okay way to be."

"You know people?"

"Not personally, but I know *of* people. I guess you're the first I've met!"

I sip my tea. It's hot, but it doesn't burn now. *An okay way to be.*

All of a sudden, I can't sit still at this table for one second longer.

"I have to go," I say, pushing back my chair so abruptly that it almost topples over. "Thanks—for the tea."

"You're welcome." Daria smiles and raises her mug to her lips. "And Lizzie?"

I turn back, my hand on the doorknob.

"We can have tea together anytime," she says.

"Thanks." I'm smiling bigger than I thought I could. "Bye!"

I burst out the door of Sarah Nan's house, and I am

walking. Before I know it, I'm at the end of their front walk, and then at the corner; each step seems to drive me forward with a power I've never known before. When the road slopes down into a hill, I feel like I could do cartwheels down it, or back handsprings—like I suddenly have the grace and strength to do things like that.

Asexual. I let out a loud breath into the air—*Hah!*—admiring the way the cloud takes shape. I can take shape, too; I exist, I have a name.

And: I finally have an idea for my CARP project.

CHAPTER 19

Ms. Faraher's long-term substitute is the same guy who substituted for her class on the day we were in the library: Mr. Le. He's young and wears a collared shirt and tie, and the first thing he tells us, after getting all of us settled and taking attendance, is that Ms. Faraher had her baby. A little boy named Rowan. He puts a picture up on the projector screen.

"Awwww!" everyone says. The baby is in one of those clear hospital bassinets with a bracelet around his tiny wrist. People always say that a baby has "his mother's nose" or something like that, but I don't see anything of Ms. Faraher there. He looks long and weird. Maybe that's what her husband looks like.

"Do *you* have kids, Mr. Le?" Chloe asks.

He laughs. "No, I think I'm still too young for that."

He turns away to begin writing on the board, and Chloe mouths to Sami across the room, *I told you.*

A little while later, when Mr. Le is struggling to present his slides on the projector screen, Sami jumps up. "I can help!"

"I don't . . . ," Mr. Le says, but Sami has already taken command of the mouse and is clicking through options.

"You have to change the display settings. There you go!"

"Thank you"—Mr. Le looks at his seating chart—"Samantha."

She grimaces. "It's Sami." But then she brightens her voice. "Samantha is okay, too."

She thinks he's cute, I realize. The words surface in my mind the same way the final answer appears at the end of a long polynomial equation—like I finally figured out x. *That's why she's acting strange.*

In front of me, Chloe is primly raising her hand, which she never did with Ms. Faraher, to offer an answer to Mr. Le's first question: "Spores?" *And she likes him, too.*

I laugh to myself, feeling like I'm suddenly in on the joke—or like it's okay for once that I'm not.

Sarah Nan and I made up over the weekend, via text. She even apologized, kind of, for telling me to grow up: I know you were bummed about Ms. Faraher leaving.

That wasn't really it, but I appreciate that she noticed.

After talking to Daria, I feel so much better about everything. I knew that asexuality was a real thing, and I knew that what I was feeling was real. But something about hearing her say, *Sure, I can understand that*, was like a lightning bolt to my core. If I want to be the way I am in the world, then more people need to know that the way I am exists. More people need to know that "asexual" is a way to be.

That's my CARP project.

Today, Mr. Le is checking in with the honors kids. We're the ones who are presenting at the CARP Expo in two more weeks. Everyone else has until January before they give their presentations to the class. I already had a ton of research on aphids and whiptails and adventitious buds; now I've added articles about asexuality as a sexual orientation for humans. I'm calling it "Solitary Species: Asexuality in the Plant and Animal Kingdoms."

This is the first time I've actually talked to anyone about my project. What will he say when he sees what I've done?

"Wow!" he exclaims when I hand him my stack of note cards. "You've definitely stayed on top of things."

"I've been working on it." I push my chair a little farther back. Mr. Le seems okay, but I still don't feel comfortable sitting too close. "Cautious contact" is what Ms. Ardvinson would call it.

He skims the first of my cards. "Aphids!" he says. "You know, there's a student in another class who's doing his project on pest control, and he's done a lot of research on aphids. Maybe you two could connect. Who was it . . . ? I'm still learning everyone's names . . ."

Now I'm not sure what to say. "It's . . . about more than aphids," I manage.

Mr. Le looks at his clipboard. "It says here you're doing apple reproduction."

That's all Ms. Faraher wrote? "Yeah. I kind of . . . changed it a bit."

Now Mr. Le studies my index cards more closely. "Did you talk to Ms. Faraher about the change?"

That afternoon when I was alone with her, she was sitting exactly where Mr. Le is now. *Humans are sexual beings, Lizzie.* "Yes."

"Okay, great." He scribbles a note on the clipboard and passes the cards back to me. "Just keep doing what you're doing. Chloe, you're next."

Back at my desk, I sit with the day's worksheet, feeling puzzled, while Michael fidgets beside me with his mechanical pencil, disassembling it piece by piece. At least he's being quiet. It's good that Mr. Le didn't have any questions or criticisms about my project, right? It's not like I *wanted* to explain to him about being asexual. Still. Now that I've told Daria, I can't help wondering how it would feel to tell other people—even someone like Mr. Le who doesn't know me well enough to really care.

My neck prickles with the feeling of being watched. Michael, his pencil fully disassembled, is now staring at me through the hollow barrel, like a telescope. It can't be more than a pinprick glimpse, but it's unnerving. What is he even looking at?

"Knock it off," I say, still focusing on my worksheet.

"What? I'm not doing anything."

I grab at the pencil and almost get it, but he wrestles it away from me. "What is *wrong* with you?" I demand, but he just cackles.

"Lizzie!" Mr. Le is glaring at us—at me. "I asked for silence."

If she wanted to, Chloe, sitting across from Mr. Le, could tell him the truth: that Michael harasses me every day, and I never do anything to stop it. She won't, though. She's glaring, too, irritated at me for interrupting whatever far-fetched scheme she has to persuade Mr. Le to wait nine years and marry her.

Michael is laughing softly. "Yeah, *Lizzie*. He asked for silence."

I return to my worksheet, hot with anger. In ten more days, I'll give my CARP presentation. I don't know if I'm brave enough to do it, but I'll have to figure out a way. I've been silent for far too long.

PE with Mr. Davis is better than it was with Ms. Ardvinson last year, but he still has the same idea on Fridays when there's nothing better to do: dodgeball.

Ms. Ardvinson blows the whistle. Her class is combined with ours for the day, so the teams are big and it's easy to hide at first, even with Michael already whipping yellow foam balls at our team from across the gym. Chloe is on my team, zipping back and forth, dodging throws and sniping idle players on the opposite side. The prospect of dodgeball for the next forty-five minutes feels like an eternity stretching out ahead of me. We play with the rule that if you catch a ball someone throws at you, one of your teammates can come back in—so even if I get out, my suffering isn't over.

There's a double thud, and Michael and Ethan both shout, "Hah!"

"No fair!" Chloe rubs her thigh, looking to Mr. Davis. "They ganged up on me!"

Mr. Davis glances up from his clipboard. He wasn't looking. Ms. Ardvinson is using a broom handle to poke loose a ball that got wedged between the basketball hoop and the backboard. "Be a good sport, Chloe," Mr. Davis says.

She stalks off to the bleachers. "Somebody better catch it!"

Everyone skitters around the court, sneakers squeaking on the polished wood. If this were self-defense, I'd be running with everyone else. There, even if the high school girls are "cool," they don't really know me. They don't think it's weird for me to care, or to try. These kids throwing foam balls at me from behind the line know what I'm really like. So do the kids on my side. It's hard to be different from what you've always been.

A feeble throw from the other side rolls across the floor and comes to a stop at my feet. The ball is pockmarked with little holes, the foam picked away over the years, probably by other kids who hated dodgeball.

"Throw it, already!" someone on my side shouts, so I do. It flies high toward a circle of chatting girls.

"Eeek!" they say, but they move in time.

"Nice one, Lizard!"

"*Michael*," Ms. Ardvinson says sharply. "One more comment like that, and you're out."

Scowling, Michael whips the ball at Ethan on his own team. Ethan jumps away, laughing.

Ms. Ardvinson's eyes meet mine. I glance away quickly, expecting disappointment, but that isn't what I saw. I look again. She lifts her arms slightly in front of her, drops one leg back. Defensive stance.

What?

With Chloe on the bench, my teammates are dropping like flies. There are more balls toward the back, gathering along the far wall. I pick one up and throw it, this time using more of my whole body for momentum, like I do with a punch against the dummy in class. The ball surges forward, then curves in, catching Ethan on the side of the leg. When he turns around and sees me there, he doesn't even move.

"You're out," I tell him.

"It didn't hit me," he says—and then I see Michael Gorman throw.

Part of why you shout, Ms. Ardvinson told us, is to empty your lungs so that you don't get the wind knocked out of you; so that if you go down, you can get back up again. *I am not going down*, I tell myself. Michael's ball drills toward me, and I don't turn away like I did on the first day of school, protecting myself but still letting it hit me. I bend my knees; I reach forward.

I catch it.

"Ha!" I shout.

"Yes!" Chloe pumps her fists and jogs back onto the court. "Lizzie, here!"

I toss her the ball, and she proceeds to pummel the other team.

Michael is still standing. "Sit down, Michael," Ms. Ardvinson says.

He wants to argue, but he can't. He trudges over to the bleachers and sits down, hard.

I was afraid Ms. Ardvinson would say, "Good, Lizzie," the way she does in self-defense class, but she must know that would embarrass me here. When I look over at her, she just smiles. I still think dodgeball is pointless. But Ms. Ardvinson knew I could do it, and she was right.

CHAPTER 20

~

"Lizzie?"

I'm at the top of the stairs at the Jacobses' house, because Sabrina can't sleep. This is the first time I've babysat the girls at night, and apparently their last babysitter used to do this all the time: sit on the top step and keep watch for monsters or robbers or bogeymen. I've spent the past twenty minutes hunched awkwardly here with my CARP note cards spread out on the rug, while Carly and Sabrina do everything but fall asleep. "What?"

Sabrina doesn't answer right away. Then: "Can I have some water?"

"You already have water."

Another pause. "I want new water."

Carly groans in the next room. "Go to *sleep*, Sabrina!"

"It's all right." I stand, twisting my spine to work the stiffness out. "I'll get it."

Down in the kitchen, I fill a new glass. Despite the interruptions, I'm making some progress on my presentation. Earlier this week, I joined AVEN, the Asexuality Visibility and Education Network, hoping to collect some firsthand data from real people. Their logo is a downward-pointing triangle representing the spectrum of sexuality; asexuality is the gray point at the bottom. *New here, just found out asexuality was a thing, so excited!!!!!* was the title of my first post.

The first response contained several cake emojis. *Welcome! So glad to have you here.*

im from massachusetts too! another person wrote. More cake.

Glad you found us, another person said. *I didn't have AVEN when I was your age.* Cake cake cake.

The cake, I figured out after the dozens of posts I read last night, is an inside joke that goes back to the founding of the forum. People welcome new members with cake emojis and pictures of elaborate cakes. Something about cake being as good as sex, or better.

I didn't share a lot about myself when I posted, but it didn't feel like I needed to. The one thing they know about me is what unifies us. Instead, I asked every question I could think of:

What do you do when your best friend starts dating?

What do you say when people ask who you "like"?

Do you ever feel like your body doesn't belong to you?

How do you deal with being alone?

I hesitated to ask that last question. I worried that it might sound sad, like I don't have friends. But being alone is part of the experience of so many asexual beings—like the whiptail lizard, which reproduces parthenogenically when other lizards aren't available for mating. I can't be the only one who feels lonely sometimes, right?

I felt disappointed somehow, though, as I read people's answers. One person wrote, *I'm an aromantic asexual, but I have close relationships with my friends.* Others talked about finding partners who were also asexual, or who found sexual partners who accepted their orientation. As I read, I kept searching for something that I couldn't find. Everyone was so honest in telling me about their own, true lives. But none of them could tell me what my own future looks like.

Out in the world, I wouldn't say that I experience sexual attraction, one person wrote, *but when I fell in love with my partner, I did feel attracted to him. We have a sexual relationship, even though I consider myself asexual.*

One of Ms. Faraher's main tenets as a scientist is not to discount data that contradicts your hypothesis—but I'm still thinking of leaving that last one out. It doesn't make sense to me. If you're asexual, how could you be in a sexual relationship?

I turn off the faucet. Faint whispers and giggles are coming from upstairs. *Oh no.* I race around the corner and find the girls at the top of the steps where I left my index cards. Carly has them fanned out like a poker hand; Sabrina says, "Eep!" and darts back to her room.

"Carly!"

"This is your project for *school*?" Carly demands, sifting through the cards. "Is this *appropriate*?"

"Give me those." I snatch the cards from her hands and gather up the remaining ones.

Carly watches me. "What even is your project about?"

"It's for science," I say, aware that that isn't really an answer.

Sabrina is sitting on top of her bed, hugging a square pillow with a face and arms that she calls her "sweet dreams pillow." It looks like the type of thing that would be hand-made by an aunt or grandmother. "You mean in science you learn about s-e-x?"

Carly rolls her eyes. "You don't even know what that is, Sabrina."

"Yes, I do! It's—"

"Stop." I stuff the cards in my pocket and direct Carly back to her room. "You don't need to worry about my project. You need to worry about being asleep before your parents get home."

"Fine." Carly climbs in bed and pulls the blankets up over her nose. I can see from her eyes that she's still laughing at what she discovered.

"Good night," I say, not very pleasantly, and shut her light off.

I go to Sabrina's room next. Her water is downstairs on the counter, but she doesn't ask for it. She's squeezing the stuffed-face pillow. Does she really know about sex already? I guess I did, by the time I was seven. I wonder how Sabrina found out. Is there a best way to learn? If I had a daughter, what would I tell her?

Back downstairs on the couch, once both girls are asleep, I slide the index cards out of my pocket and read through them again. When it's time, will I be able to talk about my project? I want to be able to explain it so that even a girl at Sabrina's age could understand. I would want her to know that there are so many different ways to be.

CHAPTER 21

~

Saturday, self-defense. While Sarah Nan is changing, I go into one of the bathroom stalls to make sure my pad is still in place. I can't think of anything more embarrassing than bleeding through. Sometimes I think maybe I should try the "moon catcher" that Daria gave me for my birthday—it's in the drawer next to my bed, where I bump into it when I go rummaging for cough drops or ibuprofen—but I still can't imagine actually putting it in. *It makes you more familiar with your own body*, Daria said. I'm still intimidated by whatever that means. During the one week of the month when my body insists on reminding me what it was made for, I try to think about what's happening as little as possible.

When I come out of the stall, Sarah Nan is standing out in the middle of the empty locker room in her racerback bra, snapping a picture of her reflection in the mirror.

"What are you doing?"

Her phone clatters to the floor. "Jesus Christ, Lizzie!" She bends hurriedly to pick it up. "A little warning would be nice!"

"Was that for Ned?"

She stands, running her thumb over the screen, assuring herself it isn't broken. She sighs and looks up at me. "Yes, okay?" She drops the phone onto a bench and pulls a T-shirt over her head. "Go ahead and judge me."

"I wasn't going to."

Her head pops out of the neckhole. "Yes, you were."

Of course, she's right. "I mean, I don't get it," I admit. "But I don't want to argue about it."

Sarah Nan seems to miss the not-arguing part. "You've never been in a relationship, so you don't know what it's like," she says. "You have to do things to keep it interesting. Otherwise the other person gets bored."

My stomach gives a little lurch at *do things*. "Is Ned bored?"

"He doesn't know what he is," Sarah Nan says, smoothing the top of her head where she's pulled the hair back into a ponytail. "He says all we ever do when we're together is make out. I told him that's what we're *supposed* to do. Then he said he couldn't see me this weekend because he was going to the arcade. What does he think this is, third grade?" She shakes her head, then checks her face in her phone, scrutinizing an invisible blemish.

Is this one of those times when I'm missing something that a sexual person would get? "Do you *have* to make out all the time?"

Sarah Nan just sighs, as if I'm hopeless. "Let's get this

over with," she says, stuffing her phone into her locker. "I hope we don't have to do any of that testicle stuff today."

"Um, Sarah?"

She shuts the locker and looks at me.

"I think that's kind of the point."

After class, Ms. Ardvinson gathers us around. "You've all come a long way," she says. "I'm actually impressed. Those of you seeking phys ed credits should have no worries about passing." A few girls give each other high fives.

"Now," she continues, "our next class, as you know, will be the dynamic simulation. Where before you practiced the moves without any real resistance, now you'll have the chance to apply them on a trained officer in a simulated attack situation."

"Hell yeah," Kendall says under her breath.

"The dynamic simulation is entirely optional," Ms. Ardvinson says. "It is not a prerequisite for passing the course. However, I recommend it, and promise that you are entirely safe. Often students find it to be an empowering experience, even if it initially seems intimidating. Do you have any questions about it?"

I *do* have a question: Can I do it? Today I felt pretty good about the moves we practiced; I could feel the strength of my legs in the snap kicks and sweep kicks. I felt like I used to back when I was younger, before *squeeeeeze*—when my body was something I could control and feel proud of. But I have a hard time imagining myself doing it for real. I mean, pretend for real.

The opportunity passes. "Have a nice weekend," Ms. Ardvinson says. The other girls break into conversation and start for the doors.

"That's messed up," Sarah Nan says, close at my side. "Fake defending yourself against a real guy? No way am I doing that."

"It's actually pretty great." Kendall, nearby, falls into step beside us. "When I took one of these classes before, we did all our practice on a trained person in gear. You feel like you can really do it."

What if I *don't* feel like I can really do it?

I look back. Ms. Ardvinson, alone, is folding and stacking the practice mats. If she were Ms. Faraher, I would go to her and tell her how I was feeling. Ms. Faraher would know what to say—or the old Ms. Faraher would have. Ms. Ardvinson would probably tell me to do more push-ups.

"You feel good after," Kendall assures us. "Anyway, see ya." The blue-haired girl is waiting. She waves from behind the glass doors, and Kendall runs to meet her.

After Sarah Nan is done in the locker room, we go to the main entrance to wait for Daria to pick us up. We're both surprised when my mom pulls up and rolls down the window.

"Your mom will be here in a few minutes, Sarah," Mom says. "I need to run an errand with Lizzie."

"No problem." Sarah Nan is back to her phone already. I climb in the passenger side and shut the door. It takes me a minute to buckle the seat belt over my bulky coat, while Mom pulls away.

"What's the errand?" I ask.

"There is no errand." Mom takes a breath. "Bonny Jacobs called this morning. I wanted to talk to you."

"Oh." Why would Mrs. Jacobs call my mom?

"She said the girls saw you working on a project for school."

I swallow. "Uh-huh."

"Apparently the project is all about sex?"

There's a bobblehead moose stuck on the dashboard that we got once on a trip to Maine. It's bobbling now, and the pothole at the foot of the driveway sends its nose bouncing wildly as if it's shaking its head, *no no no*. This isn't how it was supposed to go. "That's not all it's about."

"I know. I saw your poster."

The back of my neck feels hot. "You did?"

"I hope that was okay." Mom glances sideways at me.

It's not okay, but I don't know how to tell her that. I didn't want to show her until it was ready. Until *I* was ready.

"I thought your project was about trees."

I twist my fingers in my lap. "It started off like that. Then

I started learning about plant reproduction, and I just . . . went from there."

Mom doesn't answer for a moment. She grips the wheel. "And that's what you've been working on all this time? That's what you're going to present at the exposition next week?"

"Yes."

Mom keeps her eyes on the road. I think we're both picturing the very middle of my poster display. *Asexuality: Not Just for Plants*, it says, and then all the AVEN testimonials.

"What?" I finally say.

"What *what*?"

This whole conversation feels surreal. "What do you think about it, I guess."

She doesn't answer for a moment. "It seems like maybe this project is helping you make sense of some things about yourself."

"Yeah." Mom's got the heated seats on. I can feel the warmth creeping up the base of my spine, along with the feeling that my mom's next word is going to be *but*.

"I think that's good," Mom says. I feel the heat and the *but* building even more. "I understand that you aren't interested in boys and dating right now. I didn't have a boyfriend until later in high school. But—"

There it is. I sink lower in my seat, my arms crossed

tightly over my chest, bracing myself for something I know will hurt.

"—for you to close yourself off entirely to those kinds of relationships makes me worried. Makes me a little sad, actually. I don't want you to limit yourself."

"I'm not closing myself off," I manage to say, though my voice comes out sounding choked. "That's not what it means."

"What *does* it mean?"

"It means that I'm not—that I don't—" Why won't the words come? I press myself farther back in the seat, as if I could flatten myself into it. "Never mind. You don't get it."

"Tell me. I want to get it."

This is my project. I should be able to explain. I *have* to be able to explain in just a few more days. "Other girls—like Sarah Nan—they feel something. I can tell. But I look at a guy and I don't feel *anything*. Dating and all that stuff . . ." I can't make myself say the word *sex*. "It just doesn't interest me."

We pull up to the traffic light at the center of town.

"Are you mad?" I ask.

Mom reaches over and strokes my hair. "Sweetheart—no. I'm glad we could talk about it. I'm sorry you felt like you had to keep it a secret."

"So you believe me?"

Mom takes her hand away, brings it back to the wheel. "I believe you that this is the way you feel about yourself."

Her words strike me like a slap. "But do you believe me that it's real?"

Mom sighs. "I don't know, Lizzie . . ." We brake suddenly, both of us lurching forward as someone pulls out of the bank ahead of us; Mom's arm shoots out to block me like an extra airbag, as if that could stop me from flying forward. "To be *a*-sexual . . . I just don't see how that's biologically possible."

"Daria said it was possible."

"Daria?" We're pulling into the Maze now; I see the stone wall with its inlaid spikes. "You talked to Daria about this?"

"After Thanksgiving," I say.

"And she told you that you were asexual?"

"She told me that it was possible."

Mom nods tightly. The snow's been cleared away from the streets in our neighborhood now, the drifts already topped with gray slush from the road.

"What?"

"I think that was a little inappropriate of her, that's all," Mom says.

"What do you mean, 'inappropriate'?" I remember Daria making tea for me, how her bathrobe fell open a little bit. But that's not what Mom means by inappropriate. She means that Daria shouldn't have been talking to me about *that*.

"Daria's a single mom, just her and Sarah Nan . . . Sometimes I think she forgets who she's talking to. She treats children like adults."

"I'm fourteen," I say.

"She doesn't really even know you."

I turn away to look out the window. "She knows me better than *you* do."

The words are out, and instantly I wish I could take them back. Mom makes a sound as though she's at a loss for air.

"*Lizzie*!" she finally manages.

I'm only making it worse now, but I have this awful, tight feeling in my chest that makes me think I could explode. "At least she listened to me. At least she believed me."

"I'm just worried for you," Mom says. We're slowing down as we approach our street. "After what happened with Mr. Henckman . . ."

"*Mom*."

"That was a scary experience," Mom says. "It might take time . . ."

"This has nothing to do with that," I say.

Mom takes a breath. "The girls also told Bonny that you made them hide under a table when a man came to the door."

Carly. "That was—that doesn't—" I can't put the words together. "That was a long time ago."

"I didn't know that, because you didn't tell me."

The world feels like it's spinning. I can't believe my mom is saying these things to me. She doesn't know that she's hurting me more than Michael Gorman or any of my classmates could. Any other time in my life that I've needed her, my mom has been there to say, "It's all right"—even when her head was bleeding and Mr. Henckman was running away down the sidewalk. Why can't she say that now? Why can't she tell me this is all right?

Because it's not, a voice in me replies. *It's not all right with her.*

We're home now. Mom pulls the car into the garage, shuts off the engine.

"Lizzie," she says, but I shake my head. "Lizzie, please. Talk to me."

It's possible that I've never been so angry. I can feel it inside me, bright and hot. "You don't want to talk."

"Of course I do . . ."

"You think everyone should just talk and talk and put on a smile like you—but *you're* the one who started everything with Mr. Henckman. If *you* hadn't been so nice to him—"

Mom lays on the horn. In our small garage, it's loud. When it stops, Mom is breathing heavily.

"You cannot speak to me that way," she says.

What about the way she was speaking to me? What about when she asked, *If you ever thought you were gay, you'd tell me, right?* How is this different?

It's different because she doesn't get it.

It's different because she doesn't believe me.

It's different because for once, she doesn't know what to say.

"Fine." I get out of the car. Slam the door. Go inside.

You cannot speak to me that way. Maybe it would be better if my mom and I didn't speak at all.

Maybe we really haven't been speaking for a long, long time.

CHAPTER 22

~

On Thursday morning, Dad drops me off early at school to set up for CARP. It's cold and sleeting outside; the car was only just starting to warm up, and now it's time to get out.

"You ready?" Dad asks.

I shrug. "I think so."

"You'll be great." He leans over to kiss my cheek. "I'm proud of you."

I'm not really in the mood for affection. "I haven't even done anything yet."

"You don't have to do anything," Dad says. "That's the beauty of it! You're my daughter and I'm proud."

"*Dad.*" I go around to the back to get my trifold poster and kalanchoe plant. It's all a bit awkward to carry. I manage to clamp the poster under one arm and get the kalanchoe with my other hand, the thumb of my mitten sinking into the soil.

"Do you need help?"

"I've got it." I put everything down to shut the car door, and then I pick it up the same way.

Dad rolls the window down. "I'll be back later with Mom," he says.

"Mom's coming?"

"Of course. She got personal time off from work." Dad looks at me. "You know . . ."

"I don't want to talk about it." My feet slide a little on the already icy sidewalk. Since Mom found out about my project, we've continued almost as if the conversation never happened—except for a cold distance between us that Dad, obviously, has noticed and keeps trying to mend. Did she tell him that I'm asexual? It doesn't seem like he knows, or he would have said something. Maybe he would even say the same things she did. I don't need that.

All I need is myself.

Dad sighs. "Well, I'll see you later. Break a leg!"

I might *actually* break a leg as I slip and slide toward the main entrance, hoping the cold doesn't hurt my kalanchoe and the sleet doesn't mess up my poster. Fortunately, Mr. Le sees me coming and hurries outside.

"Careful!" he says, catching me by the elbow as I'm about to lose balance. Chloe would be jealous. I just feel embarrassed and want him to let go. He takes the poster out from under my arm. "Here, come with me. I saw which table has your name on it."

A banner extends over the cafeteria doors: *Grade 8 Capstone Research Presentations*, with a big fish—a carp—in a graduation cap. Mr. Le leads me to my table, then leaves me to set up while he goes back to the door to catch any other potential wipeouts.

More students trickle in. I unfold my poster. I hand-lettered the title myself: *Solitary Species: Asexuality in the Plant and Animal Kingdoms*. Dad used his high-quality printer at work to get me bright, clear pictures of aphids, kalanchoe leaves, and, of course, the whiptail lizard. At the center of the board is *Not Just for Plants*, the section I'll end my presentation with, which has a picture underneath of the AVEN triangle.

Mom was worried about me presenting this; she thinks I'm going to embarrass myself. But *she's* the one who's embarrassed. I'll show her when she comes, how it all makes sense. I'll show Ms. Faraher, too. There's nowhere on the board that says *I'm* asexual, but I'm laying the groundwork. I can prove that the way I feel is real.

I don't have much setup to do. Some kids, as I look around, have actual contraptions that need assembling. One girl did her project on 3D printing and has a prosthetic hand for display; a boy at the next table did acid rain and is setting up carefully labeled water samples in tiny bottles. Their posters aren't hand-lettered. They look slick and professional. Why *did* I hand-letter mine? And my only visual support is a potted plant that has barely started to grow.

More kids arrive. I tug my sleeves down, but they won't cover my wrists. I hardly ever wear this shirt. Mom told me it would look professional—black pants, white top—but other girls, smaller girls like Chloe, are wearing cute dresses and ballet flats. I feel like a caterer surrounded by all the actual guests at a party.

Am I really going to do this?

My tongue feels dead and stale in my mouth. I pop a breath freshener from a tiny tin in my backpack, and then I sit and shuffle through my cards, whispering the keywords to myself. The last card, *Not Just for Plants*, says, *Like the whiptail lizard and kalanchoe, many people identify as asexual.* Maybe I shouldn't say it that way. Technically, it isn't "many people." Just 1 percent of the human population—plus me.

"Hey."

I look up, and my mint jumps to the back of my throat. The Boy in the Skirt is standing in front of me.

"Hey." I cough, my breath burning with peppermint.

"Pretty low-tech, isn't it?" He's wearing a black skirt with his Converse today, and a short-sleeve button-down. Also black.

"What?"

He's looking around the room, not at my poster. I'm not even sure he's actually talking to me.

"My old school had a robotics convention. It was insane. Machines running all over the place. One kid built a hover-craft."

"Wow," my mouth says, while my brain thinks, *Why is he talking to me?* I've waited so long to talk to him. Now that it's happening, I can't figure out what I did to *make* it happen.

"Yeah," he agrees.

I'm afraid if I don't keep the conversation going, he'll leave. "Are you presenting?"

"Yeah. I'm all set up. Thought I'd get breakfast, check things out." He holds up a plastic-wrapped breakfast bar and an apple in one of his large hands. "Want the apple? I hate fruit."

"Sure."

He deposits it in my palm. It's small, like all school-issued fruits, and I can tell it's the kind with a tough skin that splits under your teeth to yield a mealy white inside. But then I think: *Apples*. I play it out in my head:

You have an apple tree in your yard, don't you?

How did you know that?

"Aphids," he says, pointing to my photo of tiny green bugs filing along a flower stem. "I'm doing those."

Mr. Le told me about a person doing aphids. It was him all along? "What's yours about?"

"Diatomaceous earth." He crumples the wrapper. "It's natural pest control. You sprinkle it on your plants. Microscopic spikes—it literally slashes them as they walk across it."

"Wow," I say, though truthfully, I feel a bit nauseated.

"And yours is about . . ." He leans in to look at the board more closely. "Asexual reproduction. Cool. So, like, yeast buds and parthenogenesis and all that?"

"Yeah," I say, surprised he knows the word, and how easily he says it. "And . . . also in people."

"People?"

"It's an orientation."

"I know *that*." He reaches into the pocket of his skirt and pulls out an orange juice carton that must have come with the breakfast. "Isn't that kind of different, though?"

"What do you mean?"

"A person's orientation—that's different than reproduction, right? I mean, it's not like there's a gay aphid."

"I'm not saying it's the same. I'm saying it's analogous."

"Okay." He shrugs as if he knows better.

"What?" Part of me is scared to push the conversation—but isn't that the whole reason I'm here? To explain it to people so they understand? I shouldn't miss this chance. Especially not with him.

"I mean, asexual plants literally procreate without 'getting it on.' Asexual people can't do that. Asexual people just don't *want* to get it on. It's not really analogous."

"I'm just trying to show that—" My tongue catches on the word *asexuality*. Have I actually said it aloud in front of anyone before? "That just because someone—"

The bell rings, officially opening the doors for kids to go to lockers and homeroom. "Well, good luck," he says, crushing the juice carton, "lizard girl."

I don't say good luck to him. I focus on lining up my board with the edge of the table, angling the flaps just so. Once he's gone, I collapse onto the seat, my legs shaking. *I couldn't do it.* I had my chance to explain, everything lined up perfectly, and I messed it up. What happened?

My heart races as I think through all the steps that led me here. Ms. Faraher didn't fully know what I was doing because I didn't tell her. Mr. Le barely looked at my notes. No one stopped me. And now I'm about to present this in front of everyone: my parents, Michael Gorman, Ms. Faraher, complete strangers . . . and I'm not ready. I wanted to prove that the way I am exists in nature. But Will zeroed right in on my inconsistency: I'm not really like the kalanchoe plant. Of course I'm not. The kalanchoe lives its asexual existence without thinking, without questioning. I had to figure out what I am. It exists invisibly inside me. There's no way I can prove it. The proof is what I *don't* feel, which is impossible to show.

What if Will's not the only one who tells me I'm wrong?

What if I present in front of everyone and no one believes me?

"Don't be late," one of the cafeteria staff says in the background. "Time for homeroom."

I pull up my backpack by the strap and hurry, head down, past the rows of better projects, good projects, to the main doors, where I join the crowds on their way to their lockers. *Don't listen to him, don't listen to him,* I try to tell myself. It isn't working.

"Hey, Lizzie!" Sarah Nan approaches, holding Ned by the

hand. Her hair is French braided and looks so pretty. She'll do perfectly today, like she always does. "What's wrong?"

"I can't do it." The tears are coming. "The Boy in the Skirt—Will—he told me I did it wrong, I was setting up and he was asking me questions and I wasn't ready, and now I just think the whole thing's terrible . . ." I'm choking the words out as panic seizes my lungs; Ned looks on, baffled.

"Hey, Lizzie. Hey." Sarah Nan lets go of Ned and takes me by the shoulders. "That kid doesn't know anything, okay? He shouldn't have psyched you out. Don't listen to him— your project's great."

"You don't even know what it's about." Maybe if she hadn't been so wrapped up with Ned, she would have listened. She would have listened, and she would have known it was a bad idea, and she would have stopped me. I was in my own world, doing this. I should have known it would only make sense to me.

"It's about plants, right? Okay, I don't know the rest, but I know you did a good job. You always do a good job."

I'm shaking my head now. "I can't do it. I want to go home."

"You can't go home, Lizzie."

Ned takes a bite out of a breakfast bar like the one Will had. "I mean, she *could*."

"Ned!" Sarah Nan faces me. "Look, you can do this. You don't have to be amazing at it. You just have to survive it. Right?"

214

I dry my eyes. "I guess."

"Okay, now go to homeroom."

"You got this, Lizzie," Ned says, pointing the breakfast bar at me like a royal staff. He doesn't know the first thing about me.

I start toward homeroom, but when Sarah Nan and Ned disappear around the corner, I turn back and take off down the hallway to Mr. Le's room. Anxious CARP-ers, all dressed up for today, are standing together in clumps, while the rest of his homeroom looks on in a mix of envy and relief. Mr. Le is dressed up, too, in a lavender button-down. I nearly collide with him when he turns around from handing a boy a freshly looped necktie. "Lizzie! What are you doing here?"

"I changed my mind," I say in a rush. "I don't want to present today."

"What?"

The volume in the room is so loud; I say it again. "I don't want to do CARP."

"I heard you," he says. "But, Lizzie, why? You've got your poster, you had all your notes . . . Are you nervous, is that it?"

If I say much more, I'll start crying again. "I'm not ready. My project's not ready. I need to change—some things."

Mr. Le frowns. "I won't force you to present, but . . . are you sure? You worked so hard."

I nod. Press my lips together. "I'm sure."

Another boy comes up to us. "Mr. Le, can I use the printer?"

Mr. Le turns away, probably to tell the boy to wait a minute, but I seize the opportunity to slip out of the room before Mr. Le can change his mind. Out in the hallway, I text my dad.

Don't come. I'm not presenting. Tell Mom not to come.

There.

I feel weirdly calm. I did it. I chickened out. It feels good, not caring anymore. All this time, I've been trying so hard. Trying to figure things out. Trying to understand. Trying to be stronger. Why? Other people go through their lives without questioning everything about themselves. Like Chloe, or like Michael. Maybe I should be more like them.

The bell rings, and I hurry off to homeroom, late.

When homeroom ends, I go back to the cafeteria and pick up my CARP board and kalanchoe plant. The plant goes in my locker. The board goes down to the set of trash bins in a sixth-grade hallway. The cardboard is too big to crush, so before I leave it, I tear off all the pictures and captions and the middle section, *Not Just for Plants*, that I carefully pasted on.

Now I couldn't change my mind even if I wanted to.

I'm late for math, but it doesn't matter. Everyone who's in advanced math is also doing CARP today, so Ms. Patel is basically killing time until eight thirty, when the CARP kids get dismissed to the cafeteria. I didn't think about this part: I'm the only person still sitting when everyone else gets up to leave.

"Lizzie, aren't you coming?" Sarah Nan asks as she passes my desk. I shake my head.

"What—" Chloe starts, but Sarah Nan elbows her.

"Don't worry about it, Clo."

Ms. Patel is surprised, too. She didn't expect to have anyone left to teach today. "Why don't you work on the midterm study packet?" she suggests.

I work on matrices and polynomials in silence.

I thought I could get through the rest of the day without any more CARP reminders, but our social studies teacher tells us that instead of regular class, we're going down to the cafeteria to see everyone's presentations. My stomach sinks. I don't want to go in there.

I hang back to be the last out of the classroom, and then, when we reach the cafeteria, I cut away from the line and toward a small alcove that houses a drinking fountain and the entrance to a girls' bathroom—and that's where I find Ms. Faraher.

"Lizzie!" She's filling her water bottle. She dressed up for today, too, a gray skirt and green cardigan that I remember she used to wear before she was pregnant.

"Hi." I try to think of a way out of this conversation, a lie, anything, but I can't.

She screws the lid on her bottle. "I was looking for your presentation. Which is your table?"

"Um . . . I decided not to present." My words trail off into a mumble, and I stare down at her shoes. Plain ones—she never wears heels.

"Really?" Her voice has all the surprise and disappointment I knew it would. "You're my science girl—what happened?"

I shrug. "It wasn't ready."

If Ms. Faraher is thinking of asking me more, she doesn't have the chance—because Chloe appears at the cafeteria doors. "Ms. Faraher! Didn't you bring your baby?"

The baby. I didn't even ask about her baby.

Chloe comes running over. Other kids are gathering around, too.

"I thought it might have been a bit much for Rowan," Ms. Faraher says. "But I'll bring him by class sometime, if it's okay with Mr. Le."

"Do you have pictures?" Chloe asks.

As Ms. Faraher produces her phone, I manage to back away—straight into Aidan, who's wearing a collared shirt and bow tie.

"Hey, Lizzie, where were you?" he asked. "I saw your name next to mine."

"Mind your own business," I snap, and hurry away.

The cafeteria is packed, the air filled with a mix of

conversation and whirring motors and occasional snare drumrolls from a project on percussion. All these other people could do it, but I couldn't. They're braver than me. Better than me.

I thought having a name for myself, *asexual*, would be the answer. It isn't, though. I don't just want to know myself. I want other people to know me, understand me, believe me. So that I can actually *be* myself.

I had my chance to tell everyone. But I was too afraid to even say the word.

CHAPTER 23

Dinner was supposed to be special tonight, in my honor. Instead, it's just awkward. Dad baked his sourdough bread, Mom made spaghetti and meatballs, and all of us are trying to ignore the fact that there's nothing to celebrate. I keep picturing my project board where I left it, wedged between two trash bins, stripped bare, the flaps folded in and bent from when I tried, unsuccessfully, to crush it. I'll have to start all over again before I can present to the class. Maybe I'll do apple trees, like I originally planned. I'll talk about how it takes two trees. That's what everyone wants to hear.

"Well." Mom breaks the silence. "James called me today. He said that he and Ally are getting back together."

"Oh?" Dad says, his mouth full of pasta. He doesn't seem to take this as any major kind of revelation.

I focus on twirling my fork in the noodles, but I feel Mom's eyes on me.

"You knew already?" she asks.

"I figured it out."

"Is this the same milk as usual?" Dad asks, holding up his glass to the light. We had to get a special one for him that we call the "big-nose glass," with a wide enough rim to go over his nose when he tips it back. "I thought we were getting one percent now."

"That *is* one percent," Mom says.

I roll my eyes, wanting to get back to the point. "What's wrong with James and Ally being back together?"

"Nothing," Mom says.

I never thought I'd stick up for James this way, especially after Thanksgiving, but my frustration with my mom is greater than my frustration with him. "Don't you like Ally?"

"Of course," Mom says. "I love Ally."

I'm picking an argument. I don't care. "James loves her, too."

Mom casts Dad a help-me-out-here look.

"They've been together a long time," Dad says. "It's hard to let that go."

"College is an opportunity to branch out, to meet new people," Mom says. "I don't want him to limit himself."

I look down at my plate. "That sounds familiar."

Mom turns to me. "What's that, Lizzie?"

"Nothing."

We continue eating in silence.

After dinner, Mom goes to finish some school paperwork, and Dad washes the dishes. I go upstairs to my room and flop back on the bed. Alone. This is how it's going to be from now on. I'm losing my brother. I've always thought that there must be a way to hold on to people, but maybe there isn't. Maybe it doesn't even matter. Would it matter if I just disappeared, when it already feels as though I'm stuck in place while everyone else's lives move past me? James will marry Ally; I can see myself standing off to the side in a yellow bridesmaid's dress at their wedding. They'll have two boys, my nephews, who will think their Aunt Lizzie is boring and strange. Sarah Nan won't marry Ned, but she'll go to an Ivy League school like she's always wanted and meet someone there and fall in love and she and I will talk on the phone once a year. Mom and Dad will grow old and die—and it'll just be me then, just Lizzie, alone.

I think about James and Ally when she used to join us for dinner, how they held hands under the table. I guess I sometimes wonder what it would feel like to have that kind of love.

I wonder if anyone even *could* love me.

There's the part of me that doesn't understand kissing or cuteness or attraction, and then there's the part of me that feels so lonely. How do I make sense of those two parts?

Maybe I'll never make sense of them.

Maybe I should stop trying.

All through school on Friday, I'm dreading seeing Mr. Le again. I know he's going to make me talk to him about why I bailed on CARP. But when I arrive at science last period,

Mr. Le isn't there. No teacher is there. A handful of kids, like Aidan, are in their seats, quietly waiting, while the rest are up and around, sitting on the lab tables and asking things like, "If no one comes, can we go home?"

Finally, someone does arrive: Ms. Ardvinson. "Michael, sit down" is the first thing she says.

Michael swings his legs from his perch on a table. "Why me? Other people are doing it, too."

"Michael and everyone, sit." She picks up Mr. Le's clipboard with the attendance lists. "Mr. Le is absent today. I'll be covering for him."

"Can we play dodgeball?" Ethan asks eagerly.

Ms. Ardvinson ignores him.

Mr. Le left work for us—more boring notes from those old textbooks. I hear Michael beside me, flipping through his book and snickering.

"Michael," Ms. Ardvinson says sharply, "why don't you sit up here next to me?"

That keeps him quiet.

At the end of class, Michael shoves past me, bumping my arm and knocking my lab notebook onto the floor. Aidan, on his way past, bends to pick it up.

"Thanks," I say.

Aidan doesn't meet my eyes, but drops the notebook on the table in front of me and heads for the door. I remember with a plummeting feeling how I snapped at him yesterday at CARP. Aidan always seems so unbothered by everything, and he's the only person in class who ever stuck up for me against Michael. Did I actually hurt his feelings?

"Lizzie, can you come here a second?" Ms. Ardvinson, sitting at Ms. Faraher's desk, motions me to the front of the room. Is it about Aidan? But how could she know?

I stand in front of the desk. "There's a note for you here from Mr. Le," she says. "He says he'll talk to you when he's back on Monday."

"Oh." The room behind me is emptying out; soon Ms. Ardvinson and I will be alone. "Okay, thanks."

Ms. Ardvinson studies me. If she thinks I'm going to tell her what the note is about, she's got another thing coming. "Do you have to catch a bus?" she asks suddenly.

"My mom picks me up." There's one more thing I'm not looking forward to—another silent ride.

Ms. Ardvinson returns the clipboard to the desk. "Do you have a minute to come down to the gym? I could use some help putting away the volleyball nets."

I can't think of any way out that won't seem rude. "Sure."

It's a little weird walking down the hallway with Ms. Ardvinson. With the end-of-day crush of bodies lingering at lockers and hurrying for buses, it's too loud for us to talk, so I just stay beside her, following. Once, I move aside quickly to dodge a train of girls holding on to each other's backpacks in a long line, and I accidentally lean into Ms. Ardvinson's arm a little bit. She doesn't flinch away. She keeps walking, eyes ahead.

When we get to the gym, the floor is clear. "I guess Mr. Davis took care of them already," Ms. Ardvinson says.

I hesitate. Should I leave? But something keeps me rooted in place. "Just so you know," I blurt out, "I probably won't be in self-defense tomorrow."

"Oh?"

"Yeah." I try to sound casual, like it's no big deal. "I don't want to do the dynamic thing."

"You're allowed to opt out," Ms. Ardvinson says. "That doesn't mean you need to skip class. You could support the other girls."

"I know. I just . . ." I don't know how to explain it to her. I bailed on CARP, and now I'm bailing on this. I was trying so hard to be strong. I'm sick of it.

"Let's sit down," Ms. Ardvinson says. "Here."

She lowers herself onto one of the folded mats stacked along the wall. I sit, too. It isn't very sturdy; it sinks in, sliding the two of us closer together. "You're scared," she says simply.

I nod.

"Can you tell me specifically what concerns you?"

One year ago, I could not have imagined that I would be sitting on a mat having a private conversation with Ms. Ardvinson. I thought she hated me, and I was more than willing to hate her back. She was the last person I wanted to tell anything.

There were a lot of things I couldn't have imagined a year ago.

"You know that time . . ." I swallow, feeling the words line up, getting ready. "That time I asked if we could pretend to see someone and call out to them? And you said that was a 'trick' and you wouldn't recommend it?"

Ms. Ardvinson nods. "Yes."

I fiddle with a zipper on my backpack. "I saw someone do that once. My mom. Our neighbor was breaking in, and she pretended my brother was there. She scared him away."

I can't look at Ms. Ardvinson, but I hear her exhale beside me. "When did that happen?"

"Last spring. We had to move."

"Oh, Lizzie."

That makes me look up—and when I see her face, I can't help but wonder if I've ever really looked at Ms. Ardvinson. Her white bangs fall softly over her eyebrows. Her eyes are gray. Maybe her teeth aren't *so* big.

"I wish you had told me before. I think I know why you didn't, but I wish I had known."

My cheeks color a little. She must know she wasn't my favorite person after PE last year. "I thought if I took the class . . . but I still don't know if I can do it."

Ms. Ardvinson folds her knees in a little closer. "There's

a way I think about a class like this," she says. "Part of its purpose is to teach you the skills to defend yourself. But an equal purpose, if not a greater one, is to give you the confidence that comes with recognizing your own strength. You don't have to face off with a heavily padded officer in order to prove that strength. You've already proven it."

"I have?"

"In your quiet way, yes."

Now my cheeks feel even warmer. I never imagined Ms. Ardvinson could see me that way.

"I'm not going to put a positive spin on it. I'm not going to say that an experience like the one you had ultimately makes you stronger. But we are changed by those kinds of experiences. We have to be."

I look up, wondering if she meant to say *we*.

"What makes you strong is facing that new reality. Which you did, when you took this class—whether you do the dynamic simulation or not."

She's right. As much as I might want to or try to, I'll never forget what Mr. Henckman did to my mom, to my family. I'll never forget how he made me feel. Here I've been so worried about something inside me changing—but I've already changed. I changed without realizing it. And underneath that change, I'm still me.

"I'm still kind of weird . . . around guys," I confess. "After that. It's hard."

"It *is* hard," she agrees.

She doesn't try to tell me that I might be missing out on a nice guy.

"Is that something you'd like to challenge about yourself?" she asks.

"Challenge?"

"Do you want to keep feeling that way?"

"Oh." Part of me thinks the answer should be *no*, but I'm not sure. "I guess it feels safer. Being scared."

"It feels safer not to let your guard down." Ms. Ardvinson nods. She gets it.

Is Ms. Ardvinson ever lonely, I wonder? Will I be like her someday?

"But I guess I don't want to feel that way forever." It would be nice to have a normal interaction with a boy. To just talk as human beings. Other people do that, right?

As if she can read my mind, Ms. Ardvinson says, "You're strong enough. If that's something you want to change, then you can."

I wonder if she's right. "I guess I can still come tomorrow."

"It's up to you." Ms. Ardvinson stands. "By the way," she says, "I've been meaning to tell you, I really enjoyed your CARP project yesterday."

Is she joking? But Ms. Ardvinson doesn't really joke. "You saw my project?"

"I was teaching during the exposition, but I went down

in the morning after everything was set up. I thought yours was fascinating. I never knew lizards could reproduce asexually."

"*Some* lizards," I say, shrugging into my backpack. I don't want her walking away with the wrong information.

She smiles. "Exceptional lizards."

CHAPTER 24

On the morning of our last self-defense class, Sarah Nan texts me that she doesn't feel well, so it's just Dad and me in the car on the way to the community center.

"Last early morning Saturday," Dad says as we pull out of the driveway. "Are you glad to be almost done?"

I shrug, waiting for the heat to come on. "It was a pretty good class."

"That's good." Dad raps his fingers on the steering wheel, whistling a tune I can't make out as we drive along in silence.

"Dad?" I say. The whistling stops. "Were you ever mean to girls?"

"Was I *mean*?"

"You know." I'm not sure I even know what I'm trying to ask. "When you were a kid, did you, like, tease girls and stuff."

"Well, I teased your Aunt Lisa, for sure. I used to call her 'Poodle Ears,' because of the way her hair—"

"I mean, like, girls you didn't really know. Girls at school."

"Hmm." Dad thinks about it. He's picking through memories as we drive along Main Street, and I wonder what he's seeing. "There was a girl, Sadie, who sat in front of me in fifth grade. My friend Billy sat next to me, and he would always tug her braid to get her to turn around."

I think of Michael Gorman kicking my chair, kicking and kicking. "Did you pull her braid?"

"I can't honestly remember. I might have." Dad waits for a little car to pull out of a side street before moving forward. "Why are you asking?"

I sigh. "I don't know."

"Are you disappointed in me?"

My first instinct is to protect his feelings, but that doesn't seem right after nine sessions of Women's Self-Defense. "A little."

Dad nods. "I am, too."

"Did you do it because you *liked* Sadie?"

"I think you're overestimating my self-awareness at age eleven. I'm not like you, Nugget."

The heat's coming on now. I snuggle down into my coat. "You think I'm self-aware?"

"Sure! When you want something, or when you don't want something, you know why. Not everyone has that power."

I smile. I like the way that sounds.

"You know," he says, "I understand that Mom is usually the one you go to, but I'm here, too, if there's ever any-thing . . ." He trails off, flexing his fingers against the wheel. "I just mean you can always talk to me. If you want to."

Maybe I've underestimated my dad. Maybe he wouldn't react the way Mom did if I told him about being asexual. Right now, though, I'm content keeping my thoughts to myself. "I know," I say, as the community center rises ahead of us in the distance. "Thanks, Dad."

The gymnasium is quieter today than usual. Instead of laughter and chatter where the high school girls stand around, there are whispers and nervous giggles. I join them all at center court, where a large rectangle is marked off in green tape, a two-foot-wide opening at one corner. I wonder if it's for us.

"Hey, Lizzie." Sarah Nan comes jogging up behind me, panting.

"You're here!" I could hug her, but she wouldn't like that in front of the "cool" girls. Plus, she doesn't seem in the mood for a hug. Her hair is in the messy kind of bun she usually reserves for sleepovers, and she's wearing a Martha's Vineyard sweatshirt with a small hole in the collar.

"Yeah, I decided I couldn't bail on you."

Ms. Ardvinson appears in the doorway. "Good morning, everyone!"

Another figure stands behind her, hanging back, while she claps her hands to gather us around. "Today, as you know, is our dynamic simulation. You've worked hard to prepare; this is it. This is your chance to apply what you've learned—not only to internalize the physical moves, but to do so while in an adrenalized state, which is different than the way we've practiced. Let me introduce you to Officer Monroe."

She steps aside, and in walks a tall, broad-shouldered man covered in protective gear from head to foot: a helmet with a metal grill over the face, shoulder pads, chest pad, kneepads, elbow pads, some major crotch protection, and what appear to be boxing gloves. Everything that he wears—helmet, padding, and gloves—is encased in a layer of red vinyl, like the old couch in my grandparents' basement, so that he looks like a cross between a baseball catcher and a lobster. He squeaks as he lumbers over to us.

"Officer Monroe is going to help us to stage a dynamic simulation of an attack situation, which will give you the opportunity to apply what you have learned in a more real-istic context. We're going to imagine a scenario where a stranger approaches you in a way that threatens your safety. This tape you see on the floor," Ms. Ardvinson says, motion-ing toward the square, "marks the perimeter of a closed-off space, except for that opening, which is the only exit. Each one of you will stand in this square, and when Officer Monroe attempts to abduct you, you will use whatever tech-niques you deem appropriate to escape through the exit. No running through the walls. The rest of us will be at the side-lines, cheering you on; this can be scary, so we want to be supportive. Everybody got it?"

The girls look uneasily at Officer Monroe as he takes his place in the square. Kendall's expression is flat. "Way more likely it'd be someone you know—not a total stranger," she says beside me in a low voice.

I think of Mr. Henckman. She's right. I wonder how much harder that made it for Mom to fight back—that he was our neighbor, someone we knew.

Ms. Ardvinson dumps out the contents of a burlap sack: more protective gear. For us. "Some of you may be feeling anxious or uncomfortable. Remember that everything today is optional, but the dynamic simulation is a unique opportunity to practice in a place with no repercussions. Officer Monroe is well protected, you will be well protected, and at any time you can say 'stop' and we'll stop. Is there a volunteer to go first?" she asks.

First is Alexa. Ms. Ardvinson waits for her to put on the protective vest, helmet, and gloves, then tells her to stand at the back of the square.

"Imagine you're in an ATM lobby," Ms. Ardvinson instructs.

"Ha! I *wish* I had a debit card," Alexa says as she punches in some imaginary numbers, which makes a few people laugh—until Officer Monroe comes up behind her.

"Hey, can you lend me a quarter?" he asks her. She snap kicks him in the groin.

"Okay, cut, cut," Ms. Ardvinson says, walking through

the walls of the square as Officer Monroe staggers back. "Alexa, would you do that in real life if someone asked you for a quarter?"

"I would if he were dressed like that."

More people laugh, but Ms. Ardvinson stays calm. "When we're hyper-adrenalized, we can make assumptions without all the information. You don't want that, either—not everyone is out to hurt you. Imagine he's dressed normally, and then remember some of the strategies we learned for de-escalation: Cautious contact. Defensive stance. Loud, confident voice." Ms. Ardvinson steps back from the square.

When we're hyper-adrenalized, we can make assumptions. That's what it is when I feel on edge around Mr. Le or Aidan or other guys who've given me no reason to be afraid. It's my body, adrenaline, trying to protect me after what happened with Mr. Henckman.

"Okay," Ms. Ardvinson says, "try again."

The simulations go better after that. Actually, they go really well. Everyone remembers to shout, and manages to escape after less than thirty seconds of struggle. Kendall floors her opponent the fastest, shouting, "Take that, you bastard!" Ms. Ardvinson has to remind her afterward that in a real attack situation, she would want to focus on escaping rather than giving her attacker one last kick while he's down.

When Sarah Nan's name is called, she crosses her arms over her chest and says, "No, *thank* you."

"Lizzie?" Ms. Ardvinson looks at me.

"Yeah, Lizzie!" Kendall cheers, clapping. *You're strong enough*, I hear Ms. Ardvinson saying.

In that instant, I decide. "I'll do it."

Gloves on, kneepads on, elbow pads on. I step into the taped-off square of the ATM lobby.

"Pretend to get cash," Ms. Ardvinson instructs.

I pretend to punch in numbers like Alexa did.

With the other girls, the assailant asked questions before grabbing them—*Can you tell me what time it is? Do you have any change?*—but all I get is the squeak of a footstep behind me before his arms are around my waist.

"Shin scrape! Heel stomp!" Ms. Ardvinson shouts. My heel brushes the tip of his toe—also padded—and he lets out an obliging "Oof" and stumbles back, like he's acting. I jerk my elbow. It's harder in the protective gear and doesn't feel like what we've practiced, but Officer Monroe grunts as though I've socked him.

The other girls cheer me on. "Come on, Lizzie!" I hear Kendall's voice among them: "You got this!"

. . . and suddenly the man is letting go. I feel like I can barely see from within my helmet, but I bolt for the break in the masking tape, back to the group.

Ms. Ardvinson is clapping. "Great job, Lizzie! Don't forget to shout, okay?"

I pull back the helmet. Sarah Nan is at my side. She takes my helmet and helps me strip off the padding. "I didn't do anything," I confess. "He just let go."

"It looked like you did something," she tells me.

"Is that everyone?" Ms. Ardvinson asks.

Sarah Nan raises her hand, still holding the helmet. "I'll go."

Sarah Nan fastens on the elbow pads while I help her with the kneepads. "You ready to kick some balls?" I joke. She doesn't laugh.

I stand beside Kendall while Sarah Nan enters the taped-off ATM lobby. She doesn't pretend to punch in numbers; she just faces the corner, her fists at her sides.

"Hey there," Officer Monroe says. He sounds like he's getting a bit tired of his lines. "Do you have a quarter?"

Sarah Nan turns around. She looks so small facing Officer Monroe, whose dimensions are made even huger by the protective gear. "No."

"Not even a dime?" he asks. "Come on, give me a dime."

"I—I'm sorry," Sarah Nan says, edging along the invisible wall—and that's when he grabs her.

"Go, Sarah!" the high school girls are shouting. I'm clapping along with everyone, but not saying anything as Sarah Nan nails him with a heel stomp, then slips through his grasp and darts around him for the door.

With the rest of us, when we got free, Officer Monroe just let us go. Maybe because he's trying to do his job, maybe because Sarah Nan got away so quickly, he reaches out and pulls her back again. He has her around the waist; Sarah Nan elbows him, one-two, and each blow bounces off the protective padding like moth's wings against a window-pane. He isn't stopping—the way Mr. Henckman didn't stop pushing against the door. And Sarah Nan is trying the way Mom kept trying, but the door wouldn't close and wouldn't close and he would have come into the house if Mom hadn't called out for James—James, eighteen and not big or scary at all, but Mr. Henckman was scared because James was a boy and a man and that gave him a power that Mom didn't have, that I don't have, and Sarah Nan is flail-ing and stomping and missing—and suddenly her eyes meet mine from behind the helmet grill and all I can see there is her fear.

"Stop it," I say, and then more loudly, "*Stop!*"

No one is stopping it. I rush forward, crossing the tape, and sweep my leg behind Officer Monroe's knees, sending him to the ground with a thud. Sarah Nan tumbles out of his grasp.

"Gary!" Ms. Ardvinson exclaims. "Lizzie! What . . . ?"

The other girls have fallen silent.

"Can't you see she's upset?" I demand. My heart is pounding; I feel electrified. Sarah Nan is on all fours, her head bowed. Officer Monroe awkwardly backs away as I put my hand on Sarah Nan's back. "Sarah?"

She lets out a sob, shielding her helmeted face with her arm.

"Oh—Sarah," Ms. Ardvinson says. Then: "Stay back, everyone, stay back." She steps between the concerned high school girls and our little square. "It's okay, you did great," she says softly, so only Sarah Nan and I can hear. Sarah Nan just shakes her head.

Officer Monroe—Gary—stands awkwardly off to the side. He's stripped off his helmet, and his hair is sticking up with sweat. He looks like he wants to say something, but Ms. Ardvinson turns to him with an expression that says, *Not yet.*

"Lizzie, why don't you take her outside? Help her out of the gear. I'll be right there."

Sarah Nan keeps her hands over the helmet's metal grill as I lead her out of the gymnasium. When she pulls the helmet up, her cheeks are streaked with tears.

"I couldn't do it, Lizzie," she says. "I got too scared."

I lead Sarah Nan to a bench in the lobby, where she does some deep, shaky breathing. "I was scared, too," I offer, but she doesn't reply.

Ms. Ardvinson comes out into the hallway to find us. "Lizzie, could you give us a minute?"

I try to make eye contact with Sarah Nan, to see if this is okay, but she's staring at the floor. "Sure."

Back in the gymnasium, it's all over. Officer Monroe is

giving some final tips and feedback based on our simulation with him. He's younger than I would have guessed. Alexa and Melissa are giggling and asking him questions—flirting? Or maybe, like me, they're just giddy with relief.

"That was a bitch," Kendall says, appearing beside me. "Holy crap. You think you know what you're going to do, and then—bam. He grabs you."

"I felt like I barely did anything," I admit.

"Are you kidding? You jumped in there like the Karate Kid when your friend fell apart. I should have said something, too, but I wasn't sure . . ." She shakes her head. "That's the takeaway of this class, right? Don't doubt yourself. You did a good job."

If I were Kendall's age, I wonder if she would want to kiss me in the parking lot the way she kissed the blue-haired girl.

"Hey," Kendall says—to Sarah Nan, who has appeared silently behind us. Ms. Ardvinson is back, too, inviting us all to stand in a circle the way we did on our first day.

"What did she say?" I whisper to Sarah Nan as Ms. Ardvinson gives a few last words about keeping up practice, and how we can take this same class again here for free anytime we want.

Sarah Nan shakes her head. "Just a bunch of stuff about fight-flight-freeze and how it's okay. She said I could try again, but I don't want to."

"It was a huge accomplishment for all of you just to show

up," Ms. Ardvinson is saying. "None of this is easy for me, either, and it's inspiring for me as a teacher to have such a great, supportive group. You did amazing work; don't doubt that, and don't forget it."

On the way out, a few people from the class quietly offer their reassurances to Sarah Nan:

"You did fine."

"It was scary for me, too."

Sarah Nan smiles and nods. It hurts to see how hard she's trying. Maybe she isn't as good at being fake as she thinks.

Everyone else departs quickly, leaving Sarah Nan and me alone out front as we wait for Daria to pick us up. There's a metal bench, but it's too cold to sit on. We stand side by side, breathing clouds.

"Don't tell my mom, okay?" Sarah Nan asks. Kendall's girlfriend's car pulls away, rattling onto the main road. "Or your mom."

"Why would I tell them?"

"I don't know." Sarah Nan lets out a long breath that disperses into the air in front of us. "Ned broke up with me last night."

Understanding ripples through me, along with the familiar fear that I'll say the wrong thing. "What?"

She shivers. The fur on the collar of her quilted down vest moves in the breeze and brushes against her cheek. "He said he felt like I was moving things too fast, and he just wanted to have fun." She kicks a stone, and it bounces away from us into the slushy lot. "Maybe I *was* trying to make things . . . I don't know. Serious."

"Don't blame yourself," I tell her. I'm thinking suddenly of Ms. Faraher on her last day, or James not coming home for Thanksgiving. I don't know what it's like to break up with someone, but I do know what it's like to have your heart broken. "You were together a long time. It *was* serious."

Sarah Nan glances sideways at me, surprised at my sympathy. "I just don't want to end up like my mom someday and not have anybody. You know? Things were really good with Nick and I think he wanted to marry her, but she kept saying 'not now' until he got tired of asking. She says it's always been about me first and she doesn't care whether or not she has a guy—but I don't think she really means that." Her voice wavers.

"Maybe she does. I'd pick you over a guy."

Sarah Nan laughs, wiping away a few new tears. "You'd pick a potted plant over a guy."

"True." I look at Sarah Nan then, at her profile outlined by the white snow. "I'm sorry."

"Thanks for saying that." She gives a small smile sideways at me. "I've been thinking maybe I won't date anyone for a while. I was trying so hard to be a girlfriend, I kind of forgot how to be Sarah Nan. You know?"

She called herself by her full name, not just *Sarah*. "What about your master plan?"

Sarah Nan sighs, but it's more of a huff. "Ned wasn't the right guy for that. I'm not going to do it if I don't think it's the right guy." She turns and looks at me. "Don't you know that?"

I guess I didn't. "How are you going to know who's the right guy?"

"I don't know." She shrugs, and her down vest rises and falls. "I'll feel something."

I nod. Cars rush past along the road, throwing up sprays of slush. "I don't think I'll ever feel something."

Sarah Nan is quiet, and I think I shouldn't have said it, that it was too much. "I think you will," she says at last. "But it will be different for you."

I feel my defenses going up. *Don't close yourself off. Give people a chance.* "Different how?"

She thinks for a moment. "You'll fall in love with somebody's brain," she says. "You don't care about all the stuff on the outside. Someday, you'll look straight into someone and find a big, beautiful brain. That's when you'll feel it."

A wind comes up, blowing snowflakes around us beneath the overhang. Up ahead, Daria's car pulls into the driveway. "I like that."

I don't think it's going to happen, but the fact that Sarah Nan believes it will is enough to lift my spirits as Daria pulls around to let us inside.

CHAPTER 25

Now that the CARP Exposition is over, Mr. Le is more relaxed. He's back in class on Monday, sitting backward in a chair at the front of the room while he talks to us.

"When another teacher first mentioned CARP to me, I thought it was a joke," he confesses. "I thought it was hazing the new guy or something. They really couldn't come up with a better name than 'CARP'?"

"It's always been called that," Chloe says absently. She's doodling intricate hearts in her lab notebook that say C & J.

"Does this mean you'll go easy grading us?" Ethan asks.

"After all the work you've put in? Absolutely not," Mr. Le says. "All right, take out your carbon cycle packets and see if you can finish the next few pages. You can work with the person next to you. Lizzie." He stands and goes around to his desk. "Could I talk to you?"

My stomach sinks. I can picture my board exactly where I left it by the trash bins, the flaps folded in to cover my humiliation. "Sure."

"Oooo," Michael says.

I ignore him and approach Mr. Le. His desk is bare of

anything personal, except for a small succulent that he's barely keeping on the brink of life. "So," Mr. Le says; the classroom fills with murmuring as everyone gets to work. "Tell me what happened on Thursday."

I finger one of the succulent leaves. The soil is dry and starting to pull away from the sides of the pot. "I just realized I didn't want to do it."

To my surprise, Mr. Le doesn't ask me why. He simply says, "Hm," and lowers into his swivel chair, which gives a little squeak. "Your project was about asexuality, right?"

I look up sharply. I thought he hadn't even looked at my cards. "It wasn't very good."

"Really? I could tell you did a lot of thorough research. Are you maybe being hard on yourself?"

I shake my head. "It wasn't really what I wanted it to be about."

"Is that why you threw it away?"

How did he know about that? I guess there's no sense in lying. "Yes."

Mr. Le tents his fingers thoughtfully. "You know, this is only my first CARP experience, but I have to say, I think you have something special to offer. Most of the projects I saw were very tech-heavy, not many in the natural sciences. And yours really broke it down so that people could understand. I think you *wanted* people to understand. Is that true?"

My heart beats a little faster. "I guess. Yeah."

"You're going to need to make a new board for the in-class presentation," Mr. Le says. "I tried to save your original one, but it was pretty well destroyed."

I give an embarrassed smile. "Sorry."

"You don't have to apologize to *me*," he says. "But if you're going to do an entirely new project, then you'll have to give me a proposal this week—tomorrow, really—and spend your holiday break researching so you're ready to go. Is that what you're prepared to do?"

It doesn't sound so great when he puts it that way. "I guess . . . ?"

"I can't give you an extension, but I'll put you last in the presenting order. That will give you a little extra time. Or," Mr. Le says, "the alternative is that you make your board again with your original idea. And maybe this time it *can* be what you wanted it to be."

He looks at me. How much does he know? "I'll think about it."

He nods. "I hope you will."

I know the conversation is over, but I don't sit down. I stay standing in front of him.

"Is there something else?"

I take a breath. "Yes," I say. "I don't want to sit by Michael anymore."

When I arrive at the cafeteria, it's just Sarah Nan alone at our usual table.

"Where's Chloe?"

Sarah Nan is eating a tuna sandwich on very white bread. "She and Jeremy got back together." She nods to the far corner, where Chloe and Jeremy are sharing a single seat at one of the round tables.

"Ugh," I say, before I can stop myself.

"I know, right?"

I can't remember the last time Sarah Nan and I commiserated about mushy couples together. Third grade, probably. I open my lunch box, feeling hopeful. "How's gymnastics?"

Sarah Nan acts as though she didn't hear me. "I ended up telling my mom about the dynamic simulation. You know, my meltdown."

I take a bite of my peanut butter sandwich. "It wasn't that bad."

"Please. Anyway, we're in a better place now. She knew about Ned and me kind of trying to take things too fast, but she didn't know how upset I was about Nick. She was like, 'I had no idea you wanted a dad!' Moms can be so dense."

I remember my mom: *I just don't see how that's biologically possible.* "That's for sure."

Sarah Nan looks at me as though she might ask what I'm thinking, but then she crumples up her crusts in her foil wrapper. "So, Chloe and I were planning to go to the Winter Carnival together—first as two couples, then as two single ladies. But now Chloe's a couple and I'm a single lady."

"Uh-huh." I take another bite of sandwich. Winter Carnival is the school dance that happens every January, and that's all I know about it. I've never gone.

"So . . . will you go with me?"

I laugh. "To a dance?"

"If I go by myself, I know I'll do something pathetic, like try to talk to Ned again." She clasps her hands in front of her. "Please, Lizzie? I'll feel better if you're there. We'll make fun of all the couples and stuff."

"You were *just* part of a couple."

"But now I'm not. You think I can't mock heteronormativity? Have you forgotten who my mother is?"

"Speaking of which . . ." I try to steer away from the topic of dances. "Is that ceremony still happening?"

Sarah Nan breaks open a packet of mini cookies. "Oh, it's happening. Yesterday she was chopping firewood in the backyard. We each have to carry a piece in our backpack, so leave room. And also, don't change the subject." She turns to face me. "You'll come to the dance with me, right?"

"Couldn't you just . . . not go?"

"And miss our last Winter Carnival because of stupid Ned? Come on, Lizzie. Didn't I go to three months of self-defense for you?"

"Yes, and you were so gracious about it the entire time."

"You don't have to be gracious, either. Just come. I don't want to go by myself."

It occurs to me suddenly that for all her ease with boys and friends and adults, Sarah Nan really is afraid of being alone. Just like I am. Maybe everyone is afraid of that. "If I go, you can't leave me. You have to stay with me the whole time."

"That's the point, silly!" She looks back across the cafeteria. "Ugh, she's *feeding* him french fries. How long do you think they'll last this time?"

"Two days?"

Sarah Nan laughs, elbowing me playfully in the side. I elbow her, too. I feel like I have my old friend back—or maybe she's been here all along.

Mom picks me up after school, and after our usual *how-was-your-day-fine*, we have another silent ride home. I leave her in the kitchen with the mail and go upstairs to my room to think about CARP.

The door to Mom's meditation room is closed, and light is coming through the crack at the bottom—but there's no ocean sounds or acoustic guitar. Someone is moving around inside.

I step back, almost losing my balance on the top step as the door swings open.

"Lizzie!" James stands before me in jeans and a blue hoodie. "Hey—you got taller!"

"Wha—*You* got taller," I stammer. It isn't true; James is

the same height as before. Am I actually taller? Is he actually here? "You *scared* me!"

My voice comes out more forcefully than I realize. "Whoa!" He backs up into the doorframe, laughing. "Sorry. My last exam was yesterday. It's just my final English paper that's due tonight. Gerald was leaving and offered to give me a ride, so I thought, why not finish here?"

I hug him, hard.

"You've got quite a grip there, Nugget."

A faint car smell still lingers on his sweatshirt; underneath that, the smell of boy, my brother. "You stink."

James laughs. "You'd stink, too, if you had to pay four dollars to do a load of laundry."

"Lizzie?" Mom's footsteps are moving fast toward us. "Lizzie!"

"You didn't tell Mom?" I ask, as she appears at the foot of the stairs.

"James!" Her hand goes to her chest.

"Sorry, Mom." James lets go of me and opens his arms to her. "I got a ride home early. Surprise!"

Mom is speechless, and I wonder if James knows how much he really scared both of us. I watch my mom clear away her fear, pushing it to the side the way the snowplow parted the snow last weekend. She smiles, then comes upstairs for a hug. "Welcome home, sweetheart!"

James can't talk for long; he has his English paper to

finish. "Last minute, much?" I ask.

"Ha, ha," he says, and shuts the door.

Part of me wishes I could be in there with him, spreading out my homework on the floor while he works at his desk. But I have my own project to finish now. Mr. Le said I could go last, to give me more time. That helps, I guess. I settle down on my bed and open my science notebook.

I look at the page where I first started—back when I thought I was doing something about apple trees. *Apples not true to seed*. When I was researching asexual reproduction, I learned about grafting, which is the way the most common apple varieties are propagated—not by planting them, but by cutting a branch off an existing tree and binding it to a new one. It's a delicate process. The cut branch gets slotted into the new one, then wrapped with special tape like a bandage over a wound. You wait a season to see if it takes. If it does, then the next year you'll see growth.

So much can happen in a year.

I flip through the pages. Kalanchoe, aphids, whiptail lizard. Solitary wasps, spider plants. And then, my note on mycorrhizae: *Experiments have shown that mycorrhizae greatly enhance plant growth in comparison to plants lacking fungal partners*. Partners. Not reproductive partners, but another kind. Invisible networks beneath the soil. Without them, a plant could never flourish. Even, I imagine, an asexual plant like the kalanchoe.

"Hey." My door swings open, and James leans in. "I need a break. Want to go to the diner?"

"What about your paper?"

"It'll get done. Besides, I could use sustenance. Preferably in the form of a waffle."

I shut my notebook. "Sure."

James starts downstairs ahead of me. Before I join him, I scroll through my phone for Aidan's number, which I got way back in September at the beginning of advanced math.

My finger trembles a little as I text, and I remember Ms. Ardvinson's words: *When we're hyper-adrenalized, we can make assumptions without all the information.*

Aidan is not Michael, I remind myself. *Just text him.*

Hey, it's Lizzie, I write. Sorry i snapped at you at CARP

I'm not expecting a reply anytime soon, but he writes back right away. Hey Lizzie. Thanks, it's no big deal

Yes it is, I reply. You've always been nice to me. Especially with Michael

The three-dot bubble pops up as he types his response. Michaels a prick

Whoa. Aidan never talks like that in class. I wonder what else he's hiding under the surface.

Don't let him get to you, he continues.

I won't

"Lizzie, you coming?" James calls.

"Just a sec!"

I type quickly, not wanting to keep James waiting. **You're presenting first for CARP, right?**

Yeah

My heart thuds, but I've made up my mind. I don't want to wait until the end. I can be ready—if it's okay with Aidan. **Would you mind if I switched with you?**

CHAPTER 26

~

Meet at Maple Creek Park at dusk, on the shortest day of the year.

Those were the unsurprisingly vague directions on the postcard that Daria sent Mom and me—and, presumably, Chloe and Nora and their moms—inviting us to the coming-of-age ceremony.

"Dusk?" Mom said when the invitation arrived. "What does she want us to do, check an almanac?"

I rolled my eyes. "Or you could look *online.*"

Things are still tense with my mom. On the surface, we're back to everyday conversations, but underneath is the huge gulf of what we're not talking about. *Not biologically possible*—what she said to me. *If you hadn't been so nice to him*—what I said to her. Sometimes I can tell she wants to talk to me, but how do I know we won't just say the same things to each other again?

As it turns out, on December 21, the shortest day of the year, dusk is at 4:50 p.m. The drive to Maple Creek is silent. I've got the object I was supposed to bring, the one to represent my childhood, tucked into my backpack—along with a box of graham crackers, which was what Daria asked us to contribute to the "communal feast." At Sarah Nan's warning, I left room for a stick of firewood. Mom was supposed to bring something, too, for her part of the ceremony, but she wouldn't tell me what.

When we pull into the gravel parking lot, Daria is standing by her car, waving her arms, as if we could miss her. Chloe's mom, Ginnifer, stands beside her. Sarah Nan and Chloe are inside the car, staying warm. Another car, a green station wagon, is pulled in sideways ahead of us, not officially parked. A curly haired blond passenger gets out.

"Is *that* Nora?" Mom asks. "Look at her!"

I am looking, but then Nora leans into the car, talking to someone in back. Mom cuts the engine and we get out, just in time to catch the tail end of Daria telling Nora's mom, ". . . meant it to be a mother-daughter event, you and Nora together."

"Shoot!" Nora's mom, Steffie, looks up at Daria from the driver's seat, while Nora pulls away from the back window, shrugging into her backpack. Now I can see who she was talking to: a little boy in a car seat, with two slightly bigger boys beside him.

"I totally missed that. Is there any way she could still join? I don't have anyone to watch—"

A multicolored plastic toy flies forward from the back seat and bounces off her head.

"SETTLE DOWN BACK THERE!" Steffie barks. Then

she turns back to Daria. "I know Nora was really looking forward to this."

Nora stands there with her hands in her pockets. She doesn't seem like she's looking forward to anything. This girl is different from the Play-Doh eater I remember. For one thing, she's *tall*—maybe even taller than me. She's wearing jeans tucked into boots, a yellow winter coat, and a patterned knit scarf. No hat, though. Maybe all that hair keeps her head warm.

"Of course!" Daria says. "She absolutely can join us. Come on, honey, you can put your things here in my car, you won't need them for the hike."

"Hike?" Chloe repeats, poking her head out the car door. "Isn't it getting dark?"

"So we'd better move!" Daria claps her gloved hands together. "Everybody out!"

"Bye, sweetie." Nora's mom leans her head out the window, and Nora bends to have her cheek kissed. The car pulls away, swerves a little at the end of the driveway, and turns into the street.

At the end of the parking lot, a chain extends between two concrete posts to stop cars from driving onto the trail. Footpaths on either side show the way most people go, but whenever my family came here for hikes, James and I would take a running jump over the chain. A sign hangs from the middle: No Trespassing After Dark.

"Daria," my mom says. "I don't know about this."

"My friend works for Parks and Rec," Daria says breezily. "She said no one checks in the winter."

"So when we *freeze* to death, nobody will find our bodies until the springtime," Chloe mutters. Apparently she's missing out on some party tonight and Jeremy is going without her. She's in a really bad mood.

Sarah Nan and the others walk around the post to the footpath. Nora, long-legged, just steps over the chain. In a sudden burst of inspiration, I do what James and I used to do: I take a running jump, and I hurdle it.

"Save that enthusiasm, Lizzie!" Daria calls to me. "You'll need it for the ceremony."

We all fall into step: moms in front, girls in back. The snow is mostly gone, but what's left is packed down to ice.

"What *is* this ceremony?" Nora asks as we crunch along the path into increasing darkness. "My mom couldn't really explain it."

"A big waste of time, that's what," Chloe grumbles.

Sarah Nan shrugs apologetically at Nora. "It's a coming-of-age ceremony," she says. "We're supposed to be saying goodbye to our childhoods and becoming women."

Nora nods. "Is it based on anything? Like an actual tradition?"

"I don't think so . . ." Sarah Nan hesitates. "I think she just picked stuff that she thought would be meaningful."

Chloe scoffs. "So it isn't even *real*."

"Careful!" Daria shouts. Ginnifer's legs are slipping and sliding underneath her; Mom and Daria each grab her by an elbow before she can fall down. She's wearing the wrong boots for this. Some purple, fake-leather kind.

"Watch your step here, girls," Daria calls back over her shoulder. "You might want your lights."

We dutifully take our phones out and follow along.

"The ancient peoples worshiped this day," Daria says, drawing her coat closer around her as we trudge along the path, avoiding patches of ice. "The shortest day of the year—a time for reflection and renewal!"

Chloe kicks a clump of leaf debris. "Everything is *dead*."

"Everything is a cycle," Daria corrects her. "You're a part of that cycle now. Your bodies—"

"We know, Mom," Sarah Nan says—patiently, the way she would to a child. "Save it for the ceremony."

Mom and Ginnifer laugh quietly; Daria gives a small, "Humph!"

Chloe pulls her hat down, shivering. "Anyone who wants this torture hike to be over quicker, I'm going on ahead."

She picks up the pace of her trudging—more like stomping—along the path. Sarah Nan sighs. "I'll catch up to her."

Nora keeps her same pace. I do, too.

"So," Nora says, "what have you been up to for the last eleven years?"

I give a small laugh—but she's actually waiting for an answer. "Not much, I guess," I say, which immediately sounds feeble. "I mean . . . life."

Fortunately, Nora seems better equipped for actual human conversation. "Did you have to get braces?"

"Yeah. I got them off last year. You?"

"Nope. How about your ears pierced?"

"No."

"Really?"

Other times, I would feel defensive, but Nora doesn't know me at all—and after tonight, we probably won't see each other again. "I just never felt like it."

"I got mine pierced, but the upper part," Nora says, pulling back her hair so I can see the gold ring encircling the cartilage at the top of her ear. "My mom thought I was nuts because it hurt way more, but I didn't care. I never wanted little dangly things."

"Hm," I say.

We trudge a little farther in silence. I try to think of another thing to talk about. *Do you still eat Play-Doh?*

"Do you have brothers or sisters?" Nora asks.

"Brother." I haven't actually seen much of James for the past week he's been home. He's catching up with high school friends, preparing for his upcoming internship for winter session—and, of course, spending time with Ally.

"Older or younger?"

"Older—he just started college."

"And it's just you and him?"

I sigh. "Me and him and his girlfriend."

"Whoa." Nora kicks a rock. "Someone's got some repressed rage."

"It's not rage," I say. "She's actually nice. It's just . . ."

"You don't want to share him," Nora finishes.

I look down at the trail. The beams of our phone lights make the shadows bigger, so everything looks like it's moving. "Pretty much."

"Here we are!" Daria exclaims.

I look around and recognize the park's picnic area: a clearing with a few tables, grills, and a firepit. Daria unzips her backpack and pulls out two hefty sticks of firewood.

"Girls, go see if you can collect some kindling," she says. "Laura, did you bring the newspaper?"

We manage to find some not-too-damp twigs and sticks, and when we come back, Mom is crumpling the *Wendover Gazette* while Daria stacks the firewood and some smaller sticks around it in a tent shape.

"Good," Daria says, when we show her what we found. "Stack it on there."

Soon, a small campfire is going. Chloe pulls a bag of marshmallows out of her backpack. "Can we make these now?"

"Not yet!" Daria says. "Those are for the communal feast. After the ceremony." Chloe rolls her eyes, and when Daria isn't looking, she stuffs a marshmallow in her mouth.

Daria has us all gather around the fire, moms on one side, girls opposite. It's cold; we all huddle in close. As the flames grow, they cast deeper shadows across Mom's forehead and under her eyes. I have a sudden, panicked thought: *Is that what she'll look like when she's old?*

"We are gathered here this evening to witness the coming of age of these four young women," Daria says. "It is a momentous occasion, and also a solemn one, as you each prepare to let go of a part of your childhood and accept your role as a woman in our society. Did you all bring your objects?"

Sarah Nan, Chloe, and I dig into our backpacks. Nora says, "What?"

"Here, take part of mine." Chloe pulls out a Bratz doll and yanks an arm off.

Nora dubiously takes the arm. "Thanks."

Even though Daria assured me we weren't going to burn them, I didn't totally believe her, so I picked a hand-me-down Barbie doll I didn't really care about—the older, meaner-looking kind of Barbie with heavy-lidded eyes and blue eyeshadow. Sarah Nan brought a tutu; Chloe has her Bratz doll without an arm, and Nora has the arm.

Daria, swept up in her reverie, continues. "At this time, please pass your childhood object to your mother."

As I step around the fire to Mom, I can barely make myself look at her. Mom lifts the Barbie from my hands and raises her eyebrows at me. She knows this doll doesn't mean anything to me. It's my Molly doll—or maybe an apple from the tree in our old yard—that would have represented my childhood.

"Mothers, to honor and set aside your daughter's childhood, please place the treasured object in the time capsule." Daria moves aside to reveal a large metal cylinder. "Daughters, you'll come back here fourteen years from now to open it, when you're twenty-eight."

"*I* won't be coming back here," Chloe says.

Daria ignores her, gently tucking Sarah Nan's tutu into the cylinder. Mom lowers in the Barbie, followed by Chloe's Bratz doll. Nora keeps the arm.

"Now take your places again on the side of the fire," Daria instructs. "At this time, we'll pass around the torch"— she removes a stick that has been resting in the fire, its tip glowing—"and you'll each share what it means to you to become a woman."

I didn't know we were going to have to speak. How do *I* know what it means to be a woman?

"Isn't that a little gender normative?" Nora asks.

"Well . . ." Daria starts, but falters, considering Nora's question. I don't know if she thought about how to honor womanhood without being binary. Holding the torch aloft, she reconsiders. "I suppose you could share what it means to you to be an adult. If you prefer."

Everyone nods as the firelight flickers over our faces, but still, nobody is bold enough to start.

"Sarah?" Daria asks tentatively.

Sarah Nan doesn't want to, but for her mom's sake, she puts on a smile and takes the flaming stick. "To me, being an adult means making tough decisions." She starts to pass the torch to Chloe, then takes it back. "And also respecting other people's tough decisions."

Is she just saying something to say something—or is she thinking of her mom and Nick?

Daria beams. "Chloe, your turn, sweetheart."

Chloe holds the torch away from herself. As quickly as she can, already passing it to Nora, she says, "Being a woman means always being there for your friends." Unsurprising.

Nora holds the stick. She stares at the orange glow at its tip, pondering. "I think adulthood is about responsibility," she says. "Doing things you don't always want to do."

"Like stupid ceremonies," Chloe mutters, prompting Ginnifer to snap, "*Chloe*!"

Now I have the torch. There are a few thin tongues of flame at the end; I feel the heat against my face as I hold it closer. All the obvious answers have already been taken. What else could I say that would sound good, and be true? Daria would want me to say something about cycles, about the miracle of our bodies in harmony with the moon—but I don't feel that way. Mom thinks that being a woman means being seen as a woman out in the world, and all the expectations that come with that. I don't know if she *knows* she thinks that, but she does. Sarah Nan, until recently, thought it was about having a serious boyfriend; Chloe thinks it's about knowing everything, or pretending that you do. I don't know what Nora thinks.

What do *I* think?

"For me, adulthood . . ." I look up, across the fire. We are surrounded by forest, and suddenly I find myself thinking again of mycorrhizae, the invisible network beneath the earth. Trees that otherwise might never touch are linked together by it. This circle of women feels like that. As different as we all are, we are connected—by friendship, by shared history and experiences.

"Adulthood is about relationships," I say at last. "Not just one kind of relationship, but all kinds. You figure out who you trust, and who understands you." I'm thinking about Ms. Faraher, and the Boy in the Skirt—people I thought would understand me, but didn't. Sarah Nan, the least like me, actually understands me the best. And James, bound up in the roots of who I am. Even as we grow apart, we play a role in keeping one another alive.

"All of that helps you figure out more about yourself," I finish.

"Thank you, Lizzie," Daria says, and I hand her back the torch. My face is hot, and not just from the fire, but I feel better now. Lighter. I look across the flames, and Mom is watching me, her expression unreadable.

"Let's move on to the passing of wisdom," Daria says, placing the torch back in the fire. "Mothers, please take out the gifts for your daughters. Nora, I'm sorry, honey, I'll explain it to your mom so she can do it with you later."

Nora shrugs. "It's fine."

Our moms reach into their backpacks. Ginnifer pulls out a gift bag. Daria removes a large, paper-wrapped bundle. My mom has a small box.

"Your mothers have prepared a few words for you, which they've also written on paper to go in the time capsule." She holds up three envelopes, drops them into the capsule, then reaches back into the fire for the stick and passes it to Ginnifer. "Would you like to go first?"

Ginnifer gives Chloe a pair of shoes—probably not the type of gift Daria had in mind, but Chloe loves it, of course—and talks about how Chloe was born prematurely and spent three weeks in the NICU. Daria gives Sarah Nan a quilt, gold and blue squares framed with a deep purple border. She said she's been working on it every Saturday while Sarah Nan and I were at self-defense. Sarah Nan is speechless. She hugs the quilt, and then her mom hugs her, and neither of them says anything for a long while.

Mom clears her throat. "I guess I'll go, since I'm already . . ." She holds up the torch. "Lizzie, this belonged to your great-grandmother, whose name was also Elizabeth." She passes me the box. "I've been keeping it to give to you someday."

I open the box—and inside, tucked into a velvet cushion, is a thin, silver ring.

"It was her first wedding ring," Mom continues. "She had to get another when she got older and her joints—well, anyway . . ." Mom swallows. "This is for you, right now. So you can remember the women in our family who came before you, like my grandmother Elizabeth, who would have loved you and thought you were beautiful if she could have met you."

I take the ring out of its box. It could be a wedding band if you wanted it to be, but it's thin enough that it could also just be a pretty ring—a plain, pretty ring. I slide it onto my right ring finger.

It fits.

It fits me right now, as I am.

"Thanks, Mom," I say. She takes my hand to look at the ring there, but we don't meet each other's eyes.

There's a digital *ting-ting* sound, and Ginnifer reaches into her coat for her phone.

"I believe I asked that all devices be silenced for this ceremony," Daria says, clearly irritated.

"No, it's Steffie," Ginnifer says. "She says she just read the directions in your email, she's so sorry . . . Oh! Here's what she wants to say to Nora—"

Daria snatches the phone from Ginnifer and scans the screen. She clears her throat. "'Nora, you showed *me* how to be a woman. You are my oldest child, and—'" The glow illuminating Daria's face suddenly goes dark.

"I think my battery might have been a little low," Ginnifer says.

Daria lowers the phone. For the first time tonight, she seems to really see Nora, standing there still holding a dismembered doll arm and no gift of womanhood. "Sweetheart, I'm so sorry . . ."

"It's all right," Nora says. She seems to really mean it. "I'll find out when I get home."

"Maybe now would be a good time for the communal feast?" Mom suggests.

"First, we all have to take turns digging so we can bury the capsule." Daria removes a trowel from her backpack. "Ready, everyone? Who's first?"

"Uh, Mom?" Sarah Nan says.

"Yes, sweetie?"

Sarah Nan puts a hand on Daria's shoulder. "I'm pretty sure the ground is really super frozen."

"Oh." Daria lowers the trowel. Fortunately, this only fazes her for a moment. "Well, in that case, break out the junk food!"

As far as food goes, the feast isn't really all junk food: Mom and I brought regular graham crackers, and Chloe and Ginnifer brought regular marshmallows, but Daria and Sarah Nan brought some fancy fair-trade organic chocolate and whole wheat buns, and Nora brought vegetarian hot dogs.

"I had no idea you were vegetarian!" Daria says as we begin spiking our soy dogs (except for Chloe, who says, "Bleh!" and goes straight for the marshmallows).

"I'm the only one in my family," Nora says, kneeling before the flame. "It's a little tricky sometimes, but they get it."

Sarah Nan leans over to whisper in my ear, "Is Play-Doh vegetarian, too?" I don't laugh.

Even now that we're all more relaxed around the campfire, Daria maintains the coming-of-age theme. She gives each of us paper to write a letter to our "future selves," and then our moms tell stories about us when we were little. Ginnifer tells us how Chloe, when she was still in diapers, used to go in the corner for "number two."

"*Mom*!" Chloe exclaims.

Daria talks about how I hit Sarah Nan with the Cabbage Patch doll—of course—and Mom talks about how Nora and I once unzipped the couch cushions and flung bits of their foam stuffing all over the basement. I can almost remember that. I think Nora was wearing a dress that day; I remember the foam sticking to her like snow as we threw it up in the air and watched it fall.

I'm full, but Mom's only had one s'more, so I decide to make her another. As I kneel before the coals, I see my great-grandmother's ring glinting on my hand, catching the orange light of the embers. Mom says something that makes Daria laugh; Sarah Nan puts a leaf in Chloe's hair. I think I finally know what all my CARP research has shown me: that even the most solitary of creatures is never fully alone.

CHAPTER 27

~

Back in the parking lot, after the ceremony, we make plans for how we're going to get back to Sarah Nan's for the sleepover. Daria invites Mom and Ginnifer to stay over, too ("When was the last time you had a slumber party?!"), but they politely decline. There's room for five in Daria's car. Mom says we'll go separately. She wants some time alone with me.

"Of course," Daria says.

For a long time, we drive in silence.

"Well," Mom says at last. "That was interesting."

"Yeah," I agree.

Mom glances sideways at me. "I wonder where Daria came up with all that."

"I don't know."

We aren't far behind Daria's car. When we pull up to the traffic light at the center of town, they're right in front of us. Sarah Nan, Chloe, and Nora are all sitting in back; Chloe's and Sarah Nan's heads are moving animatedly, while Nora's is still.

"I liked what you said," Mom begins abruptly. "About relationships. Figuring out who you are."

"Thanks."

"Do you think . . ." Mom trails off. "I guess what I mean is . . . you said adulthood is about figuring out who you can trust. Do you feel like you can trust me?"

The light turns, and the girls in the back of Daria's car jolt a little as she starts forward. Mom and I don't move right away. I know she wants me to say yes. How often do people say yes because they know it's what the other person needs to hear?

"Sometimes," I say finally.

It hurts to say. Mom nods. "But not other times?"

"I don't know." Except I *do* know.

"If you're mad . . ."

"I'm not mad at you." We've lost Daria's car now. It's only us. "Mom, I'm not mad at you."

"I think you *were* mad at me."

I don't answer at first. "I just wish, when I told you about being asexual . . ." I hesitate, listening for how the word lands. Mom doesn't give any hint. "I wish you'd just said 'okay.'"

"I understand that," Mom says carefully. "It *is* okay. I just want . . ."

I brace myself.

"I just want to know that you're all right. Everything with Mr. Henckman—"

"I'm not asexual because of Mr. Henckman."

"I know. I know."

We're approaching Sarah Nan's street now. Mom reaches over to rub the back of my head.

"I'm sorry we had to move. I think I never said that to you, but I am sorry. Do you understand why we did?"

"Maybe." I know my mom was afraid after what happened, like I was, but it always felt like moving was a defeat. We lost, and he won. "Not really."

She shakes her head. "You knew some of what happened, and obviously you were there when . . . But there was a lot I didn't tell you. Or James. He had my cell number—some yard sale thing a while back—and he would leave these messages. Awful, angry messages . . . worse than the one you heard. Even before he broke in, Dad and I talked about moving. We didn't want to do that to you and James, but just seeing him in the backyard would make everything inside me . . ." She shudders. "I couldn't do it. I'm sorry, Lizzie. I really am. I know you loved our house."

I don't answer right away. It scares me, what my mom just shared. That it happened, that she felt that way, and that she trusted me with it. Maybe some part of me did come of age tonight.

"Does the meditation help . . . with that feeling?" I ask.

Mom nods in the darkness. "It helps keep me in the present, if that makes sense."

"That's good," I say.

Neither of us speaks for a moment. What now?

"Did you see Nora just had a doll arm?" I ask.

Mom looks at me. Then she laughs. "Did you hear Ginnifer's *speech*? That lasted so long I wanted to throw myself in the ceremonial flames."

"Those hot dogs were disgusting."

"It was *freezing*."

"I still can't feel my toes!"

We're both laughing now. The car slows as we turn the corner, pulling closer to Sarah Nan's driveway.

"Are you sure you want to go?" Mom asks.

"I'm sure." I remember Sarah Nan's comment about the Play-Doh, and I feel bad leaving Nora alone with her and Chloe. "I'm all right."

We pull up to the curb. In the driveway, Daria is parked, and the other girls are climbing out.

"Mom?" I say.

"Hm?"

"It wasn't your fault," I tell her. "With Mr. Henckman. Just because you were nice to him, that doesn't mean . . ."

Sarah Nan is waving to me from the driveway. *Come on!* I see her calling.

"Thank you, sweetheart," Mom says. She pulls me in for a hug.

I hug her back. I don't know if we fully understand each other yet, but I'm okay with that for now. I'm strong enough to wait for us to get there.

By the time we're all set up in Sarah Nan's basement with foam mats and sleeping bags, it's past midnight. Daria says not to stay up too late and goes upstairs to bed. Of course, within five minutes, we're passing around an unfinished bag of marshmallows (which Nora declines since even those aren't vegetarian), painting our toenails, and playing truth or dare.

Sarah Nan goes first, and picks truth.

Chloe asks her, "How far did you go with Ned?"

Ugh—that question. I'm afraid to hear her answer.

Sarah Nan's face remains calm. "On top of clothes, not underneath."

Chloe shrieks, but I feel surprisingly calm. *I'm not going to do it if I don't think it's the right guy.* I underestimated Sarah Nan. I won't do that to my friend anymore—because that's what she is. My best friend. She can make out with boys if she wants to.

Nora's pretty good at truth or dare. She has Chloe stick marshmallows up her nose, and she gets Sarah Nan to confess to stealing a Snickers from the drugstore. For me, she gives an easy truth about whether I ever cheated (once, in second grade, when I copied Sarah Nan's spelling of *caterpillar*—which was wrong). Meanwhile, Sarah Nan dares Chloe to French kiss a throw pillow, so Chloe dares her back to flash us, which she won't. So then Chloe flashes us for no reason.

"Okay, I think we can agree that was completely

unnecessary," Sarah Nan says, while Chloe laughs and rearranges her pajama top. Nora has a hand over her eyes. "Whose turn is it now?"

"Lizzie's next! Lizzie's next!" Chloe points at me, as if I were trying to hide. Which, at this point in the game, maybe I am.

Sarah Nan looks at me. "Okay, Lizzie: Truth or dare?"

"Truth."

Chloe sighs and whispers, not too quietly, "*Again?*"

"Shut it, Chloe." Sarah Nan looks back at me. "Let's see, truth . . ."

My face goes hot, and I look at Sarah Nan, hoping that after fourteen years of friendship, she'll read my mind. *Please.*

"Okay," she says at last. "I want you to tell us the name of a boy you *respect.*"

Chloe snorts. "Are you kidding? Ask her who she has a crush on. Ask her who she'd rather—"

"Quiet." Sarah Nan looks at me intently. "I want to see if she can do it. And don't say your dad or your brother," she adds.

The three of them are watching me. I wish I could pull myself into my sleeping bag and not come out until tomorrow, when all this is over. "I can't think of anyone."

"Come on, Lizzie," Sarah Nan says—but not in her usual, impatient way. More like she's encouraging me. "I'm not asking who you *like.* Just who you think is an actual, decent human being."

I begin scrolling through faces in my mind. Michael Gorman—no way. Ned—he's nicer than I thought, more like a big goofy dog, but he dumped my best friend. Boy in the Skirt—I don't know what to think of him now. They all seem like creatures I can't understand. If I respected one of them, it would mean I could actually have a normal conversation with them.

"Oh my *God*." Chloe flops back against her sleeping bag. "If you're going to pick truth all the time, at least answer the *question*."

"Aidan," I say suddenly. The name pops out. "He's okay."

"Oooooh, Lizzie likes Aidan!" Chloe shrieks. She begins dancing around the basement.

"Who even is Aidan?" Nora asks. She's picking into the still-soft toenail polish already, only half paying attention to what's happening.

"Kind of a geek, but Lizzie's right, he's okay," Sarah Nan says. Then she looks at me. "Good job."

I shrug, but I kind of liked it—that Sarah Nan knew what would be hardest for me.

"All right, now that that snoozefest is over, I've got a dare for all of you," Chloe says. "I dare you to go outside and run a full lap around the house . . . *naked*."

"No *way*," Nora says, still focused on her toes.

Nora saying no makes it easier for me. "Yeah, I'm out, too."

"My mom would kill me if we got caught," Sarah Nan says. Then she grins. "Let's do it!"

The two of them race up the stairs. I hear them giggling and shushing each other at the top before everything goes quiet. Nora and I are alone.

"Nasty stuff . . . toxic fumes . . . ," Nora is muttering as she applies nail polish remover.

I take a breath. "I'm glad you said no."

She shakes her head. "These things always wind up the same. Dirty. I told my mom I didn't want to go, but she was all like, 'You knew each other when you were *babies* . . .' Yeah, well, just because you were friends when you were babies doesn't mean you're friends forever. I don't even know you guys, and I just got flashed by one of you."

"I don't really know Chloe, either," I say, not liking the way she's lumped me in with *you guys*. "Sarah Nan and I are friends, though."

Nora laughs. "Now *there's* a relationship I don't get. You seem like total opposites."

"Maybe," I admit. I remember Sarah Nan's words after the dynamic simulation. *You'll fall in love with somebody's brain.* "But we understand each other."

"Hm." Nora tosses the cotton ball away and crawls back into her sleeping bag. For pajamas, she's wearing what look like boxer shorts, but pink, with little dinosaurs. "So what was that about, Sarah Nan asking who you respected?"

"Oh." I'm lying on my back, facing the ceiling—I think I can see the Windswept Lady. Maybe it's the lingering effect of truth or dare, or maybe I don't feel like lying anymore, but

I answer, "She was giving me a hard time because sometimes I act like boys are the scum of the earth. But I'm just not attracted to them, is all."

There—I said it. It actually wasn't so hard.

Then why is my heart suddenly pounding?

"Ah." I hear Nora's arms go over her head, finding the same position as mine. "So, girls?"

"No," I say. "More like, not attracted to people in general."

Nora sighs. "Yeah, same here."

Her words take a moment to register. When they do, I think I feel my brain short-circuiting. "Wait, what?"

"What?"

I sit up. "You're asexual?"

Nora's still lying back, arms folded around her head. She turns to look at me. "What's that?"

No, no, no, no—I got it wrong. I messed up. "Never mind." I retreat into my sleeping bag.

"No—hey, wait." Nora's sitting up now. "I didn't know there was a name for it. Asexual?"

"Not experiencing sexual attraction," I mumble. "It's a thing."

"And that's what you are?"

I nod.

"Wow. Okay, cool. Asexual." She looks up slightly, toward the ceiling, as if feeling the word on her tongue. "I don't know if that's exactly what I am. I never really tried to label it. I just know that I don't get all that stuff about crushes and whatever. Seems like a waste of time."

So she doesn't think of herself as asexual. But she gets it. "One time," I say, "this kid—a boy—was kicking a paper bag at me under the table, and Sarah Nan said that meant he was flirting with me."

"*Ugh*," Nora says emphatically. "At my school, the girls have to hold a boy's arm at graduation. I'm already dreading it. Everybody else is daydreaming about who they'll get."

"I don't see how any of the boys in my grade are cute," I say. "I look at them, and I see the same obnoxious kids who chased us on the playground."

"Or did that weird thing where they make their eyeballs vibrate."

"*Exactly*," I say, and it is—exactly. Nora understands it exactly.

"Does your mom know?" I ask abruptly.

"Know what?"

"About you. About this."

Nora laughs. "You saw my mom. I'd have to bring home half a motorcycle gang before she'd have anything to say to me about boys. Am I alive? Check. Am I eating cereal for breakfast? Check. Is my report card not a total disgrace? Check. The last thing my mom is worried about is that I'm *not* dating."

"Lucky," I say, and she turns to face me. "I told my mom, and she didn't take it well."

"What does that mean?"

I lie back against my pillow. It still hurts, remembering the conversation. "She said I shouldn't make up my mind right now. She didn't want me to close myself off."

"Being asexual doesn't mean you're closed off, does it?"

I shrug. "I don't really see it happening."

"'It'?"

"Sex. Dating. Marrying some doofus."

"Huh." Nora doesn't say anything for a minute.

"What?" My guard is up again. I don't like where this conversation is headed.

"Those are kind of different things, aren't they?"

"What do you mean?"

"I mean, you can date someone and not have sex with them. You can be in a relationship and not be married—doesn't Daria have a boyfriend?"

"They broke up."

"Oh. My mom didn't know that." Nora folds her arms behind her head. "You could even be married and not have sex, right? I mean, take my parents. I have two little brothers and a foster brother. I don't exactly think they're getting any."

"Gross," I say, and Nora looks at me, confused. "I mean, to think about your parents that way."

She shrugs.

"I guess I just . . ." I hesitate. This is the biggest question—

the one I've puzzled over the most. "I know what you're saying. I'm just afraid I'll change my mind and start liking boys all of a sudden. I'm afraid something will happen to me overnight and I'll be a different person."

"Why would that make you a different person?"

It's so simple, but she has a point.

We are interrupted by pounding on the stairs and frantic shushing. Sarah Nan and Chloe come rushing in, bringing the cold with them, clutching their bundles of clothes.

"Floodlight came on—car going by—Chloe screamed!—light went on upstairs . . ."

They dive into their sleeping bags, wriggling as they pull their clothes back on. Nora and I look at each other, and when she smiles, I can tell she feels the same way I do. Like *they're* the ridiculous ones, not us.

I smile back, and we burrow down in our sleeping bags, too, just as Daria's voice calls to us from the top of the stairs, "What is going *on* down there . . . ?"

CHAPTER 28

~

The Thursday after New Year's, in-class CARP presentations begin. Most students will go later in January, and usually the people who go first are the ones who already presented at the big exposition and don't have anything new to prep—but Aidan said yes when I asked him to switch, so now, today, it's my turn.

I arrive to science with my board tucked under my arm and the kalanchoe in its pot. It's taller now, and its leaves are starting to show the tiny points that will eventually form baby kalanchoes.

I open the board and look it over, remembering what I've prepared. Most of the pictures are the same as the ones on the first board, the one that I threw out, but I rewrote all the captions to be about how asexual organisms connect with other organisms. For the whiptail lizard, I learned that their asexual parthenogenetic reproduction is often brought about by mating-like behaviors between two females. Aphids rely on ants to protect them from predators, and in exchange they convert the complex carbohydrates that they suck from plant stems into sugars that sustain the ants. And the kalanchoe, in addition to depending on mycorrhizae the way so many plants do, drops its thousands of tiny offspring in the hopes that some will survive the hard, dry months and take root—maybe somewhere nearby, maybe far away.

Lastly, at the center of the board, I have a section about AVEN—an example of community for asexual people to feel less alone, to be among others who know what it's like.

"Whoa!"

Michael stops on his way past me to his new seat. Aidan sits next to me now, and Chloe across the aisle. When Mr. Le moved Michael away from me, he moved everyone else, too. "Lizard sex? Is your project *seriously* about lizard sex?"

I ignore him and pull out my index cards to prepare. My chair jerks with a kick from behind me.

"I can't believe Lizard actually has a thing for lizards! Do you like to watch them or something? Does that get you going?"

"Michael, cut it out," Aidan says.

Michael kicks again. "So you're into animals, not people. Makes sense. Do you have a lizard boyfriend? Are you getting married? Too bad your lizard babies are going to—"

"Hey, Chloe," I say loudly, surprising her enough that she looks up from her phone in her lap. "Did I tell you I'm having my period right now?"

It's hard to say which is more gratifying: how wide Chloe's eyes go, or Michael's wordless "Uh—?"

"Yep," I say, as Chloe continues to look on in shock. "There's a lot of it. Blood, I mean. Coming out of me."

". . . Are you okay, Lizzie?" Chloe asks, probably wondering if I've been possessed. But I'm not. I'm remembering Kendall's secret weapon. *Use it if you need to.*

Michael doesn't meet my eyes, but mumbles, "Whatever . . . ," as he retreats to his seat.

"Lizzie!" Mr. Le says. "Come on up and let's get started."

I stand, leaving behind a still-speechless Chloe. Aidan is smiling to himself; I guess he wasn't uncomfortable.

At the front of the room, I open my board and steady it upright on the front table. When I share this with the class, will they tell me that it's not analogous, like Will did? Will they figure out I'm talking about myself, like my mom did, and tell me I'm wrong? Maybe. But *I* know I'm right. That's what matters.

Mr. Le quiets everyone down. "Go ahead, Lizzie."

I take a breath. I have my index cards, but I don't need to look at them as I begin. "My project is called 'Asexuality and Community in the Plant and Animal Kingdoms' . . ."

An hour before the Winter Carnival dance, I start getting ready. I take a shower even though I don't need one. When I get out, I watch myself dry off in the mirror. I practice looking. *This is me*, I think, and I try not to flinch away. It's hard, but I think it will get better.

I don't have many clothes for this type of occasion, so I put on a denim skirt, some leggings, and the top my Aunt Lisa gave me for Christmas. For jewelry, I've got a beaded bracelet and my new ring. That seems like enough. What no one can see, though I know it's there, is the Moon Catcher that Daria gave me. I put it in this morning, somewhat apprehensively, but she was right: all day, I didn't even feel it. Like it was a part of me.

Mom said she would take me, so at quarter to seven, I start downstairs. She's in the kitchen, talking to James. Actually, arguing with James, judging from their voices. I stop just shy of the doorway, listening.

"Her mom said it's fine . . . ," James is saying.

"She said that to you?"

"Ally told me she said it. Who cares? I won't see her again for three months."

"I don't know, James . . ." There's the clunk of a cupboard shutting. "I love Ally. But it worries me to see you pour so much of yourself into one person. Are you sure . . . ?"

"Mom." A chair scrapes against the floor. "Whatever you're worried about happening already happened, okay? We're nineteen."

Mom doesn't have an answer to that. I back away slowly, then stomp on the bottom stairs, pretending to be just coming down. When I come in, Mom and James are on opposite sides of the kitchen, each going about their business, pretending they weren't just having a conversation about James spending the night with Ally.

"Whoa," James says when he sees me. "Where are *you* going?"

"Winter Carnival."

"Oh, shoot, that's right!" Mom exclaims. "I'm ready—let me grab my keys . . ."

"I'll take her," James says. He scoops the car keys from their bowl on the table. "I'll drop her off on my way to Ally's."

The car is silent as we head out of the Maze and start toward the community center. I don't dance—definitely not with boys, and barely even by myself. Sarah Nan wants me there to make sure she doesn't try to get back with Ned again, but I don't really think she'll need me. I'm picturing a lot of standing around by the punch. Maybe I'll text Nora, who told me to let her know how the "Celebration of the Cis-Heteropatriarchy" went. Maybe I'll check out AVEN for tips—surely I'm not the only one who's had to survive a middle school dance.

I was on again last night, reading a thread about high school and asexuality. One person, a girl, posted about being in a relationship with another asexual person. After what Sarah Nan said to me about falling in love with a brain, I actually thought that sounded kind of nice. Maybe.

"Do you ever think Mom isn't as open-minded as she thinks she is?" I ask abruptly.

286

To my surprise, James laughs. I cross my arms over my chest, thinking he's being patronizing, treating me like the little sister who says silly things out of the blue—but then he says, "Absolutely."

"Really?"

"Didn't you hear her when I asked if I could stay the night at Ally's?"

My ears go hot. I hadn't realized he knew I was there. "I think that's different," I say. "She just wants you home."

"Mm." He doesn't sound convinced.

I ruined it. He trusted me with something important, and I said it didn't count.

"Anyway," I say, "don't you have your whole life to sleep with Ally?"

I try to say it casually, but those words, *sleep with*, and their multiple meanings make my lungs catch a little.

James looks sideways at me, then turns his gaze back to the road. "You think so?"

I'm surprised at the question in his voice—that he would ask *me*. "Sure," I say. My throat tightens as I continue. "I always thought you and Ally would wind up together. In the end."

James considers that for a long moment. "Thanks," he says at last.

"James?"

He focuses on the road as he makes a turn. "Yeah?"

"When we're grown up, and Mom and Dad are . . . I mean, when we're older, would it be okay if I . . ." I can't hide the tears from my voice. "Could I stay with you and Ally, at Christmastime?"

"Jesus Christ, Lizzie." The blinker clicks as we turn the corner. "What kind of question is that?"

"I just think I might not have anyone else," I say.

"Of course you can . . . but what do you mean, you might not have anyone else?"

I cross my arms. Look away, out the window. "I don't know."

I want to tell him what I'm thinking, all of it—but if he says the wrong thing, I don't know if I can take it. I don't know what I'll do if he doesn't understand.

I rest my chin on my hand, watching the dirty snowdrifts go by.

"Different than what?"

I look over at him. "Huh?"

"You said me sleeping at Ally's was different. Different than what?"

"Oh." I toy with the strap on my purse. I swallow. Breathe. "I told Mom that I'm asexual, and she didn't believe me."

James drives. I hold my breath. I can't look at him.

"Have you heard of it?" I finally ask.

"I have now."

"That's not what I meant."

"I know." The road splits ahead of us, and he steers left. "That seems right for you," he says at last.

"Really?" I feel myself lightening with relief. Then I narrow my eyes. "You only think that because I'm your kid sister." What older brother wants to think of his sister as a sexual being?

"It's not only that," James says. "You always seemed different. Not in a bad way. Just—you never cared about things other kids did. You had your own way."

He makes that sound like it's a *good* thing. "So you don't think I'm just . . . too young to know?"

We pull into the front lot of the community center, and around to the front doors. James puts the car in park, but neither of us moves.

"No," he says. "I don't think that."

"Really?"

People around us are filtering in, gathering at the doors. I see light coming from inside.

"I felt sure about Ally when I was fourteen," James says. "If I can be right, then you can, too."

With those words, my heart lifts. Everything in me lifts. I feel a lightness in my chest and lungs that I haven't felt for months. Maybe years.

"Are you going in?" James asks.

"I guess so." Sarah Nan is probably there already, waiting for me.

"Text me if you want to leave early," James says, peering in the doors. "These things are hell."

"I will." I step out onto the sidewalk, which crunches

with a thin layer of salted ice. Then I lean back into the car. "You and Ally aren't going to do it in *here*, are you?"

James just laughs. "Don't worry about us, Nugget. You wouldn't understand."

I stand up straight, one hand resting on the door. "That's right," I say. "I absolutely would not."

CHAPTER 29

The community center gymnasium is decorated with blue and yellow balloons and shiny streamers that drape down from the basketball hoops. *Winter Carnival*, reads a big banner above the refreshments table. Kids are packed together in clumps, mostly talking, with some swaying or bouncing in an attempt at dance. And it's *loud*. I can feel my eardrums vibrating.

I don't see Sarah Nan anywhere. After wandering the crowd for a few minutes, trying to look purposeful, my phone buzzes with a text.

In the bathroom with Chloe. Jer broke up with her again

With Chloe crying in the bathroom, there's no telling how long until Sarah Nan comes out. I knew this would happen. I knew it would end up being me by the punch.

"Hey."

The Boy in the Skirt, Will, comes up alongside me. He's wearing a different skirt today, a royal purple one with a lacy fringe at the bottom, but the same Converse underneath. He helps himself to a cup of watered-down pink.

"Hey," I say.

"How come you aren't dancing?"

"I could ask you the same thing," I point out.

"Fair." He takes a sip. "I'm not dancing because I don't want to be here. My dad made me come. He has to help chaperone some Girl Scout thing for my sister and didn't want to leave me alone at home. What's your excuse?"

"I just plain don't dance."

"Well." He raises his cup as if in a toast. "Then I guess we can not-dance together."

I raise my punch, too. This is my chance—to ask him about the skirt. To ask him why. To ask him how he knew, how he realized that he could just *do* it and nobody would care. How he himself can just not care.

But are those really questions for him? Or are they just my wishing that he might have answers to the questions I can't answer myself?

"Why did you say all that stuff at CARP?" I ask him.

He gives a small laugh. "What?"

"You said my project was all wrong. You called me 'lizard girl.'"

"You were offended by that?" A new song starts up in the background, the bass beating, *doomp, doomp,* as he stares at me, perplexed. "Obviously you're not a lizard."

"I worked really hard on that project, and you made it seem like . . ." I force myself to finish. "Like I didn't know what I was talking about."

"Why do you care what *I* think about your project?"

The strangeness of what I'm doing is threatening to overwhelm me, but I push through it. "I thought you would know what it feels like when people don't get you."

Will looks at me. All this time, I was scared to talk to him, and now I don't know why. He's just a boy in a skirt. "I don't know," he says finally. "It was early. I was bored. I hate it here. I've got Ds in everything because the teachers feel too sorry for me to give me an F."

I'm surprised he told me all that. "Well, you didn't need to take it out on *me*."

"Yeah," he agrees. Which is probably as close to an apology as I'm going to get.

"And there could be a gay aphid," I continue. "You don't know that."

"True," he says. "But that's the other thing. People always try to use science to justify the way they want to be. Like, you're allowed to be gay because penguins and dolphins can be gay, too. Why can't you just *be* whatever? You're not a plant. You don't need a plant to tell you it's okay to be who you are."

I see what he means. I don't need to go looking to the natural world for validation of what I already know is true about myself. "I guess I just like knowing it's out there," I say.

"Fair enough."

We sip our punch in silence.

"Sorry, Lizzie, I know you told me not to leave—oh, hi, Will!" Sarah Nan is back from the bathroom. Will raises a hand in silent greeting.

Sarah Nan says something to me that I can't hear over the speakers.

"What?"

"I said, you look pretty tonight!" My jaw nearly hits the glossy gym floor. "Let's get out there. Will, do you want to dance with us?"

"No, thanks." He crosses his arms and looks outward, like a man waiting for a bus. "I'll just keep living out my personal nightmare."

Sarah Nan takes me by the wrist and pulls me away. "Lizzie, you were talking to a *boy*!"

"It's no big deal," I tell her. Maybe it was—because it didn't feel like talking to a boy. It felt like talking to a person.

I wasn't sure if James really meant it when he said to text him if I wanted to get picked up, but he must have, because after about forty-five minutes, he texts *me*: Ally and I are going to Village Diner. Want to bail?

I glance over at Sarah Nan, who's laughing at the strip of silly pictures we just took in the photo booth. Can Sarah Nan come too?

It doesn't actually take much to persuade her to come with me.

Once Sarah Nan and I make it past the chaperone at the door—who asks us three times if we're *sure* we want to leave, because once we do, we can't come back—James is already there in the front turnaround.

Beside him, in the passenger seat, is Ally.

"Hi, Lizzie!" Ally gets out of the car to hug me. She's a whole head shorter than I am, and for a moment I imagine us hugging this way at some far-off holiday time, when I arrive at her and James's house bearing pie or casserole. "It's so great to see you."

"You too," I say.

Sarah Nan and I climb in back, and we pull away.

The car settles into silence, and I stare out the window at the passing neighborhoods. Some people still have their holiday ornaments up: inflatable snowmen, blinking lights on trees, one manger scene. Dad took our decorations down already. Part of me thinks maybe we should keep them up all the time—not the snowmen, but the lights. It makes the town look like a different place at night. Warmer. Welcoming. A place you're allowed to be.

"Hey, James?" I ask suddenly. We're on Main Street now, approaching the Village Diner.

"Yeah?"

"Can we go by our old house?"

No one says anything for a moment. "You mean, drive past it?"

"Yeah." My heart beats faster as an idea takes shape in my mind.

Sarah Nan pipes up beside me. "You know, I don't think I've been by your old neighborhood since Hallow—oof!" I elbow her in the side, and she shuts up.

James catches my eye in the rearview mirror. "You know we're not supposed to be there."

"He's not going to get us if we're in the *car*. He won't even see us."

James taps his thumbs against the wheel.

I pull out my phone and text Sarah Nan beside me: Help me out.

"It'll be okay, don't you think?" Ally asks. "It's dark out." Ally's taking my side?

"Plus," Sarah Nan adds, seeing my text, "how long would it take to drive around the circle? Like two minutes?"

James thinks.

"All right," he says. "But all of you are sworn to secrecy." We agree to secrecy.

What's going on? Sarah Nan texts me.

Something I have to do. I shift in my seat. Put my thumb on the seat belt button. I think my plan will work.

As we approach Deerfield Circle, Ally says, "This is the way I always rode my bike to come see you." The car rattles. "I guess they haven't fixed that pothole."

"Hey," Sarah Nan says. "I thought you two broke up."

I guess between Thanksgiving and everything else, I forgot to mention they were back together.

James and Ally share a small glance. "Nope," James says.

He puts his hand on Ally's.

"Aw," Sarah Nan says, just as James pulls onto our old road.

He goes the long way around the block so that my car window is facing the right way when we finally pass our house. The lights are off, as I expected, but a giant inflatable Santa illuminates the lawn. The Henckmans' porch light is on, and there's a glow in one second-story window.

Both houses disappear behind us.

"Can you go around again? That was too fast."

"Too fast for *what*?" James demands.

"She's right," Sarah Nan says. "We didn't really get to look."

My phone glows with another text from her. **Don't do anything stupid.**

James sighs, and around we go again. Out of irritation, he crawls along, inching past Marge's house, and the beagle ladies', and the people with the pool. Ten Christmases from now, or twenty, will I be with James and Ally? Will I be with Sarah Nan? Or will I be in my own house, decorated how I choose—and maybe with someone else? The future is hard to see.

Still no signs of movement at the Henckmans'. That's good. James speeds up a little.

"Slower," I say.

"Is *this* slow enough?" James asks, practically parking across the street from our old house. I don't answer him—because in one swift movement, I unbuckle my seat belt and throw myself out of the car, hitting the ground at a run.

"Lizzie!" all three of them shout, but none of them very loudly because we're not supposed to be here. I faintly hear them calling for me to come back, and then I don't hear anything except for the sound of my footsteps on the frozen ground.

I stay low. I keep close to the bushes. For the final, uncovered stretch, I sprint toward the edge of the woods, which is separated from the rest of the lawn by taller grass and dead leaves. If the Henckmans see me, maybe they'll think I'm Will's little sister. Does she ever play out here the way I did?

There it is.

I keep running, palms stretched out in front of me, until I slam into the apple tree the way I would when Sarah Nan and I played tag, back when this tree meant safety and home.

I'm panting. My phone buzzes in my pocket.

Lizzie, what the heck?? James demands.

Are you OK? Sarah Nan asks.

Go around again, I respond. Give me two minutes.

I don't wait for an answer. I drop to my knees, feeling around in the dry, flattened grass. There has to be one here. I felt so sure.

Finally, right in the crook of two roots, I find one: an

apple. Its skin is shriveled and a little mushy, but still intact. I stand, cupping it in my hands, waiting for James's approaching lights.

Goodbye, tree, I think.

I look up at the Henckmans' house. He took so much from my family, from me, but I wasn't going to let him take this: my chance to grow something new. It won't be the same as this tree I'm leaving behind. But unlike that first apple that fell too small, this one has lived through a season. This one, I know, has seeds that will grow.

I don't run back to the car. Instead, I zip my coat up to my chin, and I walk. The air is cold, as it should be. It prickles the inside of my nose as I inhale, but I keep my head lifted and move faster, feeling the strength of my legs propelling me forward.

I reach the curb before James comes back, so I wait until I see his headlights approaching in the distance.

All around me, the houses are warm and bright, and I think about the different lives carrying on inside them. What will my life be like one day? Maybe I'll be someone's eccentric neighbor, like Marge or the beagle ladies. Maybe I'll be like Daria, and I'll raise a daughter on my own. Maybe I'll be a teacher, like Ms. Faraher—or even Ms. Ardvinson. I'll show some other tall, quiet girl what she can be.

Then again, maybe I won't be like anyone else.

Maybe I'll just be like me.

AUTHOR'S NOTE

Dear Reader,

When I was seventeen, I opened the regional newspaper to read the "Dear Annie" advice column. "Is it possible to be nonsexual?" a reader asked, and I felt a jolt. I had been wondering the same thing about myself. When Annie responded no, and advised the person to see their doctor, I felt the way Lizzie feels when she reads the response to "Left Out": deflated, affronted, yet still convinced that what I was feeling—or rather, what I *didn't* feel—was real.

"So what am I?" I wrote in my journal. "Like I've said before, I'm not anything. Not anything there's a word for, at least. I think I'm something."

Some weeks later, another letter appeared in "Dear Annie," this time from a reader who had this to say: asexuality is an orientation, and, yes, it is possible. "As an asexual myself, I'd like to offer a few words of reassurance . . ." they wrote, and it took all the restraint I had to wait for a private moment to log on to the family computer and visit AVEN, the Asexual Visibility and Education Network, for the first time. There, everything finally clicked. My feelings made sense; I made sense to myself. I saw where I fit in the broader spectrum of sexuality and attraction—and, best of all, there were *other people like me*!

Gradually, I began telling others, wanting affirmation and acknowledgment of my feelings and experience. Sometimes I was met with understanding and acceptance, other times with disbelief or contradiction. It's invalidating to be told repeatedly that the way you feel isn't real, and while invalidation doesn't compare to the outright violence and ostracism faced by many in the LGBTQ+ community, I reached a point where I chose carefully when and to whom to reveal that side of myself.

As I became an adult, fell in love with my husband, and married him, being asexual became a less central part of my identity, and certainly a less visible one. I have a deep admiration and appreciation for anyone who has ever "come out" to anyone, at any age, because for many years I thought about how unnecessary, how irrelevant it would be if I were to let others in my life know that I identify as asexual. Really this is just another way of saying that I feared their judgment.

However, two things have now led me to share this about myself again. The first was the idea for *Just Lizzie* and wanting to put her story into the world, which I knew would mean owning the fact that some parts of it—particularly Lizzie's thoughts, questions, and doubts—come from my own experience. The second was, and is, my seventh-grade students. Lizzie's disappointing conversation with Ms. Fara-her was loosely inspired by a conversation I once had with a teacher, though fortunately not one whose opinion I valued very much. Knowing how deeply I yearned for a grown-up model of what my life could be like, and how much it would have meant to me if one of my teachers had ever said, "I'm asexual," I wanted my own students to know that about me, particularly those students who might be wondering if they are asexual themselves. This book has opened up conversations with them, and students themselves have opened up conversations that contributed to this book.

I wish I could have done justice to all the complexity and nuance that surrounds sexual identity, but one book about one girl's experience is never going to say all that there is to say. Aromanticism, for example, is an identity that is often conflated with asexuality but is quite different; for anyone looking for more information on this topic, please check out the resources that follow. In addition, Lizzie's story does not address the way that racism, poverty, and other systems of oppression intersect with sexual identity—again, the resources section offers more in this vein than I could in one book. The world needs more stories from underrepresented voices, so I encourage you to seek out other books by LGBTQ+ authors, particularly writers of color—and, perhaps one day, to write your own story.

Finally, to my adult readers: when a young person shares a part of their identity or experience with you, it is a huge honor. It means that they trust you to handle this information with sensitivity and steadiness. The best way to respond, in my experience, is to begin by saying, "Thank you for sharing this with me."

And to my young readers: trust your sense of yourself, and don't let others' fear, ignorance, or misconceptions undermine your sense of who you are. After all, who knows you better than you do?

RESOURCES

www.asexuality.org—Asexual Visibility and Education Network, or AVEN.

www.asexualityarchive.com—Articles and information about "all things ace."

www.thetrevorproject.org—Provides information and support to LGBTQ+ young people.

www.thetrevorproject.org/research-briefs/asexual-and-ace-spectrum-youth—The Trevor Projects's space for asexual/ace spectrum youth.

www.aromanticism.org/en/resources-1—Information and resources from the Aromantic-spectrum Union for Recognition, Education, and Advocacy, or AUREA.

www.glsen.org—The Gay, Lesbian & Straight Education Network, or GLSEN.

www.itgetsbetter.org—"The It Gets Better Project's mission is to uplift, empower, and connect lesbian, gay, bisexual, transgender, and queer (LGBTQ+) youth around the globe."

www.lambdalegal.org/sites/default/files/publications/downloads/fs_resources-for-lgbtq-youth-by-state_1.pdf—Resources for LGBTQ+ youth by state, from Lambda Legal.

www.pflag.org—PFLAG (Parents of Lesbians and Gays) provides resources to children, families, friends, and allies of LGBTQ+ youth.

ACKNOWLEDGMENTS

First, thank you to every student who ever asked me, "How's your book going, Ms. Wilfrid?" It meant more to me than you knew.

Thank you to my agent, Lauren Scovel, who steadily guided me on my first journey through the publishing process and assured me, long before it was anywhere close to relevant, that my book would not have a "bad cover."

To my editor, Lily Kessinger, who asked all the tough, incisive questions and pushed me toward a deeper understanding of Lizzie (and probably myself as well). Deep gratitude also to Amy Cloud, who picked up where Lily left off and guided this book (and me!) through its final stages. Thank you to the Clarion Books team at HarperCollins, especially the thoughtful and attentive copyediting by Ivy McFadden, Emily Rader, and Heather Bosch; production editor Erika West; and designer Catherine Lee. And deep thanks to Deb JJ Lee, whose beautiful cover design I loved the moment I saw it.

To all the special K–12 public school teachers who

encouraged my writing over the years, especially Helen Jones, Patty Ward, Kathleen Ambach, Sean Farrell, Mimi Paquette, and Chris Tarmey.

To the GrubStreet community, for everything you do to support writers at all stages. Special thanks to instructor Ursula DeYoung and her Novel in Progress class, and to instructor Michelle Hoover and the 2020 Novel Incubator cohort for your many reads, generous feedback, and warm encouragement: Elizabeth Bernhardt, Jessica Bird, Jane Dietzel-Cairns, Phillip Freeman, Rick Hendrie, Dan Rose, Liesl Swogger, Karen Shakman, and Mary Thomas Dibinga. Thanks also to "second reader" Linda Schlossberg for your valuable insights and feedback.

To my long-standing and outstanding writing group: Stephanie Poggi, Hathairat Sawaengsri, and Naomi Parker. Thank you for supporting me on this project from the very beginning and for being my biggest cheerleaders whenever it seemed far-fetched or impossible to continue. You are the best!

To my amazingly talented and supportive coworkers at Pollard Middle School, especially the rockstar Grade 7 ELA team: Jen Evans, Ken Lundberg, Martha Matlaw, Yolanda O'Neill, Eileen Walsh, and Manisha Patel, librarian Sue Doherty, and administrators Tamatha Bibbo and Liz Welburn. Thanks to Elissa Strauss and Pollard's GSA for welcoming me into your group, and to Erin Goodwin for generously allowing me to observe her flower dissection lab and then fact-checking my plant science. Thank you all for your unwavering support!

To my very special C-Block class of 2016–2017, for cheering me on in my first attempts to complete a manuscript and find an agent. C-LA!

A special thanks to the following students who read my completed manuscript and provided me with thoughtful and invaluable feedback: Mia Allen, Ayden Gallucci, Maggie Sharrard, and Ayla-Ryann Thompson. You are amazing writers, and I look forward to reading your books one day as well!

To Shay Orent of IMPACT Boston, for answering all my questions about self-defense courses, and to instructors Jim Watson and Meagan Anderson of IMPACT Boston's "Assertiveness and Boundary Setting" course. And to my brave classmates, E., K., C., Q., T., and L.: I wish Lizzie could have taken this class with you!

To the Putney School Summer Programs, where I wrote the first words of *Just Lizzie* during an eleven-minute free-writing prompt. Special thanks to director Tom Howe, instructors Ruth Kirschner and Ann Braden, and to my creative writing cohorts in 2016, 2017, 2018, and 2022. And to Nate Cohen: thank you for sharing late-night library writing time with me.

To Alicia, Jill, José, Catherine, Chantal, Mary, Ginny,

Sariah, and other friends near and far who have seen me through the many stages of my writing life.

To my family: my parents, Nancy Elder-Wilfrid and Dan Wilfrid, for giving me the best Christmas present ever all those years ago, which was construction paper and a stapler for my very first "books"; my brother Greg Wilfrid, for being my earliest audience and fan; and "my Johns," John Pelletier and John Gray, for honoring my writing time and for believing in me even during the long period of time when you didn't know what my book was about. And to our cat Butterscotch: you mostly slowed me down by stepping on my keyboard and meowing at me for food, but you are still the greatest.

And finally, to the James family: Tricia, Todd, Tyler, and Taylor. I could not have done this without you.